Doc heard scuffling down by his feet.

"What now? Rats, I suppose, come to feast on my flesh." He reached around for a rock to throw but found nothing. "Begone, vermin!" The scuffling got louder.

Suddenly, he heard a different sound from the same place, a distinctive sound that could not be mistaken for any other. *Giggling*.

Doc's heart hammered in his chest. He meant to snap some words of defiance to try to intimidate, but before he could, his visitor scrambled forward.

Hands grabbed hold of Doc's ankles and wrenched his legs straight with an iron grip. Then he heard a voice, high-pitched and girlish in the lightless void. "You're *mine* now. All *mine*."

And all of a sudden, there were many more hands, coming from all directions. And all of them were grabbing at him…

**Other titles in the
Deathlands saga:**

JAMES AXLER
DEATHLANDS®

CHILD OF SLAUGHTER

A GOLD EAGLE BOOK FROM
WORLDWIDE®

TORONTO • NEW YORK • LONDON
AMSTERDAM • PARIS • SYDNEY • HAMBURG
STOCKHOLM • ATHENS • TOKYO • MILAN
MADRID • WARSAW • BUDAPEST • AUCKLAND

Recycling programs
for this product may
not exist in your area.

First edition September 2015

ISBN-13: 978-0-373-62634-2

Special thanks and acknowledgment to
Robert Jeschonek for his contribution to this work.

Child of Slaughter

Copyright © 2015 by Worldwide Library

Printed in U.S.A.

Man, a mere inhabitant of earth, cannot overstep its boundaries! But though he is confined to its crust, he may penetrate into all its secrets.

—Jules Verne,
The Steam House

THE DEATHLANDS SAGA

This world is their legacy, a world born in the violent nuclear spasm of 2001 that was the bitter outcome of a struggle for global dominance.

There is no real escape from this shockscape where life always hangs in the balance, vulnerable to newly demonic nature, barbarism, lawlessness.

But they are the warrior survivalists, and they endure—in the way of the lion, the hawk and the tiger, true to nature's heart despite its ruination.

Ryan Cawdor: The privileged son of an East Coast baron. Acquainted with betrayal from a tender age, he is a master of the hard realities.

Krysty Wroth: Harmony ville's own Titian-haired beauty, a woman with the strength of tempered steel. Her premonitions and Gaia powers have been fostered by her Mother Sonja.

J. B. Dix, the Armorer: Weapons master and Ryan's close ally, he, too, honed his skills traversing the Deathlands with the legendary Trader.

Doctor Theophilus Tanner: Torn from his family and a gentler life in 1896, Doc has been thrown into a future he couldn't have imagined.

Dr. Mildred Wyeth: Her father was killed by the Ku Klux Klan, but her fate is not much lighter. Restored from predark cryogenic suspension, she brings twentieth-century healing skills to a nightmare.

Jak Lauren: A true child of the wastelands, reared on adversity, loss and danger, the albino teenager is a fierce fighter and loyal friend.

Dean Cawdor: Ryan's young son by Sharona accepts the only world he knows, and yet he is the seedling bearing the promise of tomorrow.

In a world where all was lost, they are humanity's last hope...

Chapter One

The blast took Ryan Cawdor and his companions by surprise, knocking everyone off their feet before they knew what had hit them.

As Ryan crashed to the ground, he twisted and gaped through the smoke for a glimpse of who or what had attacked them.

A slender mutie stood not fifty yards away, his crimson skin glinting in the blazing sunlight. He scowled at Ryan from behind the sights of a shoulder-mounted, jury-rigged gren launcher.

There was no time to shout a warning. The mutie's hand was on the firing mechanism.

Ryan swung up his Steyr Scout Tactical longblaster, which already had a round chambered. Sucking in a deep breath to steady his hand, he sighted on the mutie and squeezed the trigger.

The one-eyed man was an experienced marksman. His shooting skills had played a major role in his surviving for so long in the hellish Deathlands—all that was left of the United States after the world blew up in 2001. So he knew for a fact that as soon as he pulled the trigger he'd fired a kill shot.

Ryan felt an unsettling stillness all around him, like the calm that descended before a terrible storm. Then he experienced an odd sensation, a combination of powerful suction and expulsion all at once, equally balanced.

Suddenly, a wave of force slammed into him. His body buzzed and shivered as he hung in the wave's grip, caught like a moth in a spiderweb.

The wave held him there for a split second, then it let him go with a shock like a blow below the belt. As he gasped at the wrenching release, he saw the sun-scorched ground between him and the mutie ripple as if it was the surface of a lake.

A low hum started, building to a deep rumble that Ryan felt in his chest and bones. Then a flash of light exploded in front of him. When it faded, he saw that a tall rock wall now stood between him and the mutie.

It wasn't an optical illusion. Ryan grimaced at a puff of dust springing from the striated reddish-brown rock wall. It was kicked up by the bullet he'd fired, the one that had been frozen and unfrozen in midair on its way to the mutie.

"Fireblast!" Ryan cursed.

"What the hell? Where did *that* come from?" asked J. B. Dix, Ryan's longtime friend and one of his traveling companions. Known as the Armorer because of his mastery of all manner of weapons, J.B. was on the ground a few feet away. He'd been toppled by the gren blast like the rest of the team and was staying down out of the line of fire.

"Beats me." Ryan rolled over to face forward again. Fresh rounds were punching across the flat land up ahead, fired from the blasters of the muties in the trenches. For the moment, at least, the greatest danger lay in that direction.

Lining up a nearby mutie in his sights, Ryan fired his Scout, grazing the side of the enemy's head. Ryan's companions smoothly followed his lead. J.B. flung himself around on his belly and whipped up his Mini-Uzi to open fire on the nearest trench.

"Where *any* this come from?" Jak, an albino who spoke as few words as possible, flipped onto his knees and aimed his .357 Magnum Colt Python at another trench. "Land look solid before. No trenches." At the first sign of a mutie popping up, he cracked off a shot and the mutie's head exploded like a watermelon on a target range.

"Nice shot!" Ricky Morales scrambled up beside Jak. If he felt any aftereffects from the gren blast, he didn't show it.

Ricky swung up his De Lisle carbine and swept it left while Jak swept his Python right. Seconds later, both young men were filling the noonday air with sizzling lead and hitting mutie targets on opposite ends of the middle trench.

Mildred Wyeth and Doc Tanner chimed in soon enough, adding to the storm of blasterfire over the flats. That left only one member of the team whose blaster was silent.

That member was Krysty Wroth, Ryan Cawdor's life mate.

Quickly noticing the absence of the bark of her Glock 18C blaster, Ryan checked left, then right. There she was, twisting in the dust some twenty yards away, hands tangled in her long red hair.

"Krysty!" Ryan shouted over the cacophony of weapon fire, but she didn't seem to hear him.

Though the battle was in full swing, Mildred looked his way instantly. Following his gaze, she caught sight of Krysty.

Stuffing her .38-caliber ZKR 551 revolver into the waistband of her fatigue pants, Mildred scurried on hands and knees behind the firing line. A predark physician as well as a fighter, she was well used to putting her neck on the line to provide medical care for her teammates.

When she got to Krysty, though, Mildred saw no blood or bullet wounds, which was good…but that also meant the cause of her friend's distress was still unknown.

And it was getting worse by the minute, apparently. As Mildred reached for the side of Krysty's throat to get a pulse, the redhead swatted the physician's hand away.

"What's going on back there?" In the midst of the raging fight, Ryan kept looking over his shoulder at Krysty and Mildred. His right eye—he'd lost the left one long ago in a fight with his brother—was wide with concern for the red-haired beauty who made his life of constant struggle in the Deathlands worth living.

"I don't know yet!" Mildred yelled.

"Some form of seizure, perchance?" Doc suggested between blasts from his .44-caliber LeMat revolver. The blaster was a replica of a famous weapon from the mid to late 1800s—a time period, amazingly, that Doc called home. A man of the nineteenth century, he'd been snatched through time by a group of predark scientists. Then, when Doc had proved to be a difficult test subject, he was shunted to the future, to the Deathlands, where he'd been ever since.

Just then, a mutie's shot sliced past, close enough for Mildred to hear the hiss of its passing. Startled, she let out a surprised cry and fell back from her knees to her butt. "Keep me from getting killed, and you'll be the first to know!" she snapped.

Doc, who was on his belly like Ryan and J.B., pulled his blaster farther to the right and squeezed off a round. He wasn't the best shot of the group, but this time he winged a mutie's shoulder, sending the copper-skinned enemy screeching back into his trench.

"My dear Dr. Wyeth, I am doing my utmost to achieve exactly that desired outcome!"

"Less talk, more kill! That *my* desired outcome!" shouted Jak as he, too, cracked off a shot.

Ryan, meanwhile, forced himself to shut out the chaos and deepen his focus. He had to set aside his worries about Krysty and find the best way through this mess without losing his people.

The situation was pretty clear-cut, except for the apparently shifting geography. Quite simply, the day had gone sideways, as days often happened in the Deathlands.

Ryan and his companions had jumped via mat-trans to a redoubt near Ogallala, Nebraska, at the southern edge of the Sandhills. Finding the redoubt nearly stripped of supplies and transport, the companions had set out on foot, heading north in search of food. But they'd gone only a few miles when a heavily armed band of hostile muties had ambushed them.

Now the muties had Ryan and his companions pinned down; the enemy's ranks were thinning, but the companions were still outnumbered.

"J.B.!" It took all Ryan's willpower to ignore Krysty's cries and call out to the Armorer. "Let's rain down some hell on these bastards?"

J.B. grinned and unclipped a red-jacketed gren from his belt. "I like the way you think!" He tossed the bomb to Ryan, then freed up another for himself.

"Jak, Ricky," Ryan called. "You ready for an up close and personal gopher shoot?"

"You know it!" Ricky shouted.

"Enjoy flush outta holes," Jak said. "See how run."

"Move on my signal." Ryan nodded at J.B. "Count it."

"You got it."

Ryan tightened his grip on the plunger of the gren and pulled the pin with his teeth. He let loose another round from the longblaster, driving down a mutie who'd been climbing out of a trench, then rolled on his side and hauled the gren back for a big throw.

"Three!" shouted J.B., also winding up for the pitch. "Two!" He rattled off one more series of shots from the Mini-Uzi, then finished the count. *"One!"*

With that, Ryan wrenched his arm forward as hard as he could and released the gren. He saw it spin through the air, J.B.'s arcing alongside it.

Seconds after the two grens fell, a pair of explosions erupted in the trench, spraying rock and dirt and body parts in all directions. The ground shook, and screams pierced the air.

The barrage of blasterfire stopped, at least for a moment, and that was all the time Ryan's team needed. He gave his people the signal he'd promised, which in this case was to leap up and lead the charge himself, longblaster left behind and SIG-Sauer at the ready.

Muties in the rear trenches popped their heads up like rabbits, but it was too late. Ryan, J.B., Jak and Ricky were on them in a flash, racing through the cloud of smoke and dust from the explosion like avenging angels roaring through the gates of hell.

Each person cut loose with everything he had, determined to make the most of the opportunity. Now that they had the high ground and the run of the battlefield, they intended to end this conflict, which they'd never asked for in the first place.

Only two muties remained at the far ends of the first trench after the gren blast, throwing off wild shots among the burned and battered corpses of their dead brethren. These survivors went down in short order under Ryan's and J.B.'s blasters, screaming as their bodies spouted fountains of blood.

Meanwhile, Jak and Ricky vaulted the first trench without slowing and sprinted to the next. The two young fighters opened fire as soon as the barrels of their blasters crossed the rim, pelting the occupants with a shower of blistering slugs. More screams and spurting blood filled the air from below as half a dozen muties danced a jerky dance of death.

With the first trench quickly cleared and the second in the process of being scoured, Ryan and J.B. leapfrogged to the third. This time, though, they encountered opposition beyond the wild shots of panicked muties.

Just as Ryan and J.B. jumped the second trench, a mutie popped up from the third with a shotgun pointing in Ryan's direction. As the shotgun roared, the one-eyed man threw himself down hard, dodging the spread of buckshot; then he rolled over fast and came up on one knee with his SIG-Sauer P-226 searching for a target.

He didn't have to worry about the mutie with the shotgun, though, as J.B. was already peppering him with rounds from the Mini-Uzi. But as soon as that mutie dropped, two more popped up from the same trench... and five more from the next one back. All of them were armed with longblasters, revolvers or shotguns, and every blaster barrel was pointing in Ryan's or J.B.'s direction.

At that exact moment, Krysty let out a piercing shriek, the loudest yet.

Gritting his teeth, Ryan forced himself not to run to her side. Instead, he methodically fired rounds at the two nearest muties, driving one back underground and killing the other with a shot to the eye socket.

That gave the five in the fourth trench time to get off a series of shots—but the barrage didn't last. Fresh from clearing the second trench, Jak and Ricky moved up and added their blasters to the front line.

Together, the four companions unleashed their own barrage, forcing the five muties down; then they advanced. As J.B. took care of the single shooter left in the third trench, Ryan, Jak and Ricky hopped over it and darted to the rim of the fourth. Bullets flew up at them, preventing them from getting a clear look over the edge, so they settled for flicking out their blaster barrels and laying down fire where the shooting was happening.

As screams erupted and the blasterfire from below became sparser, Ryan, Jak and Ricky grew bolder and leaned over the rim for a better view. By then, only three of the muties were still on their feet; Ryan and Jak each picked off one, and J.B. joined the party and took out the third.

"Think we got 'em all?" J.B. threw down more rounds from the Mini-Uzi, making sure everyone in the trench was dead for real.

"Who know?" Jak swung up his Python and turned a slow circle, looking around. "This place full surprises."

For a moment, the landscape was quiet except for the soft trickle of settling dust in the bullet-riddled trenches.

Then, suddenly, Krysty let loose the loudest scream of all. It was so long and loud and full of pain, it could have been a howl released from the depths of torture or childbirth.

Ryan whirled in her direction, ready to run...and then he froze. A familiar stillness closed in around him, like the calm he'd felt before the rock wall had appeared between him and the grenade-launching mutie.

Once again, he had that feeling of something lurching out of place, followed by powerful suction and expulsion in perfect balance. When the balance broke, a wave of force shot through him, holding him paralyzed.

An instant later, the wave let him go. The release spun him and nearly bowled him over, but he stayed on his feet through sheer force of will, which meant he had a ringside seat to see what happened next. J.B., Jak and Ricky had fallen around him, but Ryan was upright and alert.

As he watched, dizzy and shaking, the ground at his feet rippled and changed. There were flashes of light, popping across the plain one after another like giant fireflies, and the trenches that held the corpses disappeared, becoming indistinguishable from the rest of the flatland.

Still, the ripples continued to flow forward, heading for the trio of human targets in the distance.

Heart pounding with urgency, Ryan ran toward them.

He saw Krysty continuing to writhe on the ground, flinging her head from side to side while Mildred tried in vain to restrain her. Doc stood over them both with his sword in one hand and the LeMat in the other, shouting something as he watched the ripples flow toward them.

Impact would come in mere seconds. Ryan ran as hard as he could, his legs pumping like pistons in the engine of a speeding wag, but he knew he wouldn't reach his friends in time.

"Krysty!"

The ripples on the ground rushed up ahead of him and encompassed his three friends. Krysty, Mildred and Doc all seemed to quiver at once; even the air around them seemed to vibrate.

As Ryan increased his speed, redoubling his effort to reach them in time, the quivering effect intensified. He felt the hum again, the same as before, building to a rumble in his chest and bones…in his heart. It was an irregular thrumming rhythm in counterpoint to his own pulse and footsteps, distorting his natural cadence.

Ryan fought through it, determined to reach Krysty and the others. If the effect was going to do something to them, he wanted to share the same fate. He was determined not to be separated from his lover and his friends.

Up ahead, the oscillation reached a fever pitch, accelerating until it blurred his view of his friends, creating a shivering patina of light and color in their place. Then there was a blinding flash of light.

The ground under Ryan heaved, knocking him off his feet. He landed on his back and quickly pushed himself up to see what had happened.

In that instant, he experienced a wave of panic. Instead of his three friends, all he could see was a rocky hill that had mysteriously appeared between his position and theirs.

Scrambling to his feet, Ryan ran for the hill. As he circled it, he felt a terrible sense of doom and fear that the woman he loved more than anyone in the world was gone now and forever.

His heart was slamming in his chest as he dodged around the far edge of the hill, dreading what he was about to see. His eyes zoomed to the spot where Krysty had been and he saw that she was still there, with Mildred by her side.

Instantly, a flood of relief coursed through Ryan's body. Krysty was no longer writhing and twitching on the ground. Instead, her body was limp, her face relaxed for the first time since they'd been ambushed by the band of muties.

But Ryan quickly realized that not everyone's situation had improved. Looking around, he saw that the third member of the group was nowhere to be seen.

"Where's Doc?" Ryan asked. "What happened to him?"

Mildred shook her head. "Damned if I know." She was scowling, her face crusted with dirt. "He was here just a second ago." Her brown eyes flashed to the hump of rock. "And if you ask me where *that* came from, I'll tell you the same thing. I don't know what the hell just happened."

Krysty's eyelids fluttered open, and she gazed up at Ryan. Though she was no longer rolling and screaming in pain, her green eyes still looked dazed, her face haggard. "There's something horrible here...something unnatural." Her voice was hoarse as she spoke.

"What do you mean?" Ryan asked.

She looked at him, her fiery red tresses flowing around her face like a parted veil. "Something here is warping Earth itself in a way I've never felt before. I feel as though it's killing Gaia...and me."

Chapter Two

Doc had vanished into thin air.

The companions recced the area where they'd been attacked by the muties, but they found no trace of the old man and no trace of any opening into which he might have fallen.

"Where Doc go?" Jak asked as he finished his latest search pattern and met up with Ryan. "If trapdoor or tunnel, I not see."

Ryan sighed. "People don't just disappear, Jak."

"Walls not appear, either." Jak nodded at the rock wall that had materialized during the battle. It stood not thirty feet away, as solid as if it had always been there.

The companions had examined that particular formation with great care, guessing it might hold some clue to what had happened to Doc. But they had all come to the same conclusion: if the rock wall contained any clue, it could not be detected by their senses.

Just then, Krysty approached, grimly shaking her head. "I'm coming up empty," she said. "If Doc is anywhere nearby, I can't feel the slightest trace of him."

"But you still think his disappearance is connected to the…disruption you felt?" Ryan asked.

"How could it *not* be?" Krysty shrugged. "The disturbance, the changes in the land we saw during the battle. Then Doc disappears."

"Not coincidence," Jak said. "That for sure."

"Then, what the hell is it?" Ryan gazed at the stark Nebraska landscape, watching as his friends continued to scour the area for a clue to Doc's whereabouts. They were coming up just as empty as Krysty and Jak had.

It was beyond frustrating. In the Deathlands, problems tended to be straightforward: battles in need of fighting; hardships in need of surviving; helping allies deal with tangible threats. A person had to be tough and wily and able to think outside the box…but a person didn't usually have to think outside the bounds of reality. The companions didn't usually have to face the impossible.

"What next?" Jak asked.

Ryan shifted the weight of his Steyr Scout longblaster cradled in his arms. Keeping the weapon at the ready was crucial; if the muties could take them all by surprise once, they could do it again.

"We keep looking. The land here changed before. Mebbe it'll change again, and this time we'll see where Doc went."

"Not give up on friend." Jak nodded firmly. "Always good plan."

"Something has to turn up." Ryan met Krysty's green-eyed gaze, searching for confirmation of his hope.

Krysty smiled. "It always does," she said before turning away to resume her search, leaving Ryan to wonder how much of the conviction in her voice was for his benefit.

AFTER A FEW more hours of searching, sundown came and put an end to it. Going over the same barren ground after nightfall made no sense. If the trail was nonexistent in broad daylight, it wouldn't likely become visible in the beams of flashlights.

Still, the group stayed in the area and pitched camp at the rock wall, in the hope that Doc might reappear.

The companions broke open their packs, dining on MREs they'd scrounged from the redoubt they'd jumped to.

"How long are we going to stay here?" Mildred asked as she threw down her bedroll in the dirt.

"Until we find a lead on what happened to Doc." As he said it, Ryan stole a glance at Krysty, who was also rolling out a sleeping bag. The truth was, they couldn't stay long at all, not if the place was killing Krysty. He wasn't about to risk losing her.

J.B. flashed him a look that said he could see right through him.

"I hope that lead turns up damn soon," the Armorer said.

Ryan nodded. "You and me both."

"Supplies low," Jak said, smacking the side of his backpack for emphasis.

"I know that," Ryan replied.

"Can't build fire," the albino added. "No firewood near."

Ryan nodded. He knew Jak and Ricky had looked hard for it, to no avail. This part of Nebraska—the Sandhills, according to a map in the redoubt—was rich in sand and rock and not much else. If there was a stick of wood or a growing thing anywhere in a five-mile radius, they hadn't come across it yet.

"We'll take it as it comes, like we always do." Ryan met the eyes of his companions, each in turn, projecting all the strength and confidence he could muster. "For now, we need some shut-eye." Gripping his longblaster tightly, he stared into the moonlit night. He didn't ask for anyone's opinion; he was taking the first watch, looking out for muties on the move.

So was J.B. "I kind of hope one of those damn muties shows up." Mini-Uzi in hand, the Armorer walked up to stand beside Ryan. "Mebbe he could give us a lead on Doc."

"You think the muties took him?" asked Ricky, who was sitting with his back against the base of the rock wall, cleaning his Webley Mk VI revolver.

"Good chance of it, if you ask me," J.B. stated. "They seemed to know exactly what changes were coming, and when. It was like they could read the phenomenon."

"Or control it," Mildred suggested. "If that's even possible."

"Why not?" J.B. shrugged. "We know certain people can be attuned to the Earth Mother." He glanced over his shoulder at Krysty. "Why not control her, as well?"

"Whatever they've done, whatever's happening here, it's awful." Krysty scowled and rubbed her temples. "It's wrong. Beyond wrong."

"And Doc's out there alone in the middle of it." Mildred stepped up alongside J.B. and cast her gaze into the night. "Either that, or he's…" Her voice trailed off.

No one wanted to finish her sentence.

Chapter Three

"Am I dead?"

As Doc blinked his eyes open, he could see nothing but darkness. He tossed his head one way, then the other, and the result was the same. More darkness.

But not emptiness. He could feel a solid surface beneath him, like rock, and he could sense some kind of walls around him. "Hello? If this is the afterlife, I'm really not complaining, you know. Life in the Deathlands has rather worn thin, to be perfectly honest." When he spoke, there was no echo; he could tell from the sound of his voice that he was in an enclosed space.

And more than that, he was somewhere dank and damp. He could smell moisture in the air, feel a chill against his skin.

But there was no draft of any kind, no air moving anywhere in that space, not even the faintest breeze.

Wherever he was, it didn't feel as if it was out in the open, which was odd, because that was exactly the last place he could remember being. Out in the open.

Reaching down, Doc felt a cold, damp sheet of smooth stone. Bracing against it, he boosted himself up to a sitting position, instantly regretting it when his head collided with a rock-hard ceiling.

"Ow!" He dropped back down, clutching his aching skull. "That hurt!"

At that exact moment, Doc realized two things: one, he

was still alive and, two, he was in an even smaller space than he'd expected.

These two realizations generated a terrible thought, a possibility that was starting to seem increasingly likely. If he wasn't out in the open, and he wasn't dead...

"Have I been buried alive?" The thought of it made involuntarily clench the pit of his stomach. Fear seized him, as cold and primitive as a stone ax or the plunging beak of an ancient carnivore.

Had the ground opened up and swallowed him, then closed itself over him? Was he doomed to suffocate in this tiny, dark cell in the bowels of the earth?

"Help! Somebody, help me!" As Doc cried out, he scrabbled with his fingers at the ceiling, instinctively trying to dig his way to freedom. But the ceiling was all rock, as unyielding as the stone surface on which he lay.

Panting, Doc dropped his arms at his sides. "Help me!" Even as he shouted, he knew it was in vain. Even if Ryan and the others were directly overhead, they could never hear his wailing through a layer of rock. "Please help me!"

Taking a deep breath of the chilly, damp air, he fought to get control of himself...and won, at least for the moment. He knew panic was never the answer. Calm thinking and resourcefulness were the only qualities that ever saved a person in the damnable Deathlands.

"Perhaps my tools..." Doc reached into the folds of his frock coat, seeking the holster of his LeMat revolver, with no success. Next, he rolled onto his right side, searching the stone around him for the blaster or his ebony swordstick. He did the same on his left side, with the exact same result. He found a hard rock wall within arm's reach, but no revolver and no swordstick.

"I am bereft." Slumping back on the stone, he sighed

loudly. "Without a tool to effect my escape or another mortal soul to offer solace."

Just then, Doc heard a scuffling sound in the direction of his feet. "What now?" He pushed himself up on his elbows, staying low enough that his head wouldn't hit the ceiling. "Rats, I suppose? Some other burrowing vermin come to feast on my flesh?" He reached around for a rock to throw but found nothing. "Begone, vermin!" Noise would have to suffice. "I shall not be your dinner yet!"

The scuffling came closer, got louder. Doc peered toward it but saw nothing in the pitch-blackness.

"Begone, I say!" He drew up his legs, pulling away from whatever was there. "You won't find me an easy prey, I promise you!"

Suddenly, he heard a different sound from the same place, a distinctive sound that could not be mistaken for any other.

Giggling.

Doc's mouth fell open in shock. The question was no longer what was over there—it was who.

That was no vermin scuffling in the darkness. It was a person.

Doc's heart hammered in his chest. He meant to snap out some words of defiance to try to intimidate his giggling visitor.

But before a single word could leave Doc's lips, the visitor scrambled forward. Hands grabbed hold of Doc's ankles and wrenched his legs straight with an iron grip.

Then a voice, high-pitched and girlish in the lightless void, said, "You're mine now. All mine."

Doc gathered his bravado and snapped, "Now, see here!"

But those were the only words he got out before the

person—or thing—in the night dragged him from his stony cell.

And then, all of a sudden, there were many more hands, coming from all directions. And all of them were grabbing at Doc.

Chapter Four

Krysty woke screaming from a deep sleep, her dreams shattered by a lightning bolt of pain.

Her eyes shot open, seeing predawn grayness all around. Dimly, she was aware of other bodies stirring on the ground nearby, snapped awake by the sound of her screams.

Then another bolt slashed through her mind, throwing her into a mindless seizure of agony.

As she writhed on the ground, she heard footsteps running toward her and familiar voices calling out—Ryan's, J.B.'s, Mildred's. But Krysty couldn't sort out the words they were saying or attempt to respond to them. She was too consumed with pain and the crazed need to make it stop...and one other thing.

Dread. An overwhelming feeling of dread at whatever phenomenon the pain might be signaling, just as it had signaled the earlier onslaught that had swept away Doc.

Suddenly the pain abated, and Krysty slumped. Heaving for breath, she fought to clear the haze that had shrouded her senses and stolen her ability to function normally.

"Krysty!" Ryan knelt at her left side, gazing worriedly down at her.

Krysty felt him gripping her hand and suddenly realized he'd been holding it for a while, tight enough to give her pins and needles.

"I'm okay, I'm okay." She nodded weakly. "Just another one of those attacks."

"Easy does it, Krysty." Mildred knelt at her right side, touching the back of a hand to Krysty's forehead. "Deep, slow breaths, honey. In and out, in and out."

"What coming?" Jak's voice rose up from somewhere nearby. "Last time fit, muties attack and rock wall appear."

"I don't know." Krysty closed her eyes and concentrated, focusing her mind the way she did when she called on the power of Gaia, the Earth Mother. Reaching out, she strained to find some thread of the force that had triggered her pain, some whisper of whatever had brought on the bolts of pain.

But there was nothing. Just emptiness and stillness.

Or was there something after all? As Krysty continued to strain, she felt what might have been a faint tension, pressing in the distance.

Scowling, she struggled to tighten her focus even more, to home in on whatever was out there. At the same time, she tried to steel herself against the next bolt of pain that might come.

"Look like find something," Jak said.

"Not sure yet." Krysty gritted her teeth and cast her net as wide as she could. Was she tuning something in or feeling something that wasn't there? She couldn't tell.

"Krysty." Ryan leaned closer. "We should get you out of here. You said this place is killing you."

"No, wait." Krysty sat up and raised a hand. The tension was definitely there, as if something were being pushed, or pulled...

Or stretched.

"Everybody!" Krysty snapped her eyes open and leaped to her feet. "Get out of here, *now*!"

"You heard her!" Ryan shouted. "Move! Out the way we came in!"

But it was already too late. Krysty knew it instantly,

as the tension she'd felt building suddenly released, like the string of a bow.

Or a fault line in earthquake country.

Before anyone could start running, a familiar wave of force crashed into Krysty. She hung suspended for an instant, her whole body quivering, and then the force let go, whipping her around to slam into Ryan.

As the two of them stumbled, barely holding each other erect, Krysty saw the ground in front of them flutter like a bedsheet. She heard a low hum, followed by a rumble that coursed up through her feet and shook every bone in her body.

Then a flash of light erupted before her like a second sun blazing to life. As the light faded, between the blur of spots left pulsing in her eyes, Krysty saw the thing she'd dreaded, the latest phenomenon signaled by the pain.

The ground was opening up.

"Sinkhole!" As the word left Ryan's lips, the hole expanded rapidly. In seconds, it was big enough to swallow up a good-size war wag, and still growing at breakneck speed.

The companions were on the move, scattering fast, but not fast enough. Krysty could feel the ground dropping away, disintegrating hot on her heels as she sprinted alongside Ryan.

Suddenly, the hole caught up with her. Like sand in an hourglass, the once-firm ground slid out from under her. Just like that, her feet had nothing solid beneath them, and she started to fall.

Before she could plunge into the widening chasm, though, Ryan's strong hands seized her arm and hauled her forward. It was all the help she needed. With firm footing restored—at least for the moment—Krysty was able to bolt out of reach of the hungry pit.

Mildred wasn't as lucky. She screamed in alarm, and Krysty flashed a look in her direction as she ran.

Some twenty feet away, the predark physician was almost completely in the hole. Only her head and shoulders remained above the rim. She was holding on to a hump of rock, her body dangling into the pit as it continued to grow around her.

Instantly, Krysty changed direction and raced toward her friend. She knew Ryan would follow, but she had to prepare as if she alone would mount this rescue.

Dashing toward the dissolving rim of the hole, Krysty focused her thoughts on the familiar power she drew from in times of emergency. Gaia, the Earth Mother, the world itself, provided a wellspring of energy for the few who knew how to tap it, and Krysty counted herself among their number.

Chanting her prayer quickly, she made contact with the power of Gaia, the potent force residing all around her. Embracing the power, she drew a portion of it into her, feeling it churn and crackle within her like a ball of lightning.

Then, as she and the crumbling rim raced toward each other, she let the power explode and infuse every cell of her being.

Leaping just as the rim collapsed in front of her, Krysty landed on the peak of the rock that Mildred clung to. Balancing on the balls of her feet on that peak, Krysty ducked and grabbed hold of Mildred's upper arms. With one heave, as if she was lifting a child, she pulled Mildred up.

As Mildred looped her arms tightly around Krysty's neck, the redhead turned, part of her mind wondering if she'd made a fatal error. The bank, which was still dissolving, was nearly thirty feet away.

It would be a long jump, even in her heightened, Gaia-empowered state, but it would only get longer with each second she hesitated. Her odds of survival would only get lower.

So Krysty gathered the power within her and crouched, coiling her muscles for the leap. The bank continued to recede.

Then she took a deep breath, focused the Gaia force and leaped.

Even with the weight of Mildred on her back, Krysty felt light as she sailed through the air. Miraculously, she overtook the dissolving rim and kept going, past the point where the sinkhole might take her as soon as she touched down.

When she did land, Ryan and J.B. were waiting for her. The second Krysty put down Mildred, J.B. had his arm around the woman's shoulders, urging her forward to flee the approaching pit.

Ryan did the same for Krysty. "Can you keep going?" he asked as they ran.

"Yes." Whenever Krysty tapped Gaia's power, she always went through a slump afterward, as if the superhuman exertion had unnaturally exhausted her. But perhaps because of the continued danger, she hadn't gotten to that point yet.

She and Ryan ran onward after J.B. and Mildred, trying to get past the limits of the sinkhole's expansion…if there were any. Up ahead, Jak and Ricky had stopped running and were waving their arms, urging them on.

Suddenly, a fresh bolt of pain shot through Krysty's skull, and she stumbled. She tried to keep running at full tilt, but another bolt caught her, and she stumbled again, heading for a fall.

Ryan's arms stopped her from hitting the ground. In one smooth movement, he scooped her off her feet and kept going, carrying her away from the sinkhole.

Just then, a shock wave plowed into both of them, nearly

bowling them over. Krysty saw the ground around them flow like liquid, and she knew what was coming next.

A blinding flash lit the landscape. Ryan reeled with Krysty in his arms, teetering in the light, and then the flare was suddenly snuffed out.

Instantly, Krysty could feel that the air was different. Everything was quieter and more still than before, with good reason.

The constant rushing of the collapsing ground had ended.

"It stopped." Looking back, she saw that the sinkhole had finally stopped expanding, leaving the farthest reach of the rim at about thirty feet from them.

"Best news we've had all day," Ryan said. "But why the hell did it start?"

Krysty concentrated, trying to probe their surroundings for a clue, but then the post-Gaia weakness finally struck. Her thoughts scattered like ripples from a pebble tossed into a pond, and she slumped in Ryan's arms.

Mildred was at her side in a heartbeat. "Are you all right?"

Krysty nodded weakly. "Just worn-out."

"You just let me know if you need anything." Mildred patted her cheek lightly.

"What about you?" J.B. put a hand on Mildred's shoulder, gazing at her with deep concern. "Are you all right?"

"I'm fine," Mildred said. "Not a big fan of this place, but I'm fine."

"It hellhole," Jak stated. "We stay longer, it take us like took Doc."

"Mebbe we should split up," J.B. suggested. "One group could get Krysty out of here before the next disruption while the other group stays here and keeps looking for Doc."

"Or," shouted Ricky, who was standing on the rim of

the crater, pointing into the distance, "we could all follow that."

Ryan carried Krysty to the rim, and the others joined them. As Krysty looked where Ricky was pointing, she saw what he was talking about.

J.B. blew his breath out in a low whistle. "Dark night!"

"Maybe one good thing came out of that crap storm," Mildred said.

In the distance beyond the giant sinkhole, Krysty saw that a channel now ran through the surface of the earth—a rough-hewn canal filled with a glowing red liquid. The red substance churned and bubbled, shedding plumes of rippling gray steam that revealed, at a distance, just how hot the channel's contents had to be. Meaning the red liquid could most likely be only one thing.

"Lava," Krysty said.

"Magically appearing in the middle of the Sandhills, where there's zero volcanic activity," J.B. commented.

"That we know of," Ryan corrected. But how the lava had gotten there wasn't the important part, and they all knew it. More important by far was what it might do for them.

And whom it might lead them to.

"Don't you think it could be a trail?" Ricky asked. "Mebbe it's pointing at the middle of all this."

J.B. nodded. "The epicenter of the effect."

"And that might be where they're taking Doc," Ricky added.

Ryan nodded. "Might be, at that."

"Seem like long shot to me," Jak said. "How know that where taken?"

"We don't," J.B. replied. "But we don't have any better ideas, do we?"

"I think it's worth a try." Ryan looked down at Krysty,

still resting in his arms. "But mebbe we should still get you out of here."

Krysty shook her head. "I don't want us to split up." She shifted in his grip, signaling that she wanted him to let her down, which he did. "I can handle whatever comes our way. Don't worry."

Ryan held her gaze for a long moment, reading all that remained unsaid between them. Krysty knew he was aware she was making a sacrifice, and that it would cost her, but she would gladly do it if it meant finding Doc.

And she knew he was well aware of one other fact as well: once she decided to do something, there could be no stopping her.

"All right, then." Ryan nodded. "Let's gather up what's left of our gear and get moving. The longer Doc's out there on his own, the less likely it is that we'll ever see him again."

Chapter Five

Doc blinked furiously as he was dragged from the pitch-blackness and dumped in a space awash in bright white light. For a long moment, he couldn't see a thing beyond a few dim outlines in the flaring brilliance.

Then, as his eyes adjusted, things slowly took shape around him. He saw that he was in a round, stone-walled chamber, open to the sunlight overhead. He lay on a dirt floor at the feet of a group of muties, unarmed and at their mercy.

The question was, what did they want with him? And why had they brought him here, wherever *here* was?

"Oh, dear." As Doc looked around, the muties stared back at him with great interest. They couldn't take their eyes off him; even as they giggled and tittered in childlike voices, their stares never left him for an instant.

At least they didn't seem to be exuding hostility. Doc smiled as he sat there, and many of them smiled back at him. The crimson skin of their faces crinkled around their mouths and the corners of their eyes, suggesting a response that was the polar opposite of hostile.

"Well, then." Doc slowly got to his feet. "Perhaps I have made some new friends after all. Perhaps this has all been an unfortunate mistake."

Just then, a familiar high-pitched voice piped up over the noise from the crowd. "Not a mistake at all. And we are *old* friends, not *new* ones."

Instantly, Doc recognized the voice as that of the first being who had grabbed him in the lightless stone cell. Turning to look at him, Doc saw a mutie with skin as red as a burning ember. He stood taller than the other muties by at least a head, and wore different clothing, as well. The muties in the crowd were dressed in scavenged predark clothes, while this one wore a gray uniform and boots that were practically in mint condition. Was he a leader, perhaps?

"I am afraid you have me at a disadvantage." Doc bowed quickly at the waist. "Dr. Theophilus Algernon Tanner, at your service." Straightening, he raised his eyebrows at the apparent leader of the muties. "And what shall I call *you*, pray tell?"

The leader sighed and shook his head. "What have they done to you?"

"They? They, who?"

"Your captors, of course. The ones who took you from us." The leader spread his arms wide. He held Doc's silver lion's-head swordstick in his left hand. Doc's LeMat revolver was holstered at his hip. "We took you back, but they must have done something to you first. Taken your memories or senses. I only hope they didn't ruin you for your holy work."

"What sort of holy work is that?" Doc asked, marveling at his command of the English language.

The leader just stared at him with apparent pity and worry. "Have no fear," he said coolly. "We will heal you, my friend."

Doc cleared his throat, uncertain of what to say or do next. The only thing he knew for sure what that he'd never seen these particular muties before in his life. "If, as you say, we are friends, perhaps you could humor me. Perhaps you could tell me your name."

"Though it hurts me to have to tell you, I'll do it," the

mutie said. "My name is Exo. And yours is Dr. William Hammersmith."

"I suppose it is." Doc shrugged. "What else can you tell me about myself, friend Exo?"

"You have been a naughty boy, Dr. Hammersmith." Exo ticked Doc's ebony swordstick back and forth. "It's a good thing you're so important and such a good friend."

"Naughty?" Doc straightened. Without the swordstick and LeMat revolver, he felt utterly naked. "In what way was I naughty?"

Exo pulled a stick of red-and-white-striped peppermint candy out of the vest pocket of his uniform. "You ran away. If you hadn't done that, the interlopers never would have taken you."

"I see." Doc nodded, thinking how appropriate it was that his doppelganger had a penchant for escape. Doc himself, after being snatched through time from the nineteenth century to the twentieth, had tried numerous times to get away from his whitecoat captors. "And you say these interlopers seized me against my will?"

Exo peeled back the plastic wrapper and slid the candy stick between his lips. "Why else would you have stayed away so long, leaving your critical work unfinished?"

"Hmm." Doc frowned and rubbed the gray stubble on his chin. "And what is this work to which you refer, precisely?"

"Perfecting the Shift, of course."

"Ah, the Shift." Doc nodded, then tipped his head to one side and squinted. "Which is, of course...?"

Exo took the candy stick out of his mouth and swept it in a semicircle. "All around us! The deadliest place in the Deathlands!" Stomping forward, he jabbed the swordstick at Doc's chest. "And *you* are making it even *deadlier*."

The mutie's breath was rancid enough to choke a horse, but Doc stood his ground. "Is that so?"

Exo narrowed his gaze. "I can see by the look on your face that you still don't remember it all. But no matter." The mutie reached over and cupped the right side of Doc's face in his hand. "You still have time for it to come back to you. The journey to the core will take days, and we have other business to conduct on the way."

Doc couldn't help leaning his head away from Exo's hand. "What business is that?"

Exo laughed that high giggle of his, the one that so belied his threatening personality. "Teaching your kidnappers a lesson, dear Doctor. Teaching them the price of intruding in the Shift, where they are not welcome and never will be."

He was talking about Ryan and the others, and Doc knew it. "What price is that?"

Exo paused a moment, his face completely unreadable. Then, suddenly, he lunged forward and shouted in Doc's face, "Death! Torture, mutilation and death at the hands of the shifters!"

Doc cleared his throat and took a step back. "I do not suppose you would consider letting bygones be bygones?"

Exo giggled and tossed away his candy stick. This time, when he lunged, he threw Doc down on the ground and pummeled him with his fist and the head of the swordstick until Doc started fading again.

"The Children of the Shift *never* forgive!" As Exo said it, the other muties roared in agreement. "We understand only one thing! Swift and brutal retribution without hesitation or mercy!"

It was then that Doc lost consciousness. His last thought before he went under was if this was how Exo treated his friends, then Ryan and the others were really in for it.

Chapter Six

Ricky tossed a rock into the bubbling lava and watched it melt in an instant, casting up a plume of steam.

"That's some hot stuff, man." He elbowed Jak, who walked beside him at the front of the group. "Get too close, and it'll give you a sunburn."

"No want get close." Jak was a good thirty paces from the lava channel, where he'd stayed since the team had started hiking. He was only too happy to let Ricky stay between him and the superheated flow. "Enemy not come that direction."

Ricky raised an index finger. "Unless things change again, that is. It happened before."

Jak snorted. "We ready. Learned lesson." He smiled grimly. "Expect unexpected."

Just then, Ryan trotted forward from the middle ranks. "Guys." They parted, and he formed up between them. "What's the good word?"

"All quiet for now," Ricky said.

"All *hot*," Jak added.

"What about back there?" Ricky bobbed his head toward the rest of the column. "Anything we should know about?"

Ryan shook his head. "Krysty hasn't gotten a signal since we set out. No seizures, no funny feelings, nothing."

"That good," Jak said, "for her."

"Not so good if we want to find Doc, though," Ricky

stated. "If we run out of lava channel, we'll need to find another way to pick up the trail."

"My gut tells me something will turn up." Ryan narrowed his eyes and scanned the scenery—clusters of sandy humps rolling in all directions, split up ahead by the arrow-straight river of lava. "As crazy as this place is, I'll be more surprised if something doesn't turn up soon."

Ricky kicked up a spray of sand with the toe of his boot. "Why do you think it's like that? This place? Why do you think it's so crazy?"

"If Doc was here, he'd have some kind of scientific explanation. As it is…" Ryan sighed. "Krysty says something awful happened to the earth around here, but, you know, the same could be said for much of the Deathlands."

"Skydark cause somehow?" Jak asked. "War aftereffect?"

"Or something since then?" Ricky queried. "Some kind of science project gone wrong, mebbe?"

"Any of the above." Ryan shrugged. "Right now, I guess it doesn't much matter. We just need to find Doc and get the hell out of here before the phenomenon kills Krysty."

"Survive first." Jak nodded in agreement. "Explain later."

"Hmm." Ricky stared at the lava-filled channel as he kept marching along. "What if it's all in our minds? Some kind of mass hallucination?"

"Someone mess with heads? Not first time." Jak thought about it for a moment, then pointed at the channel with the barrel of his Colt Python. "How about dip toe in there and tell if illusion?"

"You first." Ricky laughed. "But what if it *is* an illusion? We wouldn't know it, would we?"

The one-eyed man blinked at him. "Krysty might." He frowned. "Which might be the reason she keeps getting pounded by these psychic attacks, come to think of it."

"We stop attacks sooner or later." Jak popped one of his leaf-bladed throwing knives out of the spring-loaded scabbard in his right sleeve.

"Let's stay alert to all possibilities." Ryan tightened his grip on his longblaster. "Until we learn otherwise."

"My possibilities always same." Jak stabbed the air once more with a nasty flourish. "Cut and shoot till run out things to cut and shoot."

"I think I speak for all of us," Ricky stated, "when I say that's a plan we can all get behind."

Suddenly, a loud hissing noise in the distance caught everyone's attention. They swung in the direction of the noise, and they all saw the source at the same instant.

Ricky shook his head at the sight. "What the hell is that?"

"Something I'm pretty sure shouldn't be here," Ryan told him.

Some fifty yards in the distance, on the same side of the lava channel as Ricky and the others, a plume of steam shot straight up from the ground, climbing at least thirty feet into the sky.

"First lava in Nebraska, now geysers," Ryan said. "What next? A volcano?"

"Careful what wish for," Jak stated.

Just then, a second geyser erupted from the ground on the opposite side of the channel, ten yards closer than the first.

That was enough to drive Ryan into action. "Incoming!" He shouted the words over his shoulder, making sure everyone behind him could hear.

But they didn't really need to. Just as Ryan yelled his warning, Krysty let loose with her latest bloodcurdling scream.

"Form up!" Ryan charged back to Krysty's side, leaving Jak and Ricky to hold the point of the column.

"Ready test theory?" Jak cocked the Python with one hand and balanced a throwing knife by the tip with the other. "Not fight back, mebbe hallucination not kill?"

Ricky's eyes danced over the landscape, watching for the first hostile movement. "Not a chance."

"Thought you say that," Jak said. "Not believe own theory, huh?"

"I didn't say that," Ricky told him. "But even if this is all a hallucination, there's no way I'm going to let it kick my ass."

Chapter Seven

Ryan swept his longblaster left and right, waiting for whoever was coming—or whatever unnatural phenomenon was on the way, in which case, the blaster would be useless.

Behind him, Mildred supported Krysty with her left arm while brandishing her .38 ZKR 551 revolver in her right hand. "Another geyser at two o'clock."

"I see it." Ryan wondered if the geysers were a prelude to an attack or disaster...or perhaps the only manifestation of the phenomenon this time. "That makes three."

"At least we're out in the open," said J.B., who was at the rear flank with his Mini-Uzi at the ready. "Not too many hills in this spot, either. Not many places for an ambush."

"No shock wave yet..." Krysty forced out the words between clenched teeth. "No flash...of light..."

"So the worst might still be coming." J.B. checked the Smith & Wesson M-4000 scattergun slung at his back and reassured himself it would be there when he needed it. Then he straightened his fedora hat, tipping the brim up just enough to clear his line of sight.

"Oh, no." Krysty sucked in her breath. "It's coming. I *feel* it."

J.B. felt nothing, then suddenly he did. Like both times before, he felt caught between forces that were pulling and pushing him simultaneously. His heart hammered, because he knew what was next.

He tried to brace himself, but the shock wave still blew

him around and threw him down on one knee. There was a hum, then a rumble, and he squinted against the flash he knew was coming, but it did him no good. The light still caught him by surprise; he clamped his eyes shut, but it still seared his vision, replacing the texture and color of sight with a curtain of featureless white.

J.B. held his Mini-Uzi tightly, though, and listened hard for the sounds of approaching enemies. He knew his comrades' footsteps by heart; those of attacking strangers would stand out like drumbeats in a parade of flutes.

But the only new sound he heard had nothing to do with footsteps. It was a creaking sound, coming from nearby... *very* nearby. It was like the creaking of a tall tree as it bent and shifted in a stiff wind.

He listened closer as his eyes began to clear. The sound was getting louder, even closer than he had thought.

Then he felt the ground move, and he leaped aside. The creaking was as plain as day now; it had been coming from under his own feet.

His vision cleared just in time to see a spike of white stone shoot up from the ground where he'd been standing. It pushed straight upward, stopping only when it reached a height of more than ten feet.

J.B. blew out his breath in a quick sigh of relief. If he hadn't jumped when he did, he would have ended up speared on the tip of that spike.

As he stood there, he heard shouting from his teammates and spun, swinging his Mini-Uzi into firing position. But the threat they were reacting to wouldn't be fazed by a barrage of 9 mm rounds.

It was another pale pillar, bigger than the first, rising from the ground among Ryan, Krysty and Mildred. Luckily, no one had been impaled by the monstrous spike as it leaped toward the sky.

Again and again, he heard the creaking sounds, followed by the whoosh of sand giving way to climbing pillars of stone. He saw one of them flash upward near Ricky, sending him rolling toward the lava channel, his pell-mell tumble halted just in time by a sprinting Jak.

"So it's these things now?" Mildred hollered. "Stalagmites outside of a cave?"

Just as she said it, another spike shot up from the ground near J.B. He backpedaled out of its way, then turned in a circle, trying to decide where to go next. If those things could punch out of the ground anywhere without warning, there wasn't a safe place to be found.

Furthermore, what if they weren't the only threat? "Look alive!" he called out to the rest of the team. "Get ready for incoming!" He knew it was good advice. There were no signs of attacking muties, and they hadn't come when the sinkhole opened up that morning, but they'd used the upheaval once before to attack.

Looking around at the landscape, J.B. saw many more stalagmites bursting aboveground, studding the plain and even stabbing at crazy angles from distant hillsides. Before his eyes, the sparse terrain was becoming a forest of pale towers, each one gleaming like a predark bleached church spire in the blazing midday sun.

What had once been mostly open space with few places to hide was quickly turning into the perfect setting for a sneak attack by enemy forces.

In which case, J.B. and his comrades wouldn't be hard to find at all. Krysty couldn't help herself; she kept screaming as her inner torment continued.

"Anybody else get the feeling we're sitting ducks?" J.B. shouted.

Just then, Ryan opened up with his best take-charge voice. "Three groups! Krysty and Mildred in the middle! Jak and I at twelve o'clock, J.B. and Ricky at six o'clock!"

"Seen anyone yet?" Ricky asked as he took up position by the nearest stalagmite.

"Nope." J.B. set up on the other side of the same pillar, facing in the opposite direction. They needed to catch whoever came at them from either side and be ready to pivot quickly to help the others. "You?"

"Just the ones in my imagination." Ricky braced his shoulder against the stone pillar and slowly combed the barrel of his De Lisle carbine from side to side. "But they have to be coming, don't they?"

"Indubitably, as Doc might say." J.B. listened for approaching footsteps but just heard more of the distant creaking and whooshing. The stalagmite forest's growth spurt seemed to be nowhere near an end.

Then, suddenly, there was a loud creaking from just a few feet away. J.B. turned with weapon in hand, expecting another spike to erupt from the ground, but he got more than he counted on this time.

A fresh spike did indeed launch skyward with a whooshing sound of displaced sand. It was well away from J.B. and Ricky, so neither of them was at risk of being speared, but they were both in very real danger nonetheless.

For there was a crimson-skinned mutie rising up along with it, one arm wrapped around the pillar's pale girth, the other arm bracing a slightly rusted AK-47 assault longblaster that was pointing at J.B.'s head.

Chapter Eight

In predark days, Mildred had been an award-winning free shooter. Being cryogenically frozen for a century and thawed years later hadn't diminished her marksmanship skills one bit.

Which was why, when she saw her beloved J.B. in danger, she was able to move so decisively. Through a gap between stalagmites, she cranked off a fast, tricky shot with her target revolver that punched a hole dead center in the mutie's forehead.

As the mutie dropped from the stalagmite he'd been riding, J.B. whirled and waved at Mildred. Through their years of traversing the Deathlands, they'd both saved each other's lives too many times to count. It was second nature these days, something you expected from friends and comrades.

Or, in the case of Mildred and J.B., it was something you expected from lovers. Each new nightmare they faced brought them closer together and made them fight all the harder to keep what they'd found.

Even in hell itself, it turned out, it was good to have something to fight for. Ryan and Krysty certainly felt the same way.

Though at the rate Krysty was going, Mildred wondered if she would live out the day. As the predark doctor turned back to her after blowing away the mutie, she saw that Krysty had slid to the ground at the base of the closest spike. She was crouching there, screaming with eyes squeezed shut, hands gripping her temples with desperate ferocity.

Unfortunately, Mildred had no time to tend to her. Before she could drop to Krysty's side, she heard the telltale creaking and whoosh of another rising spike in her immediate vicinity.

Spinning in its direction, she saw the latest pillar shooting high and fast with a pair of crimson arms looped around it, supporting a mutie who was clinging from the other side.

As the pillar punched upward, the mutie swung around and released one hand to flash a .38 revolver from a holster on his hip. Almost instantly, he started firing, tracing a path that would soon cut a swath across Mildred's torso.

Springing into action, Mildred launched herself away from the stalagmite where Krysty huddled, drawing the mutie's fire. She heard rounds spitting into the sand behind her as she bolted for the nearest spike, intending to use it for cover.

Another mutie happened to step out from behind the spike, wielding a .380 ACP Glock pistol.

Mildred hesitated an instant, then cut suddenly left, just as the second mutie opened fire. Rounds traced her path as she ran, closing in with each shot.

With two muties blasting away at her, Mildred needed an opportunity and found one. She heard the creaking noise again, followed by the whooshing, and she pinpointed the source: ten feet away, the tip of a new spike was nosing out of the sand.

Reaching deep, Mildred picked up her pace, charging straight for the soon-to-rise spike. Bullets hissing behind her, she leaped forward just as the spike began to rise.

A second later, and she would have been pierced through the belly, but she cleared it. The spike jumped upward just as her body sailed out of its path.

As Mildred hit the ground and rolled, she heard bullets zinging off the newborn pillar. Stopping her roll, she leaped to her feet and dived behind it.

Then, popping halfway out from behind the pale spike, she quickly found the second mutie, sighted in on him and pulled the trigger. A crimson blossom erupted on his chest, and he went down.

As for the first mutie who'd swung around and driven Mildred away from Krysty, he was down for the count. Peering between pillars, Mildred saw Krysty standing over him, whaling away at him with her powerful fists.

"You go, girl." Mildred smiled grimly, then heard a sound and whipped around just in time for someone else's fist to slam into the side of her head.

Mildred's vision went dark before she could get a look at her attacker. She was dimly aware of her legs folding up underneath her, her body collapsing, and then…she was off in the nothingness, the perfect black vacuum of absolute unconsciousness.

Chapter Nine

Ryan and Jak fought back-to-back, blasting away at the muties working their way toward them through the forest of spikes.

Jak's .357 Magnum Colt Python coughed out a round, and a mutie screamed in agony. "Another bite dust." Jak spun the revolver around his index finger, then blew on the barrel as if puffing away smoke. "Jak six, muties zero."

Ryan snorted and kept sweeping his longblaster from side to side. "But the bastards keep coming." He thought he saw movement and flicked the barrel toward a spike, then realized it was a false alarm and continued his sweep. "How the hell many of them are there anyway?"

"More are, more fun for me." Jak cocked the Python and went back to combing the surroundings with his bright red eyes. "Hey, muties!" he shouted.

As if on cue, a mutie leaped between distant pillars, crossing from one to the other. Jak didn't fire, but he fixed his gaze on the mutie's new cover like a dog watching a fox's den.

Just then, Ryan heard a blaster shot fired nearby. He listened to the echo, trying to tell what specific weapon had put it out there, but the spikes upset the acoustics, and he couldn't read the weapon's signature.

"I hope the others are all right." With the shape Krysty was in, he was worrying more than usual, second-guessing his call to split up the team.

"Down one man, muties surrounding, ammo low." Jak grinned a wolf's grin. "Of course all right." The mutie twitched from behind his pillar, and Jak jerked his blaster's barrel to follow. "Just another Deathlands day."

Suddenly, a body darted from behind another spike at ten o'clock and ran into Ryan's field of vision. He caught it out of the corner of his eye, swung his longblaster around to fire…and lost his shot. Whoever was over there disappeared behind another pale column.

"More company," Ryan said quietly. "I think they're taking up position, getting ready to move."

"Want move first?" Jak asked. "Or stay sitting ducks?"

Ryan thought it over for all of a second. "Let's move out and work our way back in." He pointed toward the cover of the figure he'd glimpsed a moment ago and headed in that direction.

"Getting bored one place anyway." Jak headed in the opposite direction.

As Ryan worked his way between jutting spikes, he walked as softly as he could, keeping his longblaster at the ready. He paused at each fresh spike, ducking quickly past it to check for muties sheltering behind, then sliding around the column to take that shelter himself.

It unnerved him a little when he heard Krysty shrieking in the distance, but he kept his head and kept moving. He knew her well enough to realize that wasn't the kind of cry she made when under physical attack. The only cry she ever uttered in battle was a raging war whoop as she shattered bones and drew blood with abandon.

Ryan glided around an especially thick pillar, then stopped and flicked back behind it. Two muties were creeping past on the other side, one carrying a sawed-off shotgun, the other a remade M-16 fitted with a rusty bayonet.

Ryan breathed slowly and adjusted his grip on the Scout

longblaster. Then he eased himself around the pillar and froze. Suddenly, a bayonet and a double-barreled sawed-off were staring him in the face.

The muties had gotten the jump on him. They had to have heard or sensed him, maybe spotted his shadow, and doubled back. Now Ryan was royally screwed.

"Surrender!" the mutie with the sawed-off shouted. "Throw your weapon aside and get on the ground."

"You first." Ryan didn't blink. He had the Scout aimed squarely at the bayonet-wielding mutie's abdomen. As long as he kept it there, he still had a chance of keeping them off balance.

The mutie with the M-16 drew the blaster back, getting ready to ram the bayonet into Ryan.

At that moment, the mutie's head exploded. His body crumpled backward, dead before it hit the ground.

While the other mutie gaped, Ryan seized his opportunity. Without a heartbeat's hesitation, he cranked off a shot, putting a round right through his head.

The mutie looked at Ryan with wide-eyed amazement, making a move to raise his shotgun, but he didn't quite make it. His body slumped atop the other mutie's, splattering blood and gore in all directions.

Thirty yards off, a woman stood between two pillars.

Even from a distance, Ryan could see that she was more than six feet tall. Her black leather jumpsuit was tight enough to reveal the muscular lines of her body; her breasts were large, but otherwise she was whipcord lean.

As for her platinum blonde hair, it was tied back in a ponytail, all but for a single black braid that hung from her left temple.

Even to a man like Ryan, whose heart belonged to his soul mate, this woman was an impressive sight. Equally impressive was the weapon in her hands, though it was pointed in his direction: a Heckler & Koch G-36 automatic longblaster, complete with hundred-round drum magazine.

Without a word, she started walking toward him. She looked neither right nor left, as if she didn't fear being gunned down while leaving her cover behind. She just kept her eyes fixed on Ryan with cold and single-minded intensity.

"Nice shooting," Ryan said when she got within ten yards of him. "Thanks for the assist."

The woman did not say a word as she stalked up to him. Even when she stopped, fewer than four feet away, she remained silent.

That gave Ryan time to take in her features at close range. Her eyes were icy gray like mist, glittering in a ray of sunlight washing over her from above. Her cheekbones were high, her nose angular, her lips full, dark crimson and pressed tightly together.

"You." She was taller than he'd thought—six foot four at least—and looked down her nose at him when she spoke. "Who are you?" Her voice was deep.

"My name is Ryan Cawdor." Ryan nodded once, curtly, at her. "And who are you?"

"Why are you in the Shift?" the woman asked.

Ryan couldn't help noticing that she hadn't lowered her longblaster. "Why are *you* here?" The less he revealed at the moment, the better. For all he knew, the woman might be in league with the people who'd taken Doc.

"You brought a team." She bobbed her head to one side. "You are looking for something."

Ryan didn't know what to think of her. Was that arrogance in her eyes, suspicion or just frosty appraisal?

"What's this 'Shift' you just mentioned?"

"You're slow, aren't you?" She sneered a little, then moved her head in an arc from right to left, taking in her surroundings. "The Shift is the land of a million changes."

Ryan narrowed his eyes. "Is that so?" In that instant, he decided he didn't like her, though he still wasn't sure if she was necessarily malicious. "Thanks for finally answering one of my questions."

The woman cocked her head left like a big carnivorous bird about to pounce. "Union."

Ryan scowled. "What?"

"That is my name. So now I have answered two." Leaning closer, still with the Heckler & Koch between them, she glared at him. "And you have still answered only one, Ryan Cawdor."

Just as Ryan was starting to wonder if he might need to make some kind of deadly move, Krysty screamed again. Jerking to attention, Ryan looked in the direction of her cry.

At which point, he heard the chattering of weapons somewhere in the same vicinity.

He pushed forward, and Union backed off. "I need to go," he said, swinging up the Scout.

As he charged past her, Ryan hoped Union wouldn't shoot him in the back, and she didn't. But he did hear her running after him, her feet flicking through the sand in counterpoint to his own.

He wondered, as he ran, exactly what she had in mind and which of them was most likely to survive it.

Chapter Ten

As Krysty screamed and writhed on the ground, three hostile muties cautiously approached, staring down at her, which was exactly what she wanted them to do.

This time, her screams were all phony, and she was playing possum to draw them. Until then, they'd been hiding behind nearby spikes, popping off potshots.

But now they were out in the open, surrounding their prey, never imagining that they were her prey.

Krysty twisted in the sand, kicking and thrashing. She let out one more howl of agony, an earsplitting shriek that made the muties wince.

Then she suddenly fell still. She let herself collapse, becoming inert as if she were dead.

Keeping her eyes open but motionless, she lay there as the muties leaned closer, sizing up her condition. They were wondering what to do, if their job was done in this case or if they needed to finish her off.

One of them poked her hip with his toe. The long nail on it jabbed her, but she forced herself to remain still.

Suddenly she exploded into action.

Lashing out her left leg, she drove the heel of her boot into the bare ankle of the mutie who had kicked her. As he squealed in pain, Krysty sprang to her feet.

From that moment on, it was no-holds-barred combat. Krysty was tall and muscular, and could hold her own in any combat situation. She had holstered her Glock for the ploy, and couldn't draw it before one of the muties would get off a shot.

In a whirlwind of motion, she danced among them with arms and legs flying, chopping them down like a scythe through wheat.

Enraged, one of them came back fast, springing from the ground where she'd thrown him, but his frantic swings were no match for her rock-solid defense. Krysty dodged every blow he attempted, then knocked him back hard with a high kick to the face. This time, he didn't go down, but she could see he'd blacked out with his eyes open. She followed through with a blow to his chest, and he toppled backward, as straight as a tree.

Just like that, the tables were turned. Instead of three muties staring down at her, Krysty was staring down at them. Every one of them was out cold, and she was still fully alert and ready for more action.

Ryan charged out of the forest of spikes.

"I knew you'd be fine." He grinned as he reached her.

"I certainly hope you didn't think I needed help."

Ryan snorted. "I know better. By the way, we've got company."

A tall blonde in a black leather jumpsuit strolled out from behind a stout pillar.

"She calls herself Union." Ryan turned and watched as the woman strode toward them. "She helped me out with that automatic longblaster of hers."

Krysty got an eyeful of her big blaster and nodded once. "Good for her."

"According to her, this place is called the Shift," said Ryan. "Though she didn't tell me much more than that."

Krysty narrowed her eyes. "Whose side is she on? Did she tell you that much?"

Union looked and sounded aloof to the point of arrogance. "Whoever isn't trying to kill me, I suppose."

"And we're just supposed to trust you?" Krysty asked.

Union shrugged. Krysty could have sworn she was stifling a yawn. "Just don't try to kill me, and we'll be okay."

Krysty doubted it but shrugged in kind. "Sounds like a plan," she said, though it didn't, really. She didn't imagine for a second that Union was worthy of her trust. She didn't think the woman had any intention of allying herself with them.

But Krysty and her team were in the shit as always, and their options were limited. Trust her or back away—those were the only two choices she could think of at the moment.

"All right, then." She slumped and rested her hands on her knees. "Let's table the buddy-buddy stuff until after we put down the mutie army. Agreed?"

Union shrugged as if she couldn't care less and raised the H&K. "Go time?"

"Suit yourself." Ryan shrugged, too, then shot a wink at Krysty. "Whatever floats your boat."

Even weakened as she was, Krysty managed a chuckle at that one.

Just then, footsteps scuffed through the nearby sand. Ryan and Union whirled with weapons at the ready, but it was Jak, not a mutie, who marched out from between spikes.

"Back off the trigger," Ryan snapped, dropping the Scout's barrel. "He's with us."

Scowling, Union hesitated, then slowly lowered her weapon.

"Who this?" Jak asked.

"I was just going to ask the same question," Union said coldly.

"Jak, meet Union," Ryan said. "Union, this is Jak."

"Union Jak." Jak's smile had its own touch of frost. "Have ring to it."

"Whatever." Union sighed loudly. "If this is how you people kill muties, it's no wonder your backs are up against the wall."

Jak laughed. "You funny! All talk, no action!"

Union glared, then suddenly stomped toward him. "I don't have time for this." She paused beside him, her cold stare locking with his bright red eyes. Then she flashed a sexy smile. "So what do you say we go mow down some mutie scum, big boy?" She sashayed past him, her long-blaster swaying in perfect counterpoint with her shapely buttocks in the tight black leather jumpsuit.

Ryan watched her go, suitably stunned by the change in demeanor. He glanced at Krysty, who frowned back at him, then turned his gaze to Jak.

The albino shrugged nonchalantly. "What can say?" He raised his eyebrows. "Guess Jak irresistible." Then he spun and followed Union, disappearing into the forest of spikes.

Ryan stared at his retreating back, hoping like hell that he hadn't made a mistake in bringing Union back to the group.

Chapter Eleven

Somebody slapped Doc so hard across the face that he woke instantly from the depths of a dream and instantly wished he hadn't.

In the dream, he'd been spending a quiet Sunday at home with his wife, Emily, and their children, Rachel and Jolyon. He'd felt perfectly content in a way he never did anymore, utterly relaxed and at peace with his life and times.

Now, after that wicked slap, he was fully back in the Deathlands again, face-to-face with the current author of his misery—Exo the candy-loving mutie.

"Wake up, Dr. Hammersmith." Exo's high-pitched voice was like fingernails on a chalkboard to Doc. "Time to go, my friend."

Doc scowled and sat up, becoming aware of throbbing pain all over his body. It took him a moment to remember that he'd been asleep only because Exo had beaten him into unconsciousness. "Go where?"

"Same place we were going before your little nap." Exo pulled a purple lollipop on a thin white stick out of his mouth and waved it over his shoulder. "The core of the Shift, of course. The place where you'll finish your mission."

Gingerly touching a bruise on top of his head, Doc thought about Ryan and the rest of his comrades. "What about my…kidnappers? You said something about teaching them a lesson."

Exo laughed. "We put a hurting on them, all right." He nodded enthusiastically. "Had them running scared, that's for sure."

"Then what?" Doc asked. "How many of them did you kill?"

Exo's eyes flicked to one side, and he hesitated. It was then Doc knew that no matter what the mutie told him, Ryan and company had acquitted themselves well, as always.

"We put them in their place," Exo snapped. "They'll think twice before coming after us again."

Secretly, Doc exulted. He knew Ryan and the others well enough to know that if they were still breathing, they'd never stop coming after the muties who'd kidnapped their friend.

"Now get up." Exo stuck the lollipop back in his mouth and waved Doc's swordstick overhead. "Stop sitting there like some kind of whipped dog."

Doc struggled to his feet. When he got there, he felt wobbly and paused to steady himself. "It is hard not to, when one is whipped to the point of unconsciousness."

Exo glared at him, and Doc thought he might get beaten again, but then the glare turned into a broad grin. "Ha!" Exo clapped Doc hard on the back. "You really know how to make me laugh, Doc! Even with a faulty memory, you still crack me up."

Doc winced. Exo had struck his back on a particularly sore spot. "Glad to hear it." Though Exo had beaten him with a vengeance just a short time ago, Doc made an effort to behave in a congenial way. Trapped as he was, weaponless and without allies, he knew it would be better to play along with the moods of his captors instead of resisting.

Just then, another mutie—part of the rank and file—ran up and chattered in Exo's ear. Exo nodded without smiling and waved him aside. "Let's get moving." He met the mutie messenger's gaze and gestured in Doc's direction. "You're his babysitter, starting now." A sneer curled his lips. "Anything happens to him, you die."

As Exo walked away, the new mutie stepped up to Doc, looking tense. "So." He had a longblaster slung over his back on a leather strap; when he swung it around, Doc saw that it was a Winchester. Unlike most of the weapons carried by the hodgepodge mutie army, the Winchester was in pristine shape. The walnut stock gleamed as if it had just been polished. "I'm not happy about this."

"What is your name?" Doc lifted an eyebrow.

"Ankh." The mutie jabbed the point of the Winchester at Doc. "And if I had my way, I'd just as soon shoot you on the spot and leave you here."

Doc frowned. "And why is that, if I may ask?"

"Because I know." Ankh jabbed again. "Out of this whole gang of morons, I seem to be the only one who knows."

"Knows what?" Doc asked.

Ankh leaned closer and lowered his voice. "That you're no more Dr. William Hammersmith than I am."

Doc swallowed hard. He had the distinct impression that the only reason he was still alive was that the muties thought he was Hammersmith. If Ankh had an inkling of his true identity, how much longer could Doc expect to live?

"That's right," Ankh said. "I can see right through you."

Doc toyed with various options and decided to play dumb, at least for now. "I do not understand. Perhaps you are the one who's mistaken."

"Do you want to escape Exo and never come back, whoever you are?" Ankh asked.

"Call me Doc. And yes."

Ankh nodded. "Then, we both want the same thing." He looked both ways, then leaned closer. "And if you don't force me to kill you, mebbe we'll manage to get what we want."

Doc locked eyes with Ankh, taking his measure. Ankh's eyes were dark brown, almost black, and very steady. Whatever his true intentions might be, he seemed reasonable on the surface. Doc decided he might just be his best chance for survival and escape.

"Never let it be said that I prefer, as a rule, dying over living another day." Doc bowed his head slightly. "You have my attention, friend Ankh."

"Friend? I have no friends. Not anymore."

Doc nodded.

"I can turn an alliance with you to my advantage," Ankh said. "But make no mistake, I can turn your death to my advantage, as well."

Chapter Twelve

It was late afternoon by the time Ryan and his companions ended their sweeps of the area, satisfied that the muties had moved on. Whatever the muties' objective, other than slaughtering the outlanders, they seemed to have given up on it.

The companions—and Union—gathered at a predetermined rendezvous point a mile up the lava channel. The forest of spikes was thinner there, giving them a clearer view of the surrounding hills and flats.

From what Ryan could see, at the moment, there wasn't a mutie in sight. He and the others knew better than to think they could truly relax, but at least they could take a breath, reload their weapons and assess the situation.

"Too bad muties gone," Jak said. "Was just getting started."

"Speaking of, where in the nuking hell did they go?" J.B. took off his fedora and wiped sweat from his forehead with the back of his arm. "Place was swarming with them, and now they're all gone."

"Just like before," Mildred added. "When they took Doc."

Ryan, who'd been checking on Krysty, looked in Union's direction. Though she'd brightened up briefly once before, when she'd gone off with Jak to shoot muties, she was back to her taciturn self. Though she stood at the edge of the group, close enough to hear every word, she didn't react or participate. She just kept staring into the distance as a light breeze fluttered loose strands of her blond hair.

"Union." Ryan said her name loudly to get her attention. "You seem to know something about this place."

Union's eyes slid toward him for a moment. She made a movement that might have been a shrug, but it was hard to say for sure. Then she went back to staring into space.

Ryan shook his head at Krysty, then turned away from her. "Hey! I'm talking to you!" He walked over to stand in front of the woman, blocking her view of the landscape. "How about helping us out here?"

When she looked at him, her eyes were glacial. "I already did, didn't I? Or don't those muties I killed count?"

Ryan let the remark pass without comment. "You seem to know a few things about this place. The Shift, you called it."

This time, her shrug was plain to see. "What about it?"

"For starters, where did the muties run off to?" Ryan asked. "It was like they just disappeared."

"How should I know?" Union smirked as if his question had been a stupid one. "They could be just about anywhere."

"How so?" Ryan asked. "Some kind of underground tunnel system, maybe?"

"I can't say. The Shift never stays the same for long, and the shifters anticipate its every change."

"Shifters?" J.B. walked over to stand beside Ryan. "The muties, you mean?"

Union looked bored beyond belief. "Yes, of course. After living here for so long, they are in tune with this place. They have learned how to read it. How to ride it."

"Ride it?" Ricky chimed in. "You mean like riding freak spikes punching up from underground?"

"That is one example," Union said. "The shifters know

what is going to change and when. Then it is a simple matter of being in the right place at the right time."

"Must be nice," Ricky said. "Stand where a rock wall's about to rise up so you don't get shot."

"Also explains how they got away with Doc," J.B. stated. "Must've ducked down some rabbit hole or other that opened up in the nick of time."

Ryan nodded. The past two days were finally starting to make sense. But one question haunted him like the ringing in his ears after a big explosion.

If the Shift could change at any time, and the shifters knew how to use its changes against outlanders, how could Ryan and his team ever rescue Doc?

"So what do we do next?" Ryan asked. "What do you recommend?"

"That depends on what you're trying to accomplish."

Ryan hesitated. He hadn't shown her his cards yet, hadn't liked or trusted her from the start. But if she might be able to help, maybe the time had come for full disclosure.

"The shifters took our friend," he said. "We want him back."

Union's only answer was her usual chilly stare.

"That's the only reason we're still here," Ryan continued. "We can't leave him behind."

Union narrowed her eyes. "How do you know he isn't already dead?"

"We don't. But if he is, we might be looking for one more thing around here."

"Which is?" said Union.

"Payback." Ryan nodded curtly. "So are you going to help us or not?"

Union looked around at the group, turning from one face to the other. When she spoke, her voice was different— brighter and bouncier than before. Her expression changed, too, from a cold stare to a warm smile. "Of course I will help you find your friend."

Ryan was caught off guard. Union suddenly seemed like a different person.

"Perhaps, in turn, you might be able to help me."

"In what way?" Ryan frowned as he realized Union's voice and expression weren't the only things about her that had changed. Somehow, the single braid that hung from her left temple had changed color from black to chestnut brown.

"You'll see soon enough." Union smiled. "For now, let's just say we're traveling in the same direction."

"What direction is that?" asked Krysty, who'd appeared at Ryan's side.

"Over there." Union pointed where they'd been headed before the latest attack, along the lava channel. "That way."

"What in that direction?" Jak asked. "More shifters?"

"Oh, I'm sure of it."

"Why that? Mebbe you and shifters friends?"

"Never," Union stated. "But I know what's in that direction, and I'm sure it's the same thing they're heading for."

"So what is this thing you're trying to reach?" Mildred asked.

"The core of the Shift," Union replied. "If your Doc is still alive, you can bet the shifters are taking him there."

"So what happens when they get him there?" Ricky asked.

"That I don't know. But it won't be anything good. The shifters are a nasty bunch."

"This core," Ryan said. "Can you get us there? Can you guide us to it?"

"Sure." Union smiled at each member of the team in turn. "You seem like good people. If we watch one another's backs, we might be able to get where we're going."

"Might?" Jak scowled. "Not sound very sure of self."

"Here's the thing." Union winced. "A lot can happen between here and the core."

"Can't be worse than what's happened so far," J.B. said.

"Actually, it can. The Shift becomes more active the closer you get to the core."

"Why is that?" Mildred asked.

"Because the core is the source. It's what causes the changes in the Shift in the first place."

Ryan stared at her. He still had the feeling he was talking to someone else entirely. "How do you know so much about this core? Have you been there?"

Union smiled, but it didn't last. As Ryan watched, her expression turned grim and stiff; all warmth fled from her pale gray eyes.

Not only that, but the color of her single braid slowly changed from chestnut brown to black.

It was as if she had reverted to her original self, the one whom Ryan had first met in battle. She gazed at him with that same disdain as before, and he wondered if she would likewise go back to not answering his questions.

Surprisingly, she did not. "I lived there once." She looked down at the ground. "I have been broken ever since."

"And you're going back... Why?" Ryan wanted to know.

When Union looked up, her eyes were narrowed, her face seething with intense emotion. "To fix myself," she told him. "To put my life back together again."

With that, she put her hand on the longblaster at her hip and marched away, storming off in the direction she'd identified as that of the core of the Shift.

For a moment, Ryan and his team just watched her go. She'd given them a lot to chew on and left even more mysteries for them to consider.

"So." J.B. took off his spectacles, blew on them and

cleaned them with the hem of his shirt. "None of us has any better ideas, do we? Other than following her, I mean."

No one said a word until Ryan spoke up. "I don't like her and I don't trust her, but she's all we've got." The one-eyed man shook his head. "I hate to say it, but she might be Doc's only hope."

"Crazy woman," Jak said. "One minute one way, next minute different way."

"Yeah," Ricky agreed. "Kind of like the Shift, huh?"

"She said the shifter muties are linked to it," Mildred stated. "Maybe she is, too."

"All right then." Ryan watched Union go a moment longer, then gathered his backpack from the ground and shouldered the straps. "Let's catch up before she leaves us behind."

The rest of the companions followed his lead, pulling on their packs and getting ready to move out. In the years they'd been together, they'd followed him into danger countless times, and now here they were again.

"Okay, people." Steyr Scout longblaster in hand, Ryan nodded at his friends. "Expect the unexpected. Don't trust her for a second." He raised an index finger emphatically. "But as long as there's the slightest chance she can help us find Doc, don't give her a reason to turn against us."

"Treat crazy woman like family." Jak grinned. "Not problem. Fit in this group."

"I couldn't agree more," J.B. told him.

"Less talking, more walking," Ryan said, and then he set out after Union at a rapid clip. He didn't have to look back even once to know his companions were following close behind him.

Chapter Thirteen

That evening, Union and the companions set up camp at the base of a tall, sandy hill sheltered by an array of smaller hills.

Was it a safe location for the night? Union had no guidance to offer, but she didn't seem worried about it. At least Krysty wasn't convulsing on the ground from Shift-induced headaches, which was a positive sign.

The general conditions seemed positive, in fact. The night was warm but not stiflingly hot. The moon was full and shining down from a cloudless sky with abundant radiance.

Everything was quiet, calm and blissfully normal. The lava channel they'd been following had ended a few miles back, and there wasn't a spike to be seen in any direction. If Jak hadn't known any better, he might have believed they weren't in the Shift at all.

As he ate a hunk of deer jerky from his pack, he felt relaxed for the first time since entering the Shift. The rest of the group seemed to be on the same wavelength—except for Ryan, who patrolled the perimeter relentlessly, and Krysty, who looked as if she expected another head blast at any moment.

Then there was Union, who seemed to be out of step with all of them. Where some people might have settled in the middle of the group, getting to know everybody, Union stood thirty yards from the farthest edge of camp, looking up at the night sky.

She didn't look or act as if she wanted to be bothered, but Jak decided to bother her anyway. She was beautiful, and tough, and mysterious, with moods that seemed to change with the wind, and he wanted to get to know her.

Besides, he knew she had a friendly side; he'd seen it in action before. With any luck, maybe that side would come out to play, and they would have a nice talk.

Or not. When Jak sidled up to her, she looked at him for all of one second with the usual frigid disdain, then returned her gaze to the sky. She even folded her arms across her chest and turned her back to him, leaving no room for misinterpretation of her rejection of him.

That was not going to keep Jak from pressing his luck. "Stars not change in Shift." He sank one hand into a pocket, keeping the other wrapped around the grip of his Colt Python, and stepped up beside her. "That one good thing anyway."

Union sniffed but didn't answer. She didn't turn her back to him again, though.

Jak figured that was some kind of progress, so he might as well keep talking. "Where from originally?"

"Not here" was all she said.

"Better place?" Jak asked. "Or worse?"

For a moment, he thought she wouldn't answer, but she finally did. "Just different."

"Right." Jak nodded and shifted his gaze to another quadrant of the sky. The stars were unusually bright that night, glittering like diamond dust scattered over black velvet. "Ever been New Mexico?"

She looked at him for a moment with a quizzical expression, then looked back up at the sky. "Have you ever been to Corpus Christi?"

"Texas?" Jak frowned. "Why? That where you from?"

"Does it matter?" Union shook her head as if she thought he was an idiot. "What do you care?"

Jak refused to let her annoy him. "It called curiosity. They not have in Corpus Christi?"

Suddenly, Union whirled to face him, and she looked upset. "I'm not from there. Will you just stop?"

Jak was taken aback by her change in attitude. "Okay." He scratched his pale chin. "Stop what?"

"Antagonizing her!" Union snapped.

"Her?"

"Her!" Union's eyes widened. "She doesn't care about you. About any of you."

Jak nodded as if he had the faintest clue what she was talking about. "What she care about, then?"

"Us." She touched her fingers to her chest. "Just us."

"What you mean, 'us'?" Jak pulled his hand from his pocket and pointed a finger at her. "Only see one."

Union took her face in her hands. As she shook her head, Jak stared at her single braid, the one that hung from her left temple. He wasn't sure, but it looked bright white by the light of the moon, not the usual black.

"Now, wait." Jak started to reach over to comfort her. "Not want you get upset."

Before he could touch her shoulder, she suddenly yanked her hands from her face and lunged at him. The next thing Jak knew, Union had one hand on his .357 and the other wrapped around his throat.

"No touching!" she gritted.

Jak winced a little as she tightened her grip on his throat—not that he was in any danger whatsoever. She'd caught him off guard, and she was strong, but no match for his battle-honed fighting skills.

"Same go for you." His voice was strained as her grip tightened again. "Stop touching or I *make* stop."

She squeezed a moment more, then released him and let go of the .357. "Consider that your one and only warning! Hands off!"

"Works both ways," Jak told her.

As Union glared, she looked to him like a changed woman. Her body language was very different—twitchy, clenched, confrontational—and her features were gnarled like a knot on an oak tree. Whatever he'd done to piss her off, he had to have hit a hot button, indeed.

"So." Jak shrugged. "What do next?"

"Next?" Union's glare deepened.

"Not want fight." Jak reached out as if to shake hands, then jerked his hand away. "Whoops, forgot! No touching!"

Union's eyes twitched as she stared at his hand. "I just... I don't..."

"Not worry about it. Just want be friend."

Union shook her head as if to shake away a fly that was buzzing around it. Her braid flicked, and Jak noticed it had changed from white to auburn. "Which one?" she said, rattling the words off quickly.

"What that supposed mean?" Jak asked.

This time, she spoke just as fast but a little louder. "Which one do you want to be friends with?"

Jak still wasn't tracking. "Which one what?"

"Of us," Union snapped. "Which one of us do you want to be friends with?"

"Only see one."

"Then, you're blind. Or just plain stupe." Raising her left hand, she held up four fingers. "This is how many of us there are in here."

"Four." Jak was only a little surprised. The way she acted, changing gears so dramatically, had already primed him for the truth. "Four women, one body."

"Now you're in the ballpark, son." Union grinned and

nodded. "Still want to be friends, now that you know my secret?"

Jak stuck out his hand again. "Hell yes. More interesting this way."

Union laughed. This time, she took his hand and shook it.

Chapter Fourteen

Doc no longer wondered if the muties were crazy. He knew it to be true without a doubt.

The entire group of them—fifty strong and then some— sat cross-legged on the sand between two tall hills. They'd been there for hours now, or at least it seemed that way, sitting quietly in the light of the full moon and flickering stars.

Doc sat in the middle of the crowd, seething with a mix of utter boredom and strong curiosity. The muties seemed to be waiting for something, but he couldn't guess what, and no one would tell him. Even his babysitter, Ankh, wouldn't explain the scene; he just sat beside Doc with the Winchester aimed at the old man's belly, finger curled around the trigger.

Was it some kind of ceremony? The muties all sat in a cluster, facing the same direction, and remained silent in a way that might be considered reverent. But how could it be a ceremony without some kind of rites?

Maybe, Doc thought, they were just praying or communing with whatever gods or forces they worshipped. Or perhaps it was simple meditation or some form of regenerative rest they'd evolved since the nuclear scrambling of their DNA during skydark.

Whatever it was, he wished they'd leave him out of it. He'd just as soon catch forty winks in the lee of a dune or gaze up at the starry sky and remember simpler times. Things had been so much sweeter back then, with his family around him, the apocalypse nowhere in sight and no crazy muties to kidnap him from the handful of friends who barely made his life worth living in the Deathlands.

Doc sighed, losing patience, and immediately felt the muzzle of the Winchester poke his ribs. Glancing over, he saw Ankh's steady gaze boring into him, pitiless and unyielding...yet still the closest he had among the muties to an expression that was friendly on any level.

Ankh was Doc's only hope, at least for now. Somewhere out there in the Sandhills country, Ryan and the others had to be searching for him, but they were nowhere in sight at the moment. He couldn't depend on them to rescue him anytime soon; it was up to Doc to keep himself alive and well until that could happen.

Now, if he could just survive this exercise in tedious nonsense, he might have a chance.

Just then, he got a kink in his lower back from sitting cross-legged for too long. Grunting, he twisted and stretched, trying to work out the kink, but it only got worse.

Leaning forward, he reached back under his frock coat to knead the sore spot. But the act of reaching set off a chain of pressure points that led to a sudden spasm in the middle region of his back.

Doc cried out. He couldn't help himself. When he sat up straight, the spasm only worsened, and he cried out again.

Ankh rammed the Winchester barrel into his side, but it didn't make any difference. Doc could no more control his response to the pain than he could single-handedly defeat the mutie band in unarmed combat.

"Stop it!" Ankh hissed. "If we miss it, you're a dead man!"

Doc scowled and braced a hand on the ground. "I can't help it! I'm having a back spasm." Pushing up, he got to his knees. Getting up and stretching might break the cycle of pain, if he didn't get shot first.

"Get down!" Ankh snapped. "Get down now!"

Doc ignored him and got to his feet. Towering over the seated muties—many of whom were gaping up at him with expressions of great irritation—he straightened his back and spread his arms. The vertebrae in his spine cracked as he rolled his head from side to side, limbering up his neck. Then he leaned back slowly, extending the lower vertebrae, working to loosen up the cramp.

Gradually, he felt the spasm in his middle back let up. Leaning farther still, he heard—and felt—a midback vertebra crack into place.

Just like that, the spasm stopped. The pressure lessened, and Doc could think clearly once more.

Just in time to see the landscape before him dance with shimmering, shivering light.

"By the Three Kennedys!" he said softly, gazing raptly at the sight.

As one, the muties rolled over and lay flat on their backs in the sand—all except Ankh, who was on his feet, jamming the Winchester into Doc's gut.

"Down!" the mutie snapped. "Do as you're told!"

But Doc was lost in the vision of dancing, multicolored light. It was like an aurora of the northlands, curtains of radiance flowing and glowing hypnotically in the night. He tipped his head to one side, entranced by the beauty of it, unable to look away.

That was when Ankh finally realized the blaster wasn't going to bring him down. Swinging it over his back by its strap, he launched himself at Doc like a cougar, throwing all his weight against the taller man.

And it worked. Doc went over backward, plunging toward the sand, with Ankh coming down on top of him.

"No!" As Doc toppled, he pinwheeled his arms, instinctively trying to halt his fall. He'd just stopped the back spasm, but if he came down hard, he'd likely get it all over again.

Just as he was about to hit, however, there was a feeling of suction and repulsion all at once, and a flash of light.

Blinded, Doc did not at first realize that something had changed. But it didn't take long to sink in.

It didn't take long to realize that he should have hit the ground already, but instead was sinking gently. Something was pulling him in, dragging him inexorably downward.

Quicksand.

Tossing his head and blinking his eyes hard to clear the spots from the blinding flash, Doc saw that the muties were sinking as he was. Most of them were covered almost completely, leaving just their noses and toes exposed.

And none of them seemed to be worried. None of them were fighting the force that was drawing them down.

"Relax." Ankh, who'd rolled off Doc and now lay beside him, was only halfway covered. "You'll be fine."

But Doc didn't believe him. Frantically, he thrashed and floundered, which only made him sink faster. He grabbed for Ankh, as if holding on to the mutie might keep him aboveground, but that just pushed Ankh deeper, out of reach.

Doc yelped and thrashed some more, and then the quicksand took him down. He sucked in his last breaths with heaving desperation, watching the flickering stars through eyelashes caked with sand.

And then he was gone. The ground was empty, as if Doc and the muties had never been there at all.

Chapter Fifteen

Doc hit the icy water with a hypothermic shock and barely managed to stay afloat.

Seconds after sinking through the sand alongside the muties, he'd fallen through some kind of open space, then suddenly splashed down in water. He paddled madly now, struggling instinctively to keep from going under, though the truth was, he couldn't breathe above the surface, either. He'd inhaled enough quicksand on the way down to clog his nose and throat and lungs with smothering muck.

His eyes were wide as he thrashed and suffocated, but there was only pitch-darkness all around. If the muties were there with him, he couldn't see a trace of them.

He started to feel light-headed and heavy at the same time. One last frenzy of kicking and gyrating, and his movements began to slow; he pulled his hands in to clutch his throat, and his body drifted downward.

All sense left his oxygen-starved brain as the water rose to cover him. His vision danced with sparks, and then mysteriously cleared and brightened. He saw the faces of his wife and children from his life in the nineteenth century, beaming and waving for him to come closer.

The last expression on his face as he went under was a smile, even as his body spasmed and stiffened without air.

Then, suddenly, hands grabbed hold of his upper arms and wrenched him back up again. Dazed and almost certainly dying, Doc was barely conscious of the hands as they dragged him through the water. Was he being pulled onto some kind of surface, some kind of dry land at the edge of the water? He couldn't be sure.

Whatever was happening to him, he dropped out of consciousness like a shotgunned bird, plummeting into absolute darkness. Even the faces of Emily, Rachel and Jolyon were lost to him; he was racing finally into the limitless night, giving up the earthly suffering that had been his lot for far too long.

Or not. With the same shocking force with which he'd hit the freezing water, Doc rocketed out of the mindless blackness. Someone pounded his back again and again, and Doc gagged up quicksand in great muddy gouts.

As he retched up the garbage stuffed into his respiratory system, Doc became aware that he was on his knees on a rocky slab. He didn't have long to consider it between blows to his back, though; they came so hard and fast that they scattered his thoughts as well as ejected the gritty clods.

Finally, enough of the matter was expelled that Doc's airway opened partially. Without thinking, he sucked in a giant breath of cold air that immediately revived him.

And then the hand smacked his back again, and he continued coughing up quicksand.

Eventually, though, the hand stopped striking. Doc gagged out some more gunk, then slumped forward, breathing almost normally again.

At that moment, he heard a familiar voice in his ear. "Welcome back." It was Ankh. "You need to hold your breath better next time." He chuckled softly.

Doc turned toward him but couldn't see a thing. Wherever they were, there didn't seem to be a trace of light to be found. "What… Where…?" Forcing out words took an effort and triggered a fresh coughing jag.

When it faded, Ankh patted him on the back. "You'll see in just a moment."

As he said it, a loud boom echoed through the place, followed by a sound like the crackling of sparks from a downed power line. Off in the distance, Doc glimpsed a lonely twinkle that was quickly doused then followed by several more, flickering to life at scattered points. These guttered, too, and were replaced by others that also died, and then, suddenly, a brilliant light blazed to life.

In spite of his continued discomfort and hacking, Doc gazed in wonder at the scene before him. He was at the edge of an enormous cavern filled with a lake of crystal clear water. The walls and ceiling were lined with a web of brightly glowing filaments, the source of the illumination that had blown away the previously impenetrable darkness.

As Doc watched, the band of muties frolicked in the shallows at the fringe of a lake, laughing and splashing one another. Their weapons were spread over the upper bank of the shoreline, gleaming in the light washing over every inch of the enormous underground vault. "What... what is this place?"

"Shh." Ankh placed a crimson index finger against his lips. "Keep it down."

Doc frowned. "Why on earth would I do that?"

Ankh lowered his voice. "You're supposed to be Dr. Hammersmith, aren't you?"

Doc narrowed his eyes. "Of course."

"Well, here's the thing," Ankh said. "Dr. Hammersmith built this place."

As the implications came home to roost, Doc nodded slowly. "Ah. I see."

"It is our refuge." Ankh gestured at the cavern around them. "One of them anyway. It is underground, and it is located in a still zone."

Doc shook his head at the way the light rippled on the

surface of the lake and danced over the chiseled gray walls. He was having a hard time accepting that this had somehow been created by one man. "What is a still zone, pray tell?"

"A pocket of the Shift that does not change," Ankh explained. "It is unaffected by the energies emanating from the core. This particular still zone, in fact, is unaffected because of special shielding installed by Dr. Hammersmith. Once the quicksand pulls you belowground and fills in above you, you may rest assured that your surroundings will not undergo any sort of transformation."

"The Shift can be controlled?" Doc asked.

"Only blocked," Ankh replied. "And only in a very few locations using equipment constructed by Hammersmith. But he did believe that control might be possible. He had a theory."

"He did, did he?" Doc coughed, then swallowed hard to break the jag. "And what was it, exactly?"

"Only two people know," Ankh said. "Hammersmith is one of them, and he is…you know." He drew a finger across his throat. "As for the other, he is right over there." Ankh pointed at a single mutie who was sitting apart from the rest, contemplating with a darkling gaze the recreation going on in the water.

"Exo?" Doc coughed again. "He possesses a scientific mind?"

"I never said that." Ankh shrugged. "But Hammersmith did tell him the theory, and Exo is determined to bring it to life."

"To what end, I wonder?" Doc frowned. "Perhaps I can draw it out of him. After all, he ought to speak freely about it if I am the originator of said theory."

Ankh narrowed his dark brown eyes. "Exo has a blind spot where you're concerned, and he thinks he needs you.

But trust me, he is more than capable of making you suffer if you rub him the wrong way."

"Yes." Doc nodded grimly, recalling the beating Exo had given him. "That has been made quite clear to me."

"You ought to keep that in mind," Ankh said. "Never forget who holds the power in this society."

"An irrational creature prone to fits of extreme violence," Doc replied. "The perfect individual to seize control of the transformative nature of the Shift." Doc shook his head. "Why do your people follow him?"

"He helped us overthrow a tyrant and survive a great disaster," Ankh explained. "Though, to be honest, he was a different person then."

"In what way?"

"One without brain damage." Ankh gazed at Exo with an expression that might have been regret, then he turned away. "But that is neither here nor there."

"Brain damage?"

Ankh cut a hand through the air in a gesture of finality. "Enough." He got to his feet and dusted off the seat of his ragged camouflage pants. "If I were you, I'd enjoy this brief quiet time. There might not be another for quite a while."

"Sage advice." Doc coughed as he, too, got up from the rocky slab. "Though I believe I will ask one more question, at the risk of overtaxing your hospitality."

Ankh's expression was one of rising irritation. "What question is that?"

"If he is not the man he once was, why do *you* follow him?"

Ankh watched the muties splashing in the lake for a moment, their crimson bodies glittering in the light from the illuminated web on the walls and ceiling. Then he flashed a smirk in Doc's direction. "Who said I do?"

With that, he walked away, wading into the water

among his fellow muties, leaving Doc to ponder the possibilities that hung in the air around him.

Was Ankh unhappy with Exo's leadership? Did he represent a force for change, one that Doc might exploit to win his freedom?

Ankh had spoken of turning an alliance with Doc to his advantage. Perhaps, if Doc played his cards right, he might be able to turn Ankh and Exo against each other and escape in the chaos that followed.

That was, if Ankh's manipulations or Exo's rage didn't kill him first.

Chapter Sixteen

When the sun rose the next morning, Mildred and J.B. greeted it gladly. They had taken the last watch of the night, and now their shift was over.

"Good morning." Mildred pulled J.B. in close, so they were nearly nose to nose.

"Morning," J.B. replied, and then he closed the gap and gave her a long, warm kiss. When they broke it, he was smiling. "You're looking especially good this morning, Millie."

"You, too." Mildred chuckled. "I'd feel better after a nice, hot shower and a steaming-hot breakfast with a pot of coffee, though."

"You mean no shower and an MRE, if we're lucky?" J.B. laughed again. "Perfect start to another day."

As he said it, Union strolled around the nearest hill, which she'd kept between her and the rest of the group for most of the night. She appeared perfectly rested and alert, no different from how she'd looked at the start of the night, though every time Mildred had caught sight of her during her watch, she'd been wide-awake.

Stopping to tower over the sleeping teammates, Union met Mildred's gaze without acknowledging her. She looked briefly at J.B., then stuck two fingers in her mouth and let out a shrill whistle.

"Let's go!" she shouted. "Time to move out!"

Instantly, the companions who'd been fast asleep until

that moment sprang up from the ground, snatching and cocking weapons along the way. In a heartbeat, they were fully awake and ready for battle, all blasters pointing in the same direction, at the source of the commotion.

Just as quickly, they realized they'd been awakened by a false alarm.

"Fireblast!" Ryan snapped. "It's just you?"

"Thought muties coming," Jak said. "Almost killed you."

"What's the hell's going on?" Ricky sounded noticeably less alert than the others, still groggy though ready for combat nonetheless.

But Ryan, by far, was most annoyed. "Is this your idea of a wake-up call?"

Union shrugged. "Call it what you will. I'm just letting you know that we need to get moving if we're to have any hope of catching up with the muties."

Ryan nodded slowly, then lowered his longblaster and approached her. "I'll say this once and once only." He said the next words through clenched teeth. "You are not the leader of us. You do not call the shots." He glared at her with more than enough malice to send a very clear message. "Understand?"

Union stared at him for a moment, her expression as frigid as ever. Then, suddenly, her face changed. Her eyes widened, filling with what looked like fear and anger.

"Stop screaming at me!" She clamped her mouth shut, and her lips trembled until she burst out again. "Leave me alone!" Her voice was higher, reedy and cracking with panic. Her braid was white instead of black.

Ryan took a slow step back. He looked in Mildred's direction, seeking a cue from the resident medical doctor.

Mildred had one, too. The signs were obvious, and she'd been giving it some thought during her watch. But before she could offer any insight, Jak beat her to it.

"Four women, one body," he said. "That what she told me."

"Multiple personality disorder," Mildred added. "We're talking to someone else now."

Ryan nodded and focused his attention on Union. "I didn't mean to scream at you." He kept his voice even, his hands up with palms toward her. "And I'm not going to hurt you."

Suddenly, Union's face changed again. Her eyes narrowed, and her look of fear switched to one of fearless challenge. "You couldn't if you tried." Her voice was different, too—lower and raspier than any voice Mildred had heard her use so far. "You're outnumbered, and you don't even know it. You don't know anything."

"Then, tell us." With that, Mildred walked over to stand just behind Ryan. "Whom are we speaking to now?"

Union ignored her and kept staring at Ryan. "Has anyone ever told you what a sorry-ass bunch of losers you people are?"

"Yeah," Jak interjected. "All dead now."

Union laughed loudly. "*Him*, I like." She hiked a thumb over her shoulder in Jak's direction. "Nothing like a pasty-faced wiseass to liven things up!"

"So what name?" Jak asked. "Crazy Bitch?"

Union laughed again. "Rhonda! You can call me Rhonda!"

Then she jabbed a finger at Mildred. "But you can call me ma'am."

"Who was the other one?" Mildred asked. "The one we saw right before you?"

"Carrie." Rhonda-Union wagged her head in disgust. "But trust me, you don't want to deal with her. Talk about drama queens."

"Who's in charge?" Mildred asked. "You?"

Rhonda-Union snorted. "You couldn't pay me enough to

take that job." She tapped her left temple—where the braid had changed color from white to auburn—and grinned. "That bitch Taryn is running this loony bin, more power to her."

"Taryn?" Mildred repeated. "Who's T—"

"Enough!" As Mildred watched, Union's face shifted again. Her confrontational glare faded into a cold, stiff mask. "The more time we waste, the farther away the shifters take your friend." She spun on her heel and headed back around the hill. "I'm leaving in five minutes, with or without you!"

Mildred blew out her breath. "Well, that was interesting."

"Think know who Taryn is." Jak smirked. "Like Rhonda better."

"I don't like any of them," Ryan said.

"That you've met so far," Krysty stated. "Jak said there are four women in one body, and I only count three so far."

Mildred ticked them off in her head: Rhonda, Carrie, Taryn. Had personality number four already made an appearance and gone unnoticed?

"Unfortunately, they are…*she* is…our best chance of getting Doc back," Ryan said.

"Unless she's full of shit." J.B. adjusted the brim of his fedora. "Or even more nuts than she seems so far."

"Watch every move," Jak said. "All can do."

"The multiple personalities make her completely unpredictable," Mildred stated. "She could do anything at any time with absolutely no warning."

"So could we." Ryan nodded once and headed toward his backpack. "For now, let's do like the woman said and get moving. Pack your stuff and form up in five."

Everyone followed his order and hurriedly set about rolling up bedding and stowing equipment. Mildred and

J.B., who shared a bed, did theirs together with practiced teamwork.

But as they gathered their things, J.B. asked her a question under his breath. "She's a ticking time bomb, right?"

Mildred shrugged as she hefted her backpack. "Too soon to say. She's dangerous enough, but you already knew that. It just depends on how the balance in her head holds up under pressure."

J.B. gave her a hand adjusting the weight of her pack, then shouldered his own. "Gotta say, I'm not sure about the stability of that balance."

"Neither are any of us. Neither is she." Mildred hopped forward and pecked him on the lips. "But we've handled crazier in our day."

J.B. grinned and gave her a kiss of his own. "Some folks might say we're a little crazy ourselves."

Mildred nodded. "We need to get Doc back."

"You're right about that. We're not the same without him. Something's…off."

"He's family. We have to get him back."

"We will, Millie." J.B. clenched his jaw and nodded firmly. "We'll blow the hell out of heaven and earth if that's what it takes to get Doc back with us."

Chapter Seventeen

Doc blinked at the bright morning sunlight as he emerged from a tunnel amid the bustling shifters. After hours of frolicking and sleep in the still zone cavern, they were on the march again, continuing their journey to the core.

The muties seemed well rested, with plenty of spring in their steps, which was the opposite of the way Doc felt. He hadn't slept well in the cavern; as beautiful as it was, it had been far too cool and damp for his comfort. If he was lucky, he might have three hours of sleep under his belt, which wasn't nearly enough. He knew from experience that he could survive on that or less, but the quality of his thinking and alertness would be compromised.

Nevertheless, he would have to make do. Not only that, but he would have to excel in handling whatever came his way. His life was as much on the line as ever; minute by minute, he walked a tightrope, and one slip would be enough to take him down forever.

"You're sluggish this morning." As always, Ankh was glued to his side. His had been the first face Doc had seen when the lights had come back on in the morning.

Doc shook his head. "I assure you, this constitutional has got my blood flowing, Ankh."

Ankh cast a sidelong gaze at him, looking doubtful. "And you're not hungry, I suppose?"

Doc patted his belly. "Not a bit." The muties had offered him a portion of their rations, but he'd tactfully turned it down. The thought of sharing their squirming handfuls of live insects and worms was repulsive to him. Such food was certainly nutritionally sound, but he would have to be much hungrier to force himself to partake of it.

"Suit yourself." Ankh smirked. "Let me know if you change your mind. There's lots to go around."

Doc smiled and hoped Ankh didn't hear his stomach growling. He was determined to go without food until he found something more appetizing, like roots or berries, but the truth was, the terrain had been pretty barren so far. Finding suitable victuals in those environs could be more of a challenge than he could stand.

"No matter," Ankh said. "If you pass out from hunger at some point, we'll just drag you the rest of the way."

Doc tipped his head with faux gallantry. "Your hospitality continues to astonish me," he said.

"You'll enjoy more of it shortly," Ankh said. "We're heading for a ville inhabited by my people, the only one of its kind in the Shift."

"A ville?" Doc frowned. "How is that possible, given the changeable nature of the local landscape?"

"You'll see." Ankh adjusted the Winchester longblaster hanging from his left shoulder. "We're a good deal cleverer than you norms might believe."

"I already believe it," Doc said. "One of my best friends is a mutie, you know."

Ankh looked at him with obvious disbelief. "You're just saying that."

Doc shook his head. "I am not." There was no need to lie in this case; Krysty Wroth was indeed one of the few people he thought of as a friend in the Deathlands. "Her friendship is indisputable. She has saved my life and the lives of my 'norm' friends numerous times."

Ankh kept staring at him. "This mutie. She isn't some kind of slave or pet?"

"She is anything but. She is no one's servant or pawn, I assure you."

Finally, Ankh tore his gaze away from Doc. "Impossible," he said quietly. "Such a relationship could never exist."

Doc lowered his voice. "What about Dr. Hammersmith? I've heard Exo refer to him as a very good friend."

"More like property," Ankh said. "Though I am certain Hammersmith would tell you otherwise."

"I see. So Hammersmith is more a slave than a friend, working on behalf of Exo."

Ankh nodded. "For the best of reasons."

"And what might those reasons be?"

"The survival of our people," Ankh said. "And the extinction of all those who oppose them."

"Ah, yes." Doc folded his hands behind his back. "And here I was beginning to think your people might not be more of the same old, same old. Clearly, I was wrong."

"No, no, you were right. We can do things you have never seen before. And our vision for this place is like none other that has ever existed."

"I will take your word for it, then," Doc said.

"Oh, no." Ankh looked up at him with dark eyes gleaming from his crimson face. "You will help make it a reality before all this is done. Not for him." He gestured at Exo, who walked at the head of the ranks. "For someone more deserving and enlightened."

"Someone like you, perhaps?"

Ankh shrugged. "Time will tell, Doc. Time will tell."

Chapter Eighteen

Everyone had been hiking for two hours when Union stopped in front of a big hill and stayed there. She looked left, then right, then left again, as if she couldn't make up her mind which way to go.

She stayed that way for a full five minutes.

Krysty leaned over and whispered to Ryan, who was growing increasingly antsy. "One of the problems with having multiple personalities is that you can't always make up your mind at a fork in the road."

Ryan nodded and didn't look happy about it. "She's arguing with herself."

"Four women, one body." Krysty shrugged. "You do the math."

Ryan shook his head, cleared his throat and spoke so Union would hear him. "What happens if we go right?"

Union looked that way with eyes narrowed. Her braid, at this point, was Taryn black. "It will lead us to the core of the Shift." She looked back to the left. "That direction leads to the same place, but it's a shortcut. It will cut our time by half."

"Sounds like a no-brainer to me." Ryan took three steps to the left. "We take the shortcut."

"Wait." Union raised an index finger. "The shortcut's more dangerous. It passes through an area known as the Devil's Slaughterhouse. They say very few travelers have survived a trip through that zone."

"Huh." Ryan rubbed his chin. "How few?"

"A handful," Union replied.

"Sound like our kind shortcut," Jak stated.

"You don't understand." Union's face suddenly changed, eyes widening with terror, and her braid turned white. "There are things living in there! The Shift has changed them!"

"More delicious, I hope," Jak said. "Would kill for some fresh meat."

"They'll slaughter us! We'll be the ones who are devoured!" Union's voice continued to rise with panic. "But the others want to go that way, too! They'll doom us all!"

"Tell the others we're with them," Ryan told her. "Now can we get moving?"

Union's expression changed from fear to a sneer, and her braid went auburn. "What the fuck do you think I've been telling these dumbasses for the past fifteen minutes?"

Krysty kneaded her temples and shook her head slowly. "This is starting to give me a headache."

Ryan shot her a look with eyebrows raised.

"The old-fashioned kind," Krysty said. "Don't worry."

"All right, then." Ryan stepped back and gestured in the direction of the Devil's Slaughterhouse. "After you."

Rhonda-Union snorted and stomped past him. "Just make sure you keep up. And do as you're told! I know the critters in this little corner of hell better than you!"

"Thought only handful travelers survived Devil's Slaughterhouse," Jak said.

Rhonda-Union sneered back at him. "Including me!"

Jak trotted forward and took up position alongside her. "Then, know who I stick with."

Rhonda-Union bumped elbows with him. "Smart man, Jak. Best of this sorry bunch, if you ask me."

"Not ask. But same goes for your bunch."

At which point, Ryan looked at Krysty, who rolled her

eyes and shook her head. It was good that one of the team was hitting it off with Union…but that didn't make the budding friendship any easier to take, as Rhonda treated the rest of them like garbage.

At least Ryan understood. Reaching over, he cupped his left hand on the back of Krysty's head, pulled her close and kissed her. "We'd better get going," he said softly. "Let me know if you're in trouble."

"No problem." Krysty grinned. "Just listen for the screams of agony."

"All right, people." Ryan let go of her and looked to the rest of the companions. "Let's try to make some time."

"We will if she will." Ricky pointed at Union, who was walking away with Jak. "Tell her let's make some time."

"Sure. Just as soon as I can figure out who the hell I'm talking to."

With that, the team started marching after Union and Jak. Above them, the sky was quickly clouding up.

Krysty had a feeling that the rain, if it came, would be the least of their problems in the Devil's Slaughterhouse.

THE GROUP HADN'T been marching for long when the rain started to fall. It came down lightly at first, and Ricky didn't mind it a bit. If he had to choose between sweltering heat and cool rain, he'd pick the rain every time.

Maybe, he thought, it would even keep some of the things that were living in the Devil's Slaughterhouse from being at their most active. Still, he knew better than to relax the slightest bit while moving through the territory. He kept both hands on his De Lisle carbine and repeatedly checked his Webley revolver, making sure it was good to go in its holster.

All in all, it had been a peaceful hike, so peaceful that Ricky started to wonder if Union had lied about how bad it would be. Maybe she'd been trying to talk them into the other route, not anticipating that this was a group of people who never flinched at taking the hard way in any situation.

Or maybe the place had been awful once, but had changed. After all, it was part of the Shift, wasn't it? Maybe the creatures had become less dangerous or gone elsewhere.

That was exactly what Ricky was thinking when the fur-covered snake with the seven-foot wingspan swooped down from the gray sky and tried to snatch him up.

"Hey!" He spotted the creature at the last second and barely dodged its gleaming silver claws.

As the giant, orange-furred snake hurtled back into the heights, Ricky swung up the carbine and sighted along its length. The mutie's body, as skinny as it was, would not be an easy shot, so Ricky chose the bigger target and tugged the trigger.

He heard the thing shriek as a round punched a hole dead center through its wing. Suddenly, the beast became aerodynamically unstable, flapping frantically and whipping in a circle.

Then rounds from three other blasters—courtesy of Ricky's teammates—blew more holes in its wings, and the creature hurtled downward. It hit the ground thirty yards away with a final screech and a thud like a net full of fish being dumped on the deck of a boat.

"Wow!" Ricky shouted to the others. "That was one mean-ass—"

Before he could finish the sentence, another creature exploded from the side of a nearby hill, heading straight for him. It started as a big, gray sphere, then unfurled to reveal an underside studded with jagged white pincers and fangs.

Ricky could hear them clacking together as the creature flew straight at him through the rain. Instantly, he swung up the carbine, ready to fire, but Ryan beat him to it. The Steyr Scout belched out a round that caught the creature in the side, spinning it out of its original trajectory. As it skidded across the sand, Ricky followed up with a blast from the carbine, blowing it apart like a watermelon.

Before he could take a breath, he caught sight of another creature galloping toward him from fifty yards away—and this one was much bigger than either of the other two. It looked like a cross between a hippopotamus and a porcupine, studded with spines and roaring belligerently from an enormous maw full of multiple concentric rows of inward-pointing, razor-sharp teeth.

Smoothly, Ricky spun and sighted his carbine at the beast. He squeezed the trigger, and a round crossed the distance in a heartbeat. He knew before it hit that it would be a perfect head shot.

Which it was. But what he didn't expect was that the bullet would zing from the creature's forehead without leaving a scratch.

The hippo-porcupine kept charging, and Ricky quickly realized how ugly his situation had just gotten. Glancing around, he saw his teammates were all occupied with bizarre creatures of their own. No one else was aiming a weapon at the stampeding monstrosity.

No one else was going to come to his rescue. If Ricky hoped to survive, he would have to make it happen on his own.

He squeezed off another shot, and it, too, deflected from the beast's skull. Then, as the hammering hoofbeats pounded ever closer, Ricky did something he rarely did during the many conflicts he faced in the Deathlands.

He ran for his life.

Chapter Nineteen

In his years roaming the irradiated wastelands of what had once been the United States of America, Ryan had dealt with some horrifically mutated wildlife. He'd met, and put down, some truly twisted animals that in some cases were so warped, he hadn't been able to identify what species they'd originally been.

But the thing that was facing him now through what had become a soaking downpour really took the cake. It was like someone had crossed a giant tarantula with an armadillo...and a barrel of hydrochloric acid.

The creature was seven feet tall, with the bulbous body and eight hairy legs of a tarantula. But the body and legs were clad in overlapping armor plates like those of an armadillo. Only its head, with its huge, curving fangs and clusters of eyes, was unshielded.

Not that the armor was its only defense. As Ryan darted to one side, the creature shot a stream of fluid from between its fangs; the stream struck the spot where he'd been standing, dissolving the sandy ground with a loud hiss.

Heart pumping hard, Ryan bolted around behind the creature, out of range of its acid jet, and reloaded the Steyr Scout. He had to take the monster down fast, but how? It was built like a tank.

Whatever he did, he would have to do it soon. His teammates were all under attack by the hellish local fauna, which seemed to have awakened all at once. From what he could see, all of his companions were all equally endangered, though some were having worse luck than others.

MILDRED CLAWED AT the ground, but the thorny tendrils kept dragging her by the ankles. Looking back over her shoulder through the rain, she saw what they were dragging her toward, and that inspired her to redouble her efforts.

An amorphous, gelatinous blob like an overgrown amoeba kept its glistening mouth wide-open in her direction. The tendrils didn't seem to be part of it—they were connected instead to a giant green pod squatting nearby—but they yanked her inexorably toward the blob nevertheless.

As she slid across the muddy surface, she watched her ZKR 551 get farther away. She'd dropped it after pumping two shots into both the blob and the pod, without killing either one. Now the weapon was twenty feet away and getting more out of reach with each passing moment.

With a cry of frustration, Mildred scrabbled for any kind of handhold, to no avail. The tendrils dragged her another three feet, bringing her to within ten feet of the blob.

She could hear it smacking and slurping behind her, and she realized she couldn't avoid it. Her only chance, it seemed, would be to confront the organism head-on, with her bare hands.

If it didn't devour her first.

JAK HURLED ONE of his leaf-bladed throwing knives into the eye of the pouncing see-through lion, interrupting its leap. The great cat landed on its feet, roaring in pain, and then it grew another eye beside the ruined one.

Through the animal's transparent skin, he could see the damage done by the blade. Blood poured from an artery, gushing inside and outside the wound. When the lion roared again, the wound widened, increasing the damage and blood flow.

But within seconds, the bleeding stopped. Another artery grew beside the first, twining its way through the tangle of blood vessels and ligaments in the creature's neck.

"Just got interesting." Jak drew a blade in each hand. He flexed his grip on both handles, took a deep breath and steeled himself for what he was about to do. "Wonder if limit how much can regrow?"

As if in reply, the lion let out a loud roar.

Jak twirled the knives in his hands. "Not worry, cat." He stopped twirling and tightened his hold on them. "Find out fun way. Cut cat down to size, see if new one grows."

With that, he let out a roar of his own and charged at the lion, blades flashing in the rainy gray daylight.

KRYSTY STOOD STOCK-STILL as the swarm of piranha wasps surrounded her, their wings emitting an earsplitting whine.

Each wasp had a head like a carnivorous fish—its maw packed with gnashing fangs—and an ebony body with a massive black-and-yellow-striped stinger. The creatures were big, the size of Krysty's fist, and hovered menacingly all around her.

Sweat beaded her forehead as they cut off all escape routes, even filling in the space above so she couldn't leap clear. Heart racing, she watched their multifaceted black eyes, which appeared to be blank.

Their intentions, she had no doubt, were nothing but hostile. The only real question remaining at that moment was *when*, not *if*, they were going to attack.

Through gaps in the swarm, she glimpsed Ryan. He wasn't more than twenty yards away, but he would be no help to her. He was busy facing an enemy of his own, some kind of enormous armored tarantula creature.

Breathing deeply, Krysty shifted her stance to a crouch.

As soon as she moved, the piranha-wasps inched toward her and buzzed louder.

When she froze again, they moved no closer, nor did they give up the ground they'd just gained. Krysty was convinced: once she started moving in earnest, the capsule of creatures would collapse inward all at once, doing their worst to her.

Still, she could think of no better idea. She would have to commit herself to the plan and hope she survived it.

Slowly, she lowered her hand to the butt of the Glock 18C in the holster at her hip. The piranha-wasps twitched inward at the motion, then stopped when she stilled her hand.

At that point, at the most, the creatures were two feet away from her. It would not take much for them to make contact.

Soaked by the rain pouring through the gaps between bugs, Krysty took a deep breath and prepared herself. Her only chance was to once again call on Gaia, the Earth Mother, to come to her aid in her hour of need. She began her prayer, reaching out to the Gaia force in the world around her, triggering the cycle that would light her up like a Roman candle.

There was a good chance she wouldn't live through the next five minutes, and she knew it. She made her mental goodbyes to Ryan, and then she threw open the gates within her.

It was as if the insect creatures could sense the power when it flooded into her. The whine of their wings grew louder as they closed in on her body.

J.B. FIRED BLIND, cranking off shots from the Mini-Uzi in an arc around him. Did a single round make contact with the creature that had been attacking him?

He couldn't tell, because he couldn't see it in the first place.

Then, suddenly, he realized the creature was still very much alive. Something heavy and rubbery slammed into him, knocking him off his feet and sending the gun flying from his grip.

"Nuking hell!" J.B. went down hard on the wet sand, then scrambled to his knees. He quickly caught sight of the Mini-Uzi and launched himself after it, determined to regain what little advantage he had.

But his invisible enemy, whatever it was, swatted him from behind and took him down again. This time, the fall knocked the wind out of J.B. and left him dazed.

"What *is* this damn thing?" Sitting up, he shook his head hard, trying to clear the cobwebs. As he did, he heard a hissing sound passing alongside him, and he leaped to his feet.

The hairs on the back of his neck stood at attention as he looked for some sign of the unseen creature…and found it. Right where he'd heard the hissing sound, he saw the sand compressed in a track like a shallow, rounded ditch, as if something tubular were moving through it. It looked like the kind of trail a giant snakelike creature might make, except for the star-shaped claw-prints pressed into the sand on each side of it. Each print had five sharp points grouped around a circular central pad; the span from claw tip to claw tip was at least ten inches.

And it was impossible to tell how many feet were making those impressions. From what little J.B. could see, there might be two, or four, or even six. And they provided no real clues about the creature's anatomy. Was he dealing with a mammal, a reptile, an insect or something else?

All he really knew was that it was toying with him. From the tracks and the hissing, he could tell it was circling him from four feet away. It had to know it could strike at any moment, and he would be at its mercy.

Not that he was going to go down without a fight, even against an invisible whatever it was.

Watching the tracks and listening, J.B. swung around his Smith & Wesson M-4000 scattergun and pumped the magazine, loading a shell in the chamber. When he thought he knew the beast's location, he aimed at the thin air there and pulled the trigger.

He was rewarded with a monstrous howl from the same direction. He heard thrashing, saw the wet sand churn and moved to follow up the first tag with another.

But before he could pull the trigger, something heavy crashed into him from behind, and he went down. As he hit, he heard a blistering roar, saw fresh tracks from another direction and he suddenly realized something that made a chill rush through his body. The game, which had been difficult enough to begin with, had taken a turn for the worse.

Because there were two invisible creatures trying to kill him instead of just one.

Chapter Twenty

When Doc topped the latest in a long line of hills, he found himself staring down through the pouring rain at a ville unlike any he'd seen before.

It was located in a depression in the sand, a bowl rimmed by tall hills that provided shelter from the rest of the Shift. From above, it looked like a tumble of wreckage, a cluster of corrugated metal and plastic sheets, wooden timbers, broken glass, canvas and cardboard strewed over the wet, dark sand.

But as Doc peered into the ramshackle mess, he soon saw people going about their business down there—muties with the same crimson skin as Ankh and the other shifters. They moved easily among the ruins, darting in and out of half-buried doorways, clambering over smashed rooftops and into shattered windows, leaping from collapsed stairways and diving into pipes and ductwork.

There was activity everywhere, in fact. What looked like jumbled wreckage was actually a thriving community, a veritable anthill of mutie endeavor.

"This is it," Ankh said. "The ville I told you about."

"Incredible." As the rest of the shifters swarmed past him down the hill, Doc stayed at the crest and gaped with open fascination. "It looks as if it has been destroyed and rebuilt numerous times."

"Too many times to count," Ankh told him. "What you see before you is a record of our people's struggle to survive the elements. Which is why the place is called Struggle, of course."

"Why don't they rebuild somewhere else?" Doc asked. "In a still zone or somewhere outside the Shift, perhaps?"

"Because this is home."

Doc frowned. "What about moving some of Hammersmith's equipment here and making this a still zone, then?"

"We don't know how to make it work," Ankh said. "Only Hammersmith could do that."

"All this damage," Doc said. "And all the deaths, past and future. Yet they still will not consider moving?"

"They aren't like you." Ankh sniffed. "You wouldn't understand."

Just then, a high-pitched voice broke in from behind them. "Ankh is right." Exo had slipped to the back of the ranks when Doc hadn't been paying attention. He approached them now, a fresh red-and-white-striped candy cane protruding from between his lips. "Only a shifter can truly grasp the importance of this place."

Instantly, Doc went on guard. The presence of the unpredictable leader of the shifters made his heart race, his muscles tense and the hackles on the back of his neck rise.

As if sensing the tension, Exo clapped a hand on Doc's shoulder, making him tense even more. "But you, of all the humans I have known, came closest to understanding." Exo sank his fingers into Doc's flesh, clamping down with a grip so tight it was almost painful. "Didn't you once tell me this place inspired you?"

Doc wondered if the question was a trap but knew he didn't have long to consider it. "My memory's been faulty lately, but this, I remember." He smiled as he gazed out at the ville of Struggle. "It is very moving indeed. A testament to the resilience of the shifters in the face of great adversity."

Suddenly, Exo's grip tightened, and Doc nearly cried out. Had he said the wrong thing?

But then Exo merely leaned closer and patted his chest. "You do understand." He smiled around the root of the peppermint stick and nodded. "We thrive on defeat. We are destined to rise up and rule, no matter how many times we are crushed."

"An indomitable spirit indeed," Doc said. "Your people are to be commended."

"Commended?" Exo laughed and let go of Doc's shoulder, then hauled back Doc's swordstick and plowed the head of it into Doc's belly. "Bowed down to, is more like it." Next, he smacked Doc hard across the face with his open hand. "We will settle for nothing less!"

Doc stumbled away from Exo, wanting more than anything to strike back at him and end the abuse once and for all, but realizing that to do so could lead to his death.

"Enough talk," Exo said. "We have delayed our arrival too long already."

With that, he ran down the side of the hill toward Struggle, on the heels of the rest of the shifters. That left only Doc and Ankh at the top, staring after the departing leader.

"Why do I always feel like I am on the verge of being killed every time I talk to him?" Doc asked, taking deep, measured breaths to fight the pain from Exo's strikes.

"Because he's always on the verge of killing you every time he talks to you," Ankh replied. "But if it's any consolation, he's like that with everyone."

Doc frowned. "Surely you would save me to ensure your future plans."

Ankh shrugged. "If it makes you feel better, go right on thinking that."

And then the two of them started down the hill toward Struggle.

As Exo AND his troop of shifters strolled into the ville, their mutie brethren came out of the woodwork to greet them. Crimson muties emerged from makeshift shelters, piles of junk and holes in the ground, scurrying through the rain to surround the new arrivals.

They treated Exo and his forces like conquering heroes, showering them with garlands of what looked to Doc like feathers and crumpled newspaper and colored cotton balls. They hugged and kissed the shifters and chanted Exo's name, dancing as they did so with arms upraised.

But when it came to Doc, the locals kept their distance. As he entered the ville, they fanned out around him, staring and whispering. One of them threw a rotten vegetable, which bounced off his frock coat and left a smear.

In this place, Exo was the hero, and Doc was the unwelcome outlander. He would find no relief from his captivity here; he might actually be in greater danger than ever.

For what could have been the millionth time, he looked at his swordstick in Exo's grasp and the LeMat revolver holstered at his hip. Doc was certain that Ryan or Jak or any of the others would have taken them back by now, or at least tried. Sometimes he wished he was more of a man of action like them, more of a physical threat to the savages of the Deathlands. But he was so nonthreatening, apparently, that the shifters hadn't even bothered to restrain him.

And taking on Exo to get back his weapons was a fight Doc didn't think he could win, especially in a crowd of Exo's followers. If Doc wanted a way out, he would have to find it by another avenue.

Another mutie tossed something, a tomato, and Doc stepped aside just in time to avoid being hit. An angry murmur began to build, and Doc felt nervous sweat trickle down his back.

Ankh, who had gotten a little ahead of him, suddenly

turned back and grabbed Doc's arm. "You need to keep up. Here, you are considered an enemy outlander."

"I had not noticed." Doc's sardonic tone belied his deep worry in the face of the mob. He thought it might be worse to be torn apart by the assembled muties' dozens of claws than beaten to a pulp by his own swordstick at Exo's hands.

"The changing landscape of the Shift has not been the only cause of their suffering," Ankh stated. "Bands of marauders have been known to come through these lands, raping and pillaging as they go…at least until the Shift's transformations take their lives or drive them out."

"These people," Doc said. "The shifters of Struggle. Can they read the Shift like you and your people?"

"Yes. Even better."

"Then, why do they not use their foreknowledge to prepare to face the changes?" Doc asked. "To construct countermeasures or reinforce structures to withstand the transformations?"

"The transformations often arise too quickly," Ankh explained. "We don't always have time to plan and act as you suggest."

"I see." As Doc continued through the wrecked shantytown, he marveled that much of it was still standing. Half-collapsed walls leaned at precarious angles, propped up by lengths of rusty rebar and splintered utility poles. Sheds built of sheet metal and plastic tarpaulins sagged and tipped from the weight of the rain. Stacked plywood crates with privacy flaps made from tacked-up old black trash bags teetered in the wind, even as mutie shifters clambered up and down and in and out of them.

It was like one big house of cards, just waiting for the right tremor or gust of wind to knock it down. Yet, somehow, the residents kept it from complete disintegration in what had to be one of the most unstable regions of the Deathlands. It would be worth closer study, to determine what techniques they were using to ensure the ville's survival.

If Doc had had the time to study it instead of just trying to stay alive, of course.

"At least it's a quiet day today," Ankh said. "So far anyway."

Doc nodded, watching as a shack built from cardboard and duct tape fell apart twenty yards away, collapsing inward. Its two occupants had to dig their way out, cursing in high-pitched voices as they pushed aside cardboard sheets that were soaked through from the rain.

Just then, a shrill whistle from up ahead captured Doc's full attention. Looking in the direction of the sound, he saw a crowd gathering around a cobbled-together platform at the end of the muddy street through the middle of town. The street held dozens of shifters—Exo's men plus Struggle residents—but there was only a single figure on the platform: Exo himself, waving Doc's swordstick in the air.

"Let's go." Ankh tipped his head toward the action. "Show's about to start."

As Doc and Ankh drew up to the rear of the crowd, Exo was in the middle of a rousing speech about making the Shift a mutie paradise. The audience responded to his shouted pronouncements and dramatic waving of the swordstick with enthusiastic cheers and wild applause.

Then, when Exo caught sight of the newcomers watching from the back, he focused on Doc. "You! Come up here!" Exo gestured for Doc to join him on the stage. "Let's tell our friends about the future of the Shift!"

All eyes locked on Doc, and he smiled nervously. "Wonderful," he muttered. "What can I say to avoid getting bludgeoned in front of a hundred shifters?"

"Improvise," Ankh said.

"You have been so helpful," Doc said sarcastically.

With that, he started for the platform. The gathered

shifters parted to make way, glaring and whispering as he passed.

"At least no one is throwing rotten vegetables," Doc said to himself. "Not yet anyway."

Smiling halfheartedly, he ascended the unevenly stacked cinder block steps to the platform, which consisted of several sheets of plywood supported by cinder block pillars. As Doc walked across it, he felt the plywood bounce a little under his feet. It wouldn't take much, he thought, to make the whole setup collapse.

"Here he is!" Exo stomped over to meet him, making the platform bounce even more. "This is the man who will make our glorious new destiny possible!" He threw his arm around Doc as if they were best friends. "Ladies and gentlemen, Dr. William Hammersmith!"

The crowd clapped with limited enthusiasm. Doc smiled and nodded, as stiff with tension as a steel girder.

"This man!" Exo touched the head of the swordstick to Doc's chest. "This man is our hope for tomorrow!"

The crowd clapped with slightly more interest, and much of the grumbling ceased. Exo had their attention.

"Dr. Hammersmith has developed a technique for harnessing the power of the Shift!" Exo looked around, meeting the eyes of several shifters in the crowd as he let his words sink in. "With his help, we will control the transformations of this place! The forces that have made our lives a struggle for survival will finally be within our grasp!"

The crowd liked what it was hearing. The clapping got louder, and scattered cheers arose.

"We will use this power against our enemies, to drive them from our lands!" Exo said. "We will use it to reshape the land to suit us! And we will stabilize it so places like this will never again undergo random disasters!"

That part really got the crowd excited. This time, they applauded long and loud, and the cheering was widespread.

Not everyone shared the spirit, though. Casting his gaze to the rear of the crowd, Doc saw Ankh standing with his arms folded across his chest, his expression one of cool detachment.

"Not only that!" Exo's voice kept getting louder and higher as he keyed on the crowd's growing excitement. "Not only that, but we will expand our power beyond the bounds of the Shift! We will use it to change the world outside to our liking!"

As Doc listened, he wondered if Exo's outsize promises had any basis in reality whatsoever. Hammersmith had theorized some form of control over the Shift, apparently, but had he found a way to extend the Shift's transformative qualities to locations beyond the Sandhills? Such a capability would give the shifters a very formidable weapon indeed...if there had been such a theory, that is.

And if Hammersmith had still been alive to implement it.

"With the power of the Shift at our command, we will carve out an empire," Exo went on. "We will never fear or suffer or go hungry again, for the world will be ours for the taking!"

That did it. Finally, Exo had pushed the audience over the top, sending them into a flurry of wild exuberance. They clapped like maniacs, shrieked with delight and danced ecstatically, causing quite a scene of unbridled support. Instead of glaring at Doc, they beamed and waved at him; some of them even chanted his name, or what they thought was his name. "Hammersmith! Hammersmith! Hammersmith!"

For Doc, it was an unreal moment. Even as he smiled back at the capering muties, he felt as if he was in some kind of strange dream in which he'd swapped bodies with someone else and was praying that no one realized the deception.

"William! Doctor Hammersmith!" With a flourish, Exo tapped Doc's shoulder with the swordstick. The muties calmed and quieted as he spoke. "Please say a few words to these people whose lives you're about to make so much better!"

Doc looked out at the crowd and wondered what he could say that might be appropriate without being a groundless claim. The shifters waited quietly, all eyes glued to Doc as if he was some kind of graven idol they were all worshipping dutifully.

Doc cleared his throat. "Yes, yes, thank you." He nodded and smiled, reaching for inspiring words like the ones Ryan often came up with in times of trouble. "My friends." He cleared his throat again. "Your hearts are my heart. Your pain is my pain." He paused. "Your dreams are my dreams."

The audience rippled with applause and a scattering of cheers and whistles.

Doc kept talking. "We are bound together by this place and its unique properties. It has shaped our lives in the past, and we will shape *its* destiny in the future."

Loud whoops and cries and chants told Doc he'd struck a chord with the shifters, though he hadn't really said anything of substance.

"Will you join me in shaping that future?" Doc asked. "Will you all help me to create a brighter tomorrow here in the Shift?"

The crowd roared in approval; the continued rain could not dampen their high spirits. The shifters, including Exo's own troops, jumped up and down and howled with unconditional support.

The waves of their appreciation washed over Doc, giving him a thrilling shiver. He'd forgotten how good it could feel, performing in front of an audience.

As another shiver coursed through him, he opened his

mouth to continue his speech and was cut off by Exo, who stepped up to drown him out.

"Do you see how inspiring this man is?" Exo waved the lion's-head top of the swordstick at Doc. "He was sent to us for a reason. He was put here to unleash our true greatness. And we will do everything in our power to live up to his great expectations!"

That did it. Everyone in the crowd except Ankh went crazy, whooping and hugging and spinning and singing in the rain. It was a scene of absolute jubilation, ecstatic enough to move Doc's own heart, though he was a prisoner with no stake in their celebration and no hope of escape.

This time, Exo didn't try to interrupt the party with more pronouncements. Grinning, he walked to the front edge of the stage, shaking hands with the audience below. When he wasn't doing that, he was pumping his fists in the air and getting the "Hammersmith" chant going again.

As for Doc, he just hung back and kept smiling, though his situation was completely out of control. Those cheering muties… What would they do when they discovered he was an impostor? How would they react when he failed to produce the results that Exo had promised?

Doc's eyes flashed across the crowd to Ankh, who seemed as close to an ally as he was likely to find. Ankh had his own dark motives and secrets, but perhaps he could keep Doc alive long enough for Ryan and the others to liberate him.

Just then, Doc felt his stomach tighten. It bothered him that yet again he was relying on the kindness of others to save him from a scrape. How often had he faced a similar dynamic, in which he wasn't able to rescue himself for one reason or another and someone else had to pull his fat out of the fire? It was not an uncommon occurrence, though it didn't usually bother him to this extent.

Now that he was on his own amid the shifters, his lack

of self-reliance was eating at him. He was starting to feel as if it was high time he stepped up and saved himself for once. But he couldn't, for the life of him, see a way to do it that lay within his capabilities and limitations.

Suddenly, Exo pranced back to him, grabbed his hand and reeled around in a giddy dance. Doc would have preferred to trip him and send him sprawling on the plywood, but instead he played along...a little. He let Exo turn him one way and then the other as the crowd clapped out a sprightly rhythm. He even bobbed his head a bit to the beat, trying to seem like a good sport to the assembled shifters.

Finally, Exo stopped, turned to the crowd and thrust Doc's hand in the air. The muties shrieked and shook their own fists overhead in a gesture of joyous solidarity.

"We have said our piece! The future is ours for the taking!" Exo dropped Doc's hand and gave the swordstick a graceful twirl. "Now let the feasting begin!"

As the locals in the crowd scattered, Doc wondered what their version of a feast could possibly consist of. He envisioned buckets brimming with squirming centipedes and maggots, skewers of still-twitching crickets, bowls of clattering, skittering cockroaches sprinkled with bristly fire ants.

Before he could find out exactly what was on the menu, however, Doc heard a deep rumbling noise from afar. Frowning, he heard it get closer, and then he could feel it shaking the plywood platform.

Earthquake.

Immediately Doc charged toward the cinder block steps. He was not yet on the ground when the shaking intensified, knocking him off the last block at a bad angle.

He came down in the wet sand on his right hip. Wincing, he lay there as the earth kept moving, rocking him inside as well as out.

Then he heard a creaking noise and looked toward it.

Just as his eyes found the source of the noise, he wished they hadn't.

Less than twenty feet away, a mutie tower jury-rigged from rusty plumbing, automobile panels and zip ties was teetering from the quake. Worst of all, the tower was thirty feet tall and teetering in Doc's direction.

His eyes widened, and his heart raced. If the tower fell, it would come down on top of him. It would likely crush him under the weight of the metal panels and plumbing.

Doc clenched his teeth and tried to get up, but the quake surged and threw him back down. Just as he hit the ground again, the tower creaked louder than ever and began to collapse, falling straight toward him.

Chapter Twenty-One

Ricky ran in a zigzag pattern over the wet sand of the Devil's Slaughterhouse, barely staying out of reach of the charging hippo-porcupine.

How much longer until the creature overtook him, or Ricky simply ran out of steam? He had to do something soon to end the chase while he could still survive it.

The De Lisle had a round in the chamber, and Ricky could shoot it just fine on the run, but bullets bounced off that beast with no effect. Whatever its weak spot, Ricky wouldn't have nearly enough ammo or time to find it.

He cut a sharp right around a steep hill, and the monster swerved to follow him. Ricky had tried the same thing enough times to know he couldn't lose the beast with that trick.

But there was one maneuver he hadn't tried yet.

Heart and feet and arms still hammering, Ricky swung an even sharper right and bolted up the hill. He gave it all the juice he had left, launching himself as far as he could up the sandy slope.

He heard the hippo-porcupine roar behind him, felt the thudding of its hooves on the base of the hill, and then heard another roar. This one came from the same low altitude as the first, and Ricky knew why.

Stopping at the halfway point, he turned and saw the creature still at the bottom, pawing at the sand. The angle of the hillside was just too steep for the hippo-porcupine to climb.

Looking down from the safety of the heights, Ricky considered various possible weak points on the animal's body and settled on the eyes. Sitting back, he braced himself on the sand and sighted the carbine, fighting to keep a lock on the creature's left eye while it roared and thrashed its head.

He timed the shot just right. When he squeezed the trigger, the round slid right into the hippo-porcupine's eye socket.

The creature wailed and toppled over on its right side, making the ground shake a little when it hit. Ricky took a moment to catch his breath and wipe the sweat off his forehead.

Then he started looking around for someone to help.

WHEN THE SEVEN-FOOT-TALL armored tarantula lunged to face Ryan, he darted around to its backside yet again, staying out of range of the beast's front-mounted acid jets.

Ryan knew he'd only bought himself another couple of seconds, but he was determined to put them to use. Armor plated and acid spewing the creature might be, but Ryan had an idea of how it might be vulnerable in a way he could exploit.

Taking a deep breath, he got ready, then sprinted around to one of the armored tarantula's front legs. "Hey!" he shouted for attention, and banged on the leg's plating with the butt of the Steyr Scout. "Hey, stupid!"

In response, the creature's black-furred head rotated down to pin him in its unblinking, many-eyed gaze.

Ryan watched for the familiar twitching of the fangs that always signaled a release of acid. "Yeah! I'm talking to you!"

The beast twisted its head back a little farther and made a sound like a belch crossed with a sneeze. Ryan tensed, ready to explode from the spot at any second.

Then he saw the fangs twitch, and he knew what was coming. He lingered half a heartbeat more, then bolted away in the nick of time, just as the acid spray shot out of the creature's maw.

The acid splashed over the tarantula's armored leg, bathing the lower knee thoroughly. Ryan, watching from behind the creature's enormous body, held his breath. He'd known from the start that his plan might be faulty; it made sense that the monster's armor would be resistant to its own acid.

As the acid ran down the leg, the metallic plating sizzled and smoked. The acid was burning its way through to whatever vulnerable parts were within.

Clenching his teeth, Ryan darted to his next objective—the front leg on the other side. "Hey! Hey, dummy!" Again, he banged on the armor with the butt of his rifle.

And again, the tarantuladillo craned its dark face around to look his way. This time, the noise it made was a loud buzzing interspersed with guttural clicks. Whatever it meant, Ryan didn't give a damn.

But when its fangs twitched, all his attention zeroed in on them. Every muscle in his body coiled, ready to spring, and he waited just a second more.

Then he sprung. As before, he bolted away just in time, as the beast's powerful acid washed over its armor-plated leg. He heard the metallic material hissing as the powerful spray ate it away, exposing the once-protected parts underneath.

His face etched with grim determination, Ryan ran around the great beast to the first front leg, which had been cooking just long enough in its acid bath. Swinging up the Steyr Scout, he pumped three rounds into the heart of the damage in quick succession.

Then, as he back stepped, the knee buckled with a loud crunch like a toppling tree. The tarantuladillo thumped down hard on that side, cracking another two legs in the process.

Ryan raced around behind it to the front leg on the other side and repeated the process. The Steyr Scout blasted three rounds dead in the middle of the sizzling hole in the creature's armor.

After which, that side of the beast crumpled, too. It now sprawled flat on the wet sand, alternately mewling and screeching as its own acid continued to eat away at it.

That was when Ryan walked up onto its back as if he was stepping onto a stone. He jammed the longblaster's barrel against the top of the beast's head and cranked the trigger.

The round he fired blew a hole straight through the tarantuladillo's skull, ejecting its sizzling, acid-soaked innards onto the sand below.

"Damn spider." Ryan hopped off the creature's back and immediately scanned the area for whoever needed his help the most.

Quickly choosing his next target, he raced off through the rain, reloading the Steyr Scout along the way.

THE THORNY GREEN tendrils gave Mildred another tug, bringing her to within four feet of the amoeba-like blob. One more pull and she'd be hoisted into its slavering maw, ready to be devoured.

It was time to make her move, the only move she could think of. Unarmed, with her ankles bound by tough tendrils, her options were narrowed down to one. The only alternative she could imagine was death.

So in the brief interval before the next tug, she gathered her strength as best she could, drew in a deep, bracing breath and got ready. There was just enough slack in the tendrils for her to dig her heels into the wet sand. She pushed herself down so her knees were bent, and all her weight was focused on the foothold she'd dug.

Here goes nothing, she thought.

When the tendrils jolted her forward again, Mildred used the foothold as a pivot point and let the force of the jolt slingshot her up and over. Instead of being dragged into the blob's maw, she shot to one side of it and came down hard on the big green pod that controlled the tendrils.

The pod made a kind of whistling sound, like a deflating balloon, and compressed under her weight. At the same time, the tendrils relaxed their grip on her ankles.

Mildred kicked her legs free and scrambled off the pod just as it puffed back up to its former size. Its tendrils thrashed wildly, writhing around in an effort to regain their grip on Mildred.

But she was already bolting across the sand, going after her ZKR 551 revolver.

Mildred could hear the tendrils slithering after her as she ran, close behind. She could swear she felt the tips of them tickling the backs of her legs, just about to make a grab.

She dived for the weapon, then rolled and came up with it in her hands. She opened fire on the tendrils, blasting them back though they were still too tough to blow apart.

Then, after a few more rounds, she leaped up and ran, hoping the tendrils weren't infinitely expandable.

They weren't. Mildred sprinted another thirty yards before they finally stretched to their limit. They flopped on the ground then, pulled taut and quivering after Mildred as if they thought they might still be able to reach her.

At last, Mildred was able to stop running and catch her breath. She slumped forward, panting and sweating, with her hands on her knees.

But she didn't stay that way for long. Moments later, she straightened and looked around for any of her friends in need of help.

JAK STOOD, PANTING, his arms painted in blood up to the elbows. Moments ago, he'd wondered if there was a limit to how much damage the see-through lion's body could repair on its own. If Jak kept hacking it up, would the animal continue to regrow and replace whatever was hurt or missing?

He finally had his answer, and he didn't like it one bit. He'd stabbed and slashed his way through the beast as if there was no tomorrow, butchering it between dodging snaps of its jaws and swipes of its giant paws. There was hardly an inch he hadn't cut with his blade, often plunging it in up to the hilt and twisting with a vengeance, yet…

Yet the lion was still alive and baring its teeth, glaring at him with its glittering dark eyes.

"Hey, kitty." Jak stood six feet back from the big cat but was ready to run at the first sign of pouncing. "Thought supposed have nine lives only."

The lion roared in reply and licked its muzzle, the same muzzle Jak had slashed to ribbons two minutes ago.

Jak shook his head. "Starting bore me." He slid the knife into its sheath at his hip and reached for the .357 Colt Python holstered beside it. "Been fun, but fun wearing off."

As the lion roared again, Jak swung up the Python and cocked it in one smooth motion. Squinting, he drew a bead on the middle of the creature's forehead and squeezed the trigger.

In that same instant, the see-through lion lunged to one side, so the round caught him in his left shoulder instead of his forehead. The impact blew apart flesh and bone, blasting them in all directions.

With a strangled cry, the lion flew back to the ground, hitting like a sack of cement. It lay there, thrashing and groaning, as Jak approached with the handblaster held out before him.

"Still not give up?" As Jak watched, the obliterated shoulder writhed, transparent shredded tissue kneading and reforming into new muscle and tendons. "Survivor like me. Kindred spirit." He raised the .357. "Guess already know who walks away."

The lion mustered a final roar and scrambled to try to regain its feet, then crashed back down. Its body was fixing itself, but not fast enough to save its life.

Unless, of course, a bullet wouldn't be enough to kill it permanently. Jak knew it was a possibility, but what else could he do?

Pulling the trigger, he blasted a round into the animal's head, blowing it to pieces. Then he kept firing rounds into other critical parts, exploding the chest and abdomen with shot after shot.

He stopped only when he ran out of ammo. That was when he took a closer look and realized the lion was still trying to resurrect itself. The little bits of it were twitching and pulsing on the sand, some squirming together and merging into larger pieces.

Jak thought of kicking the lion's remains as far apart as he could get them, then changed his mind. "If manage to rise from dead after that," he said, "deserve second chance."

As THE PIRANHA-WASPS closed in from all around her, Krysty leaped into action. Surging with the power of Gaia, she spun and swept her fist in a circle, smashing away a swath of the creatures with one swipe.

With the accelerated movement and heightened reflexes that came with the power, Krysty flashed this way and that, swatting aside bugs. But even as the ones she struck careened through the air, spinning like meteors to crash down on the wet sand, others jammed their stingers into her flesh.

Blazing-hot bolts of venom shot into her, sizzling through her veins like napalm. Even as Gaia let her fight past it, pushing it back to the depths of her awareness, she knew a world of pain awaited her when the power faded. She just had to hope there wasn't enough poison in those shots to take her life, or the battle she now fought would all be for nothing.

When a cluster of the vicious fish-bugs went for her face, she clubbed it out of the way with the butt of the Glock. Then she pistol-whipped more of the things on her arms and legs and sides. It was better to leave bruises from the blaster's butt than take more hits of venom from the creatures' stingers.

Speaking of which, though she wasn't feeling much pain in her Gaia-empowered state, she had a sudden realization that she couldn't take much more venom. A deep sickness was building in her gut and nerves and brain, and something told her she was nearing her limit.

Krysty marshaled all her strength and speed and cut loose in a graceful, brutal frenzy. She batted and kicked away bugs, whacked them with the blaster's butt, then spun the weapon around and blew a clump of them into chunks and goo.

She continued that way for as long as she could, fending off the swarm until finally there were no more piranha-wasps attached to her body, driving their stingers in deep.

As soon as she stopped, she could feel the Gaia force begin to taper off. She started her descent from the peak of her powers, knowing all too well the venom-induced pain that awaited her. At least there would be no fresh injections of it; at least she had stopped the bug things from overwhelming her.

That was what she was thinking when she heard the buzzing. Turning toward it, she saw the swarm—what was left of it—hovering some thirty feet away, half its original size, but still enough to surround her.

And without Gaia's power surging through her, Krysty knew she wouldn't have a chance of survival.

She took a long, deep breath and tried to steady herself. Warrior that she was, she would go down fighting.

"Come and get me," she grated. "What are you waiting for?"

As if in response to her words, the swarm started gliding toward her.

Then, suddenly, a blastershot boomed from nearby. A round blasted through the swarm, blowing several of the piranha-wasps out of formation. Another shot followed from the same direction, kicking out a few more.

Looking toward the source of the shots, Krysty saw Ricky taking aim with his Webley. He saw her looking and grinned as he pulled the trigger once more, throwing another round into the swarm.

Just then, another shot echoed from a different direction, and Krysty looked that way, too. This time, she saw Jak pointing his Colt Python at the swarm. His arms and torso were soaked with blood, but he otherwise looked to be unharmed from whatever threat he'd been confronting.

As Jak and Ricky fired more shots, Krysty heard yet another blaster in action. This time, the familiar sound of the weapon was enough to make her heart skip a beat, in a good way.

Even before she turned toward the latest blasterfire, she knew who was making it happen. She knew he'd emerged unscathed from yet another battle in the Deathlands, and that meant everything to her.

As Ryan rattled off rounds from his SIG-Sauer P-226, he glanced for an instant in Krysty's direction. His expres-

sion was as grim and intense as ever, completely focused
on his brutal work.

But she knew how he felt about her, and that was all
that mattered. The one-eyed man might not be smiling,
but he was there, and he was doing what he could for her.

Not that she had any intention of letting him do all the
work. Clenching her teeth against the weakness and pain
surging into her as the Gaia power faded, she raised her
Glock and fired at what was left of the swarm. The shot
pegged one of the piranha-wasps dead-on, sending it spi-
raling down to the sand like a crashing plane.

Smiling with a death's-head grimness that was the equal
of her man's, Krysty fired again, knocking down another
bug. And then she fired once more, emptying the blaster
just as the last of her energy ran out, and she collapsed to
the ground.

As one invisible creature swatted J.B.'s back, the other
bashed his front, pasting a heavy blow across his chest. J.B.
gasped at the impact and let himself fall to one side, but the
angle was intentional. He still had a hold of his M-4000
scattergun, and now he had a range on the two beasts he'd
been fighting, one of which he'd already tagged once.

When he hit the ground, he flipped over on his back and
blasted away to the right and to the left, where he knew
the creatures had been just seconds ago.

But they weren't there now, at least not in the path of
his rounds. He heard thrashing but no roars of agony, saw
a muddle of tracks but no imprint of a falling body in the
sand.

Cursing, he scuttled back and scrambled to his feet.
Watching the sand, he saw the tracks of the two creatures
fan right and left around him, resuming their ominous
circling pattern like invisible vultures around a doomed
animal.

If only he could better pinpoint their size and shape, he'd have a better chance of landing a shot. As it was, he thought he had a good idea of the outlines of their undersides and feet, and little else. They kept hitting him with some kind of limb or flipper or pseudopod, but even the extent of that extremity was not clear to him.

As if in response to his thoughts, one of those very limbs thudded into the back of his head. It was then he realized there had to be a third creature in the mix, because the other two were still leaving tracks on each side of him.

"Damn it!" Whirling, he kept a tight grip on the scattergun, listening and watching for traces of the third creature. He heard a rustling from the left, thought he saw the sand dimple and popped rounds in that vicinity but with no discernible contact.

By the time he heard the louder noise—a growling from the right—it was already too late. The thing lurking there plowed its limb across his face, stunning him senseless.

J.B. dropped the scattergun and toppled backward. He hit like deadweight, and blacked out for a moment.

He was snapped back to consciousness by the roar of blasterfire.

Staying low, he looked up and saw Mildred standing twenty yards away, firing her .38 revolver in his direction. She threw three more shots, then stopped to reload.

But the sound of blasterfire instantly resumed from another direction. Only this time, it was the sound of round after round jackhammering from a fully automatic assault blaster.

Twisting, J.B. saw Union blasting away from Mildred's three o'clock, filling the air with a hail of projectiles. It seemed like a solid approach to him; Union's Heckler & Koch outpowered every weapon on the field, laying down enough constant fire that it stood a better chance of ventilating the invisible creatures.

Sure enough, J.B. heard the screams of at least one of the beasts erupting from nearby. He heard a thump and saw the sand compress into an odd-shaped dish under the body of one of the monsters.

Briefly, J.B. considered trying to retrieve his own scattergun and rejoin the fight, but for once, he thought the best strategy might be to let someone else do the shooting.

Meanwhile, Union never let up. She just kept blasting out rapid-fire rounds from the H&K's drum magazine, sweeping the area with hurtling bits of metal that were bound to hit something invisible sooner or later.

Sure enough, another creature howled in pain and thumped to the ground, this time about twenty feet from J.B. Moments later, he heard a third cry and thump from farther away, some thirty yards.

And then he heard a wild shrieking from Mildred's direction. He twisted just in time to see her open fire with the .38, shooting at what looked like thin air right in front of her.

But the thudding sound J.B. heard after Mildred's second shot told him the air over there wasn't so thin after all. There had been a fourth creature, and Mildred had put it down.

Was that all of them? For all he knew, there might be a whole pack of them out there, lurking among the raindrops.

Whether that was true, J.B. was sick and tired of staying out of the line of fire. As soon as he saw Union lower her weapon, he jumped to his feet.

By then, Mildred was rushing up to him with a smile on her face.

"I'm so glad you're all right," Mildred said softly, leaning back to meet his gaze.

"The feeling is mutual." He nodded and drew her in for a hug. After the fight he'd been through, he was happier than usual to still be alive.

"We shouldn't linger," Union said as she stalked toward them, stiff backed and imperious. The braid at her temple was black, meaning Taryn was running the show. "There could be more of those things around, or other things that are even worse."

"No kidding," Mildred agreed. "I've got to hand it to you, Union. You weren't exaggerating about the local wild-life."

"Actually, it's been somewhat worse than I remembered." Union looked around warily. "I've seen some, if not all, of these creatures before, but never in this kind of concentration."

"Could it be this bad up ahead?" Mildred asked.

Union's shrug was barely perceptible. "It's never *not* bad in the Devil's Slaughterhouse."

"Then, I guess you were right," Mildred stated. "About us getting slaughtered, I mean."

Union scowled, somehow taken aback by the comment. Was it possible the Taryn personality didn't remember things that had been said or heard by another personality? Or was it just that she didn't approve of what Carrie had said?

"Hey!" At that moment, Jak ran over with Ricky in tow. "Having second thoughts 'bout shortcut!"

"You were warned, weren't you?" Union said.

"That not point," Jak snapped. "Losing Krysty!"

Without hesitation, Mildred ran after him.

"Damn!" J.B. took off after the two of them, mentally kicking himself for losing track of Ryan and Krysty. If only he hadn't been so wrapped up in his own battle and the aftermath.

If only none of them had entered the Devil's Slaughter-house in the first place.

Looking back over his shoulder, he saw that Union wasn't following them. She was just standing there, watching them all rush away from her. Was she being indecisive again, torn between her multiple personalities? Or was something else going on with her, something far more ominous?

What if she wasn't following because she didn't care if Krysty lived or died? More than that, what if she didn't care if any of them lived or died?

It was something J.B. had known from the start might be true.

Though, whatever Union's intentions were, J.B. already knew one thing for a fact. If Union did go all the way dark at some point, J.B. and his friends would have a hell of a time putting her down before she could do the same to them.

Chapter Twenty-Two

As an earthquake rocked the ville of Struggle, Doc lay in the path of a toppling tower. If the structure came down on top of him, it would likely crush him in an instant.

There were times in his life when he might have frozen in such a situation, times when he might have panicked or had a flashback and required a rescue. But this wasn't one of them.

Adrenaline blazed in his bloodstream, impelling him to action. Throwing himself to the side, he rolled fast across the ground, hurtling out of the path of the tower.

The quick action saved his life, though he wasn't completely unscathed. The rickety structure crashed down beside him, the heavy metal car doors that formed its walls slamming down with such force that all their windows shattered at once. As for the framework of rusty plumbing that had been holding it all together, the impact blew it apart. Broken lengths of copper and iron pipe sprang from the wreckage, flying outward—and one pipe collided with the middle of Doc's back. He cried out when it hit, though at least his spine was spared; the hunk of metal struck to one side of the spinal cord, mostly catching the flesh around his ribs.

The injury stung, but it could have been worse. Gingerly, Doc rubbed the impact site, glad the projectile hadn't smashed into his skull instead.

Then he heard someone else crying out, and he sat up.

Listening and looking around, he quickly identified the source: the plaintive shouts were coming from another collapsed building, one that had fallen across the street from the jury-rigged tower.

Getting to his feet, Doc realized that most of the shifters were focused on other buildings in the center of town. No one seemed to be paying any attention to the crumbled brick-and-timber blockhouse from which the nearest cries for help came.

The thought of turning away never entered his mind. Setting his jaw, Doc hurried across the street and started picking his way through the blockhouse rubble.

"Help!" The voice from within was high-pitched, a child's. "Please, somebody help me! I'm trapped!"

"Help is on the way, my friend," Doc shouted in reply. "I hope to have you out of there in three shakes of a lamb's tail."

"Please hurry!" The voice sounded close, as if the child were a short distance inside the crumbled walls. "My mama isn't breathing!"

"Hold tight, friend." Doc's movements took on added urgency as he pushed aside broken timbers that were blocking the front entrance of the building. Grunting, he picked up bricks that were piled in the doorway and dropped them to one side. His back injury pinged repeatedly, and he kept working through the pain, determined to dig his way inside.

A few more moments and he'd cleared a path into the wreckage. Carefully, he stepped through the doorway and moved down a short passage, stopping twice to push more timbers out of his way.

"Hello?" the child called. "Are you still out there?"

"Yes, my dear." Doc had to ease his way around a heavy timber that was wedged between ceiling and floor and wouldn't budge. "Rest assured, I am still moving in your direction."

"Please hurry!" the child urged.

Doc ducked under another collapsed timber, stepped over a pile of dust and debris, and came to a doorway on his right. He had to contort himself to get through it, setting off his back injury, and then he was in the same room as the child.

He saw now that the shifter child was a little boy, no older than five or six. "You're here!" The boy's eyes widened and lit up from across the rubble-strewn room, where he was squatting on the floor beside his mother's supine body. "You came!"

"There was never any doubt, child." Doc smiled as he picked his way through the rubble.

"My name is Cardy," said the boy. "Can you help my mama?"

"I will certainly try." Doc lowered himself to kneel at the unconscious woman's side. Her skin was pink; the usual deep red color common to shifters had faded.

Cardy had been right: she wasn't breathing. But when Doc pressed his fingers into the artery in her neck, he felt a thready pulse. Maybe it wasn't too late to save her.

"Can you help her?" The boy's face was streaked with tears.

Doc didn't want to get his hopes up. "I will try." With that, he checked her airway, which was clear, and started administering cardiopulmonary resuscitation. It was a technique he had learned from the whitecoats who'd time-trawled him to the 1990s; at least they'd taught him one thing of lasting value during his captivity.

Doc performed chest compressions on the boy's mother, then tipped her head back, pinched her nose shut and puffed breath into her lungs. Her chest rose, then fell, and he blew in another breath.

As he resumed chest compressions, he heard a creaking sound and looked up at the ceiling. He saw a single splintered beam buckling under the weight of sagging wallboard; it was only a matter of time until the entire ceiling collapsed.

After administering another series of breaths, Doc applied more compressions. "Go outside, Cardy," he told the boy. "Go ahead, and I'll meet you shortly with your mama."

"No!" Cardy shook his head vehemently. "I won't leave her!"

"Please," said Doc. "You must."

"No!" Cardy placed a hand protectively on the woman's shoulder. "Just help her!"

Dust from the wallboard ceiling trickled down around Doc. "Go!" he snapped, trying to jolt the boy into getting clear of the imminent ceiling collapse. "Get out of here!"

The boy just shook his head, more tears pouring down his cheeks.

Again, Doc repeated the breaths and compressions, and again the woman didn't respond.

Was Doc going to have to tell the boy that his mother was dead? The thought of it propelled him through another round of CPR. He knew just how it felt to have a loved one torn away, to never see that person again because of the mistakes of others.

More ceiling dust trickled down, and the creaking of the beam grew louder. Doc's heart hammered, and his stomach twisted painfully.

Then, suddenly, the woman inhaled on her own. Breath rushed into her lungs, and she coughed.

"Mama!" Cardy lit up with joy. "Mama, you're alive!"

Just then, the beam above them creaked again, louder than ever. Doc knew they were all out of time. "Let's go!"

Cardy was hugging his mother around the neck, and

Doc pushed him off her. Getting to his feet, Doc scooped the woman up with some trouble, ignoring the protests of his injured back.

"We need to get out of here!" Doc nodded toward the doorway through which he'd entered. "You first!"

Cardy hesitated. "But my mama…" He didn't seem aware of the fact that the beam was about to snap.

"Just do it!" Doc hollered. "Unless you want all this to be for nothing!"

Cardy scowled as if he might cry. "What do you mean, for nothing?"

Doc was exasperated. "Just go!" He said it with the most commanding voice he could, hoping he would cut through the little boy's confusion.

It worked. With a hurt and angry glare, Cardy spun and charged out of the room. As young and nimble as he was, he sidestepped the debris in his path as if it didn't exist.

Doc hurried after him as fast as he could, praying the ceiling would hold up for another few seconds. Navigating the wreckage, he followed Cardy's footsteps through the doorway and into the passage beyond.

Doc was most of the way down the hall when he heard the ceiling collapse behind him. The crash was like a thunderclap to Doc, seemingly all the louder because it signified the death he'd just escaped.

By the time he maneuvered out the door with the woman in his arms, following on the heels of Cardy, an audience had gathered. Five shifters ringed the doorway, watching with wide eyes as Doc emerged from the destruction.

The shifters all cheered for him at once, then surged forward to help him with the woman. By the time they were done, Doc was standing there empty-handed, but not for long.

"Thank you!" Cardy leaped at him and hugged him tight around the middle. "Thank you for saving my mama!"

Doc had to admit, he felt choked up at that particular moment. The boy's gratitude was overwhelming.

So was Doc's surprise and delight at what he'd done. As the reality of it sank in, he relished the thought that he'd acted so decisively and saved someone's life without help or guidance. He'd done it all on his own, with no prodding, and it made him feel good.

He liked being the rescuer much better than being the one being rescued.

"CONGRATULATIONS," ANKH TOLD him later. "You've made quite an impression on the people of Struggle."

Doc was working on a young patient in the middle of the street, setting a broken bone in her arm with a makeshift splint. "I assure you, such was not my intention."

"The result is all that matters," Ankh said. "And the result is that you are a hero to them."

Doc snorted as he wrapped cloth tightly around the splint. "A hero is something I have never been, nor will I ever be."

"Good, good." Ankh smiled. "If there's one thing the people like more than a hero, it's a reluctant hero."

Doc looked up at him, thought about arguing further, then decided against it. Perhaps his apparent heroism fit into some plan of Ankh's that would mean freedom for them both.

"You did something wonderful," Ankh told him. "You, an outlander, risked your life to save the lives of a shifter mother and child. I don't think you realize how profound a statement that is."

"Any decent person would have done the same thing." Doc finished winding the cloth around the splint and clipped the end with a safety pin he'd been carrying.

"But you're not just any person, are you, Dr. Hammersmith?" Ankh winked.

Just then, Exo's high-pitched voice interrupted. "No, he is not."

Ankh raised his eyebrows and stepped back. Whatever his plans were, he deferred to the leader as always.

"Ah, William." Exo stormed over with a pink-and-blue candy stick in his mouth. "We are in your debt, as always. We can never repay you."

Doc helped up the girl whose broken arm he'd set and nodded for her to leave, thinking that Exo could repay him by letting him go.

"Thank you." Looking nervous, she quietly uttered the words and hurried away, skirting heaps of wreckage piled in the street by cleanup crews.

When the girl left, Exo threw his arm around Doc's shoulders. "We do have a reward that I think you'll appreciate, though."

"What might that be?" Doc asked.

"Final revenge against your abductors." Exo grinned. "The people of Struggle were so moved by your heroism, they have volunteered to send an army to wipe out the scoundrels who kidnapped you."

It took an effort for Doc not to show his alarm. Exo had just announced that an army was going to wipe out his companions all because of Doc and his heroism.

"What do you think of that?" Exo squeezed Doc's shoulder so hard, he made Doc wince. "Isn't it a noble sacrifice?"

Doc clenched his teeth against the words he really wanted to say. Looking askance, he caught sight of Ankh, who was nodding forcefully and staring intently in his direction.

"Yes," Doc said finally. "A noble sacrifice indeed."

"This quake has galvanized them against the outlanders," Exo said.

"But the outlanders didn't cause it, did they?" Doc asked.

"Who can say?" Exo shrugged. "Their presence alone might be enough to disrupt the delicate balance of the Shift and spur such disasters.

"But don't worry." Exo swung his arm from around Doc's shoulder and punched him in the biceps. "You won't have to face them, my friend. You'll be far from that battlefront."

Doc frowned. "How far?"

"Dozens of miles in the opposite direction," Exo said. "While the kidnappers are getting their just deserts, you'll be heading straight for the core to finish your work."

Doc cleared his throat. "Maybe I would rather see my kidnappers suffer first. Clear the air, so to speak."

"Can't be helped." Exo shook his head. "We need you to work your magic in the core, or this empire of ours will never get off the ground." With that, he smacked Doc in the middle of the back, hitting the exact spot where his injury hurt the most. "How does it feel to be in demand?"

Doc sucked in his breath at the wild shot of pain. "It feels...good." His eyes watered, but he didn't let himself cry out or show the extent of his discomfort. He was too afraid of what Exo's twisted reaction might be.

"Excellent!" Exo pulled the candy stick from his mouth and waved it in Doc's face. "You're going to change the world, my dear Dr. Hammersmith! In a thousand years, they'll still be singing songs about you and how you made my empire possible!"

Doc smiled and gave him a thumbs-up gesture while choking back his reaction to the still-throbbing back injury. "Wonderful." He hoped Exo didn't pick up on the strain in his voice, the sign of weakness that might invite his vicious scrutiny.

"They'll sing about how you saved that woman and her

child," Exo said. "And they'll sing about how the shifters repaid you with the blood of your abductors."

"Lovely," Doc grunted.

"Now go get ready to see off the army," Exo ordered. "They march within the hour. And make no mistake, they will bring you that blood you seek. The shifters of Struggle are the most elite shock troops in all of the Shift. They cannot be stopped, especially on a vengeance quest like this one."

Doc looked at Ankh, who nodded firmly. Apparently, the Struggle troops lived up to their billing from Exo.

"They will bring you plenty of blood," Exo promised. "And whatever you want from the corpses of those outlander scum. Though, I have to say—" he chuckled "—I cannot personally guarantee what condition they'll be in when they get to you." He laughed, finding the thought of it hilarious.

Then he rushed off down the street, still laughing uproariously.

When Exo was out of earshot, Doc spoke to Ankh. "He should not send those troops. It is a mistake."

"How so?" Ankh asked. "Don't let this ramshackle ville of theirs fool you. They are every bit as deadly as he says."

"My friends…" Doc shook his head slowly. "They will blow them to kingdom come."

"Save your idle threats," Ankh said, and then he shrugged. "Though, if your people are that dangerous… Oh, well."

Doc stared at him. "What do you mean?"

Ankh shrugged again. "If this army was out of the picture, it wouldn't be a bad thing for either of us. That's all I'm saying."

Doc frowned as the implications became clear. Taking the army of Struggle off the board was something Ankh desired, however permanent their absence from the game might turn out to be.

It was a cold-blooded strategy, but the Deathlands was a cold-blooded place.

And bloodshed, all too often, was the only way to survive its brutal climes.

"Don't be so gloomy, Doc." Ankh grinned and reached over to pat Doc's shoulder. "Thanks to you inspiring the people of Struggle with your heroism, their troops—which are intensely loyal to Exo—will be miles away from the core when it most matters."

Doc raised his eyebrows. "And when will it most matter, exactly?"

"When we are there," Ankh said. "And the future is ours for the taking."

Chapter Twenty-Three

"I can't believe she's not dead." Mildred leaned back from Krysty, who was lying on the ground, and wiped sweat from her own forehead with the back of her arm. "She shouldn't be alive after all those stings. Her system is flooded with poison."

Ryan was kneeling at the other side of Krysty's body, gently holding her hand. It was one part of her that hadn't been stung by the vicious bugs. "The Gaia power..."

"It doesn't make her poison-proof," Mildred said. "Unless maybe this place has changed the way she processes the power, or altered her physiology somehow."

"Shift hard on her," Jak said. "Mebbe forced her adapt."

"Whatever's keeping her alive, she's not out of the woods yet," Mildred told them. "She's in some kind of comatose state. Her pulse is so low, it's almost nonexistent."

"She needs medical care." Ryan said it without looking up from Krysty's face.

"More than I can give under these conditions." Mildred's stomach tightened. So many lives had slipped through her fingers since her arrival in the Deathlands, but Krysty's death would haunt her forever.

Krysty was a true friend as well as a teammate; as the only two women in the group, they had bonded on a deep level, supporting each other through the Deathlands' endless challenges and celebrating the few and far between good times, as well. They had become like sisters to each other.

"Okay, then." Ricky turned to Union, who was hovering, as usual, at the fringe of the group. "So where's the nearest place of healing in these parts?"

"What're you smokin', kid?" From the way Union snapped out the words—and the auburn color of her braid—it was clear that Rhonda was in the driver's seat at that moment. "We're in the middle of the Devil's Slaughterhouse! There's nothing here!"

"What about some kind of shelter, at least?" J.B. asked. "Some place to hole up?"

"How the hell should I know?" Union spread her arms wide to take in her surroundings. "This place is constantly changing."

"Choice clear." Jak crouched at Krysty's feet. "Need carry her back way came. Retreat to last redoubt."

"Redoubt?" Union frowned.

Jak ignored her. "I take first shift. Move now. Running out daylight."

"It's a long way back," J.B. said. "And we'll be in deep shit if the terrain starts changing again."

"What alternative?" Jak snapped. "Let die?"

"That isn't going to happen," Ryan said darkly.

"And what about Doc?" J.B. asked. "If we hump back out of here, we're giving up on him, plain and simple."

"We'll split up," Ryan told them. "Just like we talked about before, when we were going to get Krysty away from the source of the seizures."

"Worth a try." J.B. nodded. "And we were talking about backing out of the Devil's Slaughterhouse anyway, so we don't have to split up yet."

"We can talk about who goes where on the way to the split," Ryan said. "Good thing we've got an extra body along."

He looked at Union, and so did the others. She just kept staring into space with an icy gaze, as if the black braid at her temple wasn't proof enough that Taryn was in charge.

The team made preparations to leave, and Mildred checked Krysty's pulse one more time. It was so faint, she almost couldn't find it.

"Come on, honey," Mildred said softly, pitching her voice so only Krysty could hear it. "You've got to keep it together. We're all doing our best here, but you have to keep fighting, too."

Just then, Ryan returned from prepping his gear and crouched alongside Krysty. "Is she good to go?"

Mildred nodded. "Ready to roll."

"I guess it goes without saying, but you're not leaving her side, Mildred."

"The only way I leave this patient is if I'm dead." Mildred met his eyes with grim determination. "We can't lose her, Ryan. We can't let it happen."

"You think I don't know that?" Ryan slid one hand under the middle of Krysty back and the other hand under her knees. "Nobody and nothing's taking her away from us." With a grunt, he lifted her off the ground and stood. "That's just how it is."

Suddenly, Mildred heard a strange sound in the distance—a thunderous pounding of the ground. Seconds later, she felt a pummeling tremor reach deep inside her, shaking her from within.

"What the hell now?" Whipping around toward the sound, she saw its source: a herd of black, horned animals stampeding in a vast mass over the horizon.

"Buffalo!" The nearest sandhill was at least fifty yards away, and Ryan hurried straight for it. Protecting Krysty was his top priority.

As for Mildred, she drew her .38 ZKR and joined the others, who were forming a line facing the buffalo.

"Let's see if we can knock enough down that it'll turn

the herd." The hoofbeats were so loud by now that J.B. had to holler to be heard. "On my mark! Ready!"

Everyone along the line flicked off safeties and chambered rounds.

But as the animals got closer, Mildred wondered if the team's arsenal would be enough. Like every other creature they'd encountered so far in the Devil's Slaughterhouse, these buffalo had been changed in an unnatural way.

Specifically, they all had an extra horn in the middle of their heads, a bone-white spike sparking with electrical current. The closer they got, the more clearly Mildred could see that all the horns were connected by dancing streamers of force, linked in a crackling golden network.

"Aim!" J.B. shouted.

"Aim?" Jak laughed. "Hard to miss."

Still, the wall of electrified buffalo rumbled closer. They were less than a hundred yards away now.

Mildred swallowed hard. If she and her teammates couldn't turn the herd aside, they would surely be trampled to death. The air she was inhaling could very well be the last she ever breathed before her body shut down forever.

Her finger tightened on the trigger. Electrical bolts zapped the ground ahead of the herd, coming perilously close.

Then, suddenly, she heard an unexpected sound over the thunder and crackle. A shrill whistle pierced the air, punching through the interference and instantly getting her attention.

Looking over her left shoulder, she saw Ryan standing in front of the hill where he'd taken Krysty…only Krysty was no longer in his arms. Instead of carrying her, he was waving his arms over his head, gesturing emphatically for her to join him. J.B. was about to order the firing line to open up on the herd when Mildred started shouting.

"It's Ryan!" she yelled. "Look, over there!"

Everyone looked at once. Over by the hill, Ryan stuck his fingers in his mouth and whistled again, then waved some more.

"Let's go!" Mildred said. "He's calling us over!"

"But what about target practice?" Jak shouted. "Like shooting buffalo in barrel!"

Just then, an electrical blast scorched the ground at his fcct, and Jak jumped back.

"Stun guns on the hoof, is more like it!" hollered Ricky.

"Come on!" Mildred didn't wait for a group vote. Whirling, she broke into a full-tilt run, sprinting as fast as she could for the hill.

Were the other three behind her? She was certain they were. J.B., especially, would never let his girlfriend get away from him in the heat of danger.

Trying not to think about the buffalo stampede, though it made the ground under her feet quake with each running step, she charged toward the hill. Yard after yard flicked past as she hurtled over the wet sand, crossing the midpoint and gathering her strength for a hardcore kick to the finish.

Mildred got a stitch in her side and pushed past it. Ryan was waving with increasing urgency; this was no time to give in to pain.

As she closed the gap to twenty yards, then ten, she felt as if the buffalo were right on top of her. Reaching deep, she found her last reserves of energy and tapped them, powering a final furious dash.

When she got to Ryan, he caught her, spinning around with the force of her momentum. "Get inside!" he shouted. "Go around!" Letting go, he pushed her by the shoulders, shoving her around the curve of the hill.

Without thinking, she followed his orders. She looped around the bend of the hill, looking for some kind of access point, and spotted an open hatch that was low to the ground and half her height.

The thunderous hoofbeats pounded closer. Mildred needed no further incentive to duck into the hatch and out of the path of the electrified herd.

Chapter Twenty-Four

Jak was the last one through the hatch, following on Ryan's heels. By then, the front rank of the buffalo herd was hammering past, sending teeth-rattling tremors surging up from the quaking earth.

Jak slammed the hatch door shut behind him, then straightened and looked around. Until that moment, he hadn't given much thought to what awaited him inside the hill; if it was good enough for Ryan to summon him, it had to be safe enough for Jak and the others to enter.

What Jak saw when he scanned his surroundings didn't give him a lot of answers, though. He was standing at the edge of a laboratory, purpose unknown. Stainless-steel counters and equipment gleamed in the white light from fluorescent tubes mounted on the ceiling. Computer screens danced with video, electronic waveforms and columns of numbers. Glass beakers and racks of test tubes crowded counters and shelves, tinkling from the percussion of the buffalo herd's hooves.

But what interested him the most was the examination table in the middle of the room. Krysty lay on that silver surface, still unconscious, as a man in a dirty white lab coat leaned over her, injecting her arm with something from a syringe.

Ryan stood a few feet back from that table, watching the proceedings with intense interest. Jak stepped up, touched his shoulder and asked a question in a quiet voice. "Who?"

"*Duh.* A doctor, obviously." The man snapped out the words in the gravelly voice of a longtime smoker. "But you can call me, 'Thank you, sir, for saving my life.'"

Jak wasn't sure if he should be more pissed off or amused, but the doctor was working on Krysty, so he went with amused.

"Funny guy." Jak chuckled. "No manners, but funny."

Suddenly, the doctor swung up the syringe and brandished it like a weapon. "Do not underestimate me!"

Jak smirked. "If say so."

The doctor was squat—no taller than five-three—and not visibly muscular. He had a face that resembled a chimpanzee's, with close-set eyes, a broad, flat nose and a muzzle like half a grapefruit. His ears stuck out of the sides of his head like cup handles, and his hair was a thinning black decal, glistening with oil and split down the middle.

He didn't look like much, but Jak had learned long ago just how deceiving looks could be. This middle-aged whitecoat could be full of unsupported bluster or the deadliest foe that Jak and the others had ever encountered.

"I can toss you back out into the Slaughterhouse just like that." The doctor snapped his fingers.

"Like see try."

The doctor frowned at Ryan. "What's with the way this guy talks?" He pointed the syringe at Jak. "Is he simple or something?"

Jak laughed. "Heard about actions, Doc?"

The doctor's frown deepened. "What in the hell are you talking about, Casper?"

"Actions." Jak let a sadistic grin spread over his features. He drew one of his leaf-bladed throwing knives and spun it around his finger. "Louder than words. And not Casper."

At that moment, Ryan caught Jak's gaze. "Dial it back." His one-eyed stare was dead serious. "Let the man work."

"Yeah, Casper." The doctor sneered and stuck up both middle fingers in a double salute intended for Jak.

Before Jak could respond, Ryan stepped closer to the table and snapped out a question. "What's her condition?"

Instantly, the doctor switched to professional mode. "I have her stabilized for now. Lucky for you, I keep plenty of epinephrine on hand. Never know when you're gonna need it with those fish-wasps around."

"Wait." Mildred, who'd been observing but hanging back on the doctor's side of the table, pushed forward. "What else did you give her? I saw you administer the epi, but what was the other injection?"

"Antivenom." The doctor grinned and waggled his busy black caterpillar eyebrows. "My own special recipe." He leaned closer to Mildred. "You'd be surprised at what I can cook up, honeybunch."

Mildred didn't flinch. "Know what I think is adorable?"

The doctor's grin widened. "What's that?"

"A man who doesn't realize he's about to get his ass kicked." Mildred nodded emphatically and elbowed him aside.

"I love a woman who plays hard to get!" The doctor rubbed his hands together briskly. His laugh was a stuttering, wheezing snicker from deep in his throat. "Though, y'know, if you wanted to throw yourself at me in gratitude for pulling your ass out of the fire, that'd be okay, too." He gave her a broad wink as he scuttled away from the exam table. "Let's just say I've been alone in the Devil's Shit-House for a long time, sweet-knees."

"How did you end up out here in the first place?" Ricky asked.

"I might ask the same of you, rug rat," the doctor said, "if I were a nosy person. Just like I told tall, dark and one-eyed when he dragged his girlfriend in here—it's for me to know and for you to find out."

As the doctor wobbled toward a counter across the lab, Jak turned to Ryan. "This guy nasty," he said under his breath. "Not trust him."

"Mebbe." Ryan nodded, also speaking softly. "But he could've left us out there to die. He didn't have to open the hatch and invite us in."

Jak narrowed his ruby eyes and snorted. Ryan had a point, but he didn't have to like it, and it wouldn't keep him from disliking his so-called host.

Fortunately, a welcome distraction took his mind off the doctor just then. The rhythmic tremors that had been rattling the place since his arrival were fading.

"Buffalo herd finally past," he said. "All clear out there."

"*Clear* is a relative term," the doctor said as he retrieved a red coffee can from the counter and peeled off the black plastic lid. "*Clear* in the Devil's Shit-House and *clear* in the rest of the world are two very different things." Plunging his pudgy hand into the can, he pulled out a small plastic bag full of dried green buds and a packet of rolling papers. "But if you want to channel your inner morons and go out for an afternoon stroll, don't let me stop you."

"Say, Doc," J.B. said, "you don't have a lot of friends, do you?"

The doctor held a rolling paper between thumb and forefinger and sprinkled crushed bits of green bud into it. "I'm not really what you'd call a people person."

"Then, why the hell did you invite us in here?" J.B. asked.

"You really don't know?" The doctor put down the plastic bag, then rolled the paper and crushed buds into a skinny cigarette. With practiced ease, he swiftly licked the gummed edge of the paper, sealing the joint. "It's all because of that one." He said it matter-of-factly and pointed the end of the joint in the general direction of the group.

"That one who?" Jak asked.

"The Iron Maiden, of course." The doctor pulled a pre-dark butane lighter from a pocket of his lab coat, then used it to ignite the tip of the joint while inhaling deeply. He held the smoke in his lungs for a moment before letting it out with a cough. "We have a history together."

As one, the teammates all turned and stared at Union, who was standing stiffly near the hatch. She stared back at them with icy detachment.

"I guess she hasn't told you about the skeletons in her closet yet." The doctor snickered. "I'm sure she was getting around to it, though. Right, metal britches?"

"It's true," Union said without changing her expression in the slightest. "We do share a history."

Again, the doctor snickered. "You gotta love this chick, am I right?" Then he lifted the joint for another puff. "Don't expect to get too much out of her, though. She's a woman of few words."

"Actually—" Union slowly turned her head and focused her glacial gaze on him "—you might be interested to know that he's the architect of the Shift. This place exists because of his reckless experimentation."

The doctor choked on his latest lungful. "Well, I'll be damned! I didn't see that coming!"

"And his name," said Union, "is Dr. William Hammersmith."

"Well, shit." Hammersmith giggled and shrugged. "I guess the jig is up."

"And," Union said, "he's supposed to be dead."

Chapter Twenty-Five

"Dr. Hammersmith!" Exo shouted. "Provide the benediction for these brave men and women as they depart on their holy mission!"

Doc Tanner, who stood beside Exo on the makeshift reviewing stand in the middle of the town of Struggle, cleared his throat. Gazing at the army of shifters arrayed in the street before him, he found it hard to think of a blessing he wanted to give them.

After all, they were setting out to kill Doc's only true friends in the world. And they were legion; he counted hundreds in their ranks. He hadn't imagined there were so many people in the little wrecked town, nor that so many of them were soldiers.

As formidable as Ryan and the others were, could even they withstand such numbers? Could they survive the big artillery cannon parked at the edge of town, which the shifters would take with them into the fight? And once the terrain started shifting—as it seemed it inevitably would—how could normal humans hope to triumph over muties who could read and ride the transformations?

"Go ahead, William." Exo reached over and pinched Doc's leg so hard, he almost cried out. "They await your inspirational message."

"Yes, yes." Doc cleared his throat again and smiled. "My friends!" He raised his voice and spread his arms. "May the blessings of your creator keep you safe on your journey!"

The crowd cheered, but their hearts weren't really in it.

Exo kept grinning around his latest peppermint stick as he pinched Doc's leg even harder. "Step it up!" he whispered. "You can do better than that!"

Doc winced from the pain of the pinch, then spoke to the crowd again. "May you comport yourselves well on the field of battle, meeting all challengers with staunch reserve and unyielding…"

This time, Exo jabbed him in the kidney with the head of his own swordstick. Doc actually jerked forward and let out a gasp against the pain.

"Kill them all!" Doc shouted. "Murder the bums!"

And that, finally, was what the crowd—and Exo— wanted to hear. Everyone howled and hooted with savage delight, rhythmically pumping their longblasters and swords in the air as if in a choreographed production number.

"Yeah!" Exo wailed. "Kill! Kill! Kill! Kill!"

The army sang along and stomped its feet. Watching them, Doc felt sick to his stomach. Hundreds of shifters were getting ready to hunt down and slaughter his friends, and he had helped them get in the spirit.

"Go get 'em!" Exo swung the swordstick overhead with joyous abandon. "Bring back buckets of their blood for your children to bathe in!"

The crowd cheered louder than ever, chanting, "Blood! Blood! Blood! Blood! Blood!"

"Now go!" Exo shrieked, pointing the swordstick at the far edge of town. "Carry out your sacred mission and make us all proud!"

Still chanting, the army marched off down the street, their heavy footsteps carrying them into the hilly wasteland beyond.

Meanwhile, behind them, their children watched from

ruined hovels, quake-damaged shanties that looked ready to collapse at any moment.

"What about the children?" Doc asked as the troops flowed off into the distance.

Exo shrugged. "Not my kids." With that, he turned and jogged down the reviewing stand steps—a precarious stack of mismatched wooden crates. "Now pack up your shit! We leave in one hour!"

Doc sighed. He had no shit to pack up, not these days, and he wasn't looking forward to another forced march through the Sandhills.

But then, as he considered the best way down those rickety crates, his mood improved considerably. Looking in all directions, he realized something had changed... changed for the better.

For the first time since his abduction, the first time in days, he was on his own. No one was watching him.

HEART POUNDING, DOC crouched in the shadow of a toppled building. He knew it wouldn't be long until one of the shifters came looking for him. What could he possibly accomplish in that limited amount of time?

Escape was impossible. No matter which way he went, there was nothing outside the ville but open ground and low, sandy hills.

Hiding in the ruins of the ville wouldn't make any sense, either. The shifters seemed to know the place inside out, even after the earthquake had shaken it to pieces.

That left him with very few options to take advantage of a rapidly closing window of time.

What would Ryan Cawdor do? As soon as the question fluttered into his mind, he shooed it out again. What Ryan would do involved the methodical murder of shifters, the seizure of their weapons and a blazing shootout that ended with every last one of the enemy bleeding to death on the sand.

Asking himself what his other companions would do produced similar results. Yet again, he wished he were more adept at lethal action, better suited to survival in the perpetual blood-soaked melee of the Deathlands.

Kicking at scattered debris, he cast about for something that could aid his quest for freedom. The whole time, his heart hammered with increasing speed; he knew his time alone was running out. He could practically sense Ankh sniffing the air, picking up his scent.

Suddenly, something in the rubble caught Doc's eye. Bending, he fished it from the dirt and held it up for closer inspection.

It was thin and rectangular, a metal strip about an inch long by a half inch wide, with a slit down the middle. When he wiped off the dust on the sleeve of his coat, he could see polished sharp edges on the long sides of the strip.

A razor blade.

Doc frowned. He had no doubt that Ryan or Jak could have used it to kill their way out of captivity, but to him, it wasn't much. Though he acquitted himself well with his sword or revolver in hand, he lacked his comrades' stealth and skill in close-quarters combat. He couldn't imagine the razor blade would be much good to him.

Still, it was better than nothing. He slipped it into a hidden pouch in the lining of his coat, already thinking of how he might put it to use.

No sooner had he done that than Ankh came around the corner. "There you are!"

Doc had his back to him, and an idea presented itself. He pretended to fumble with the buttons of his trousers, then slowly turned. "My apologies," Doc said. "I needed a moment of privacy."

Ankh chuckled. "Not the preferred protocol for relieving oneself in the ville, but no one seems to have witnessed your breach."

"Thank you." Doc nodded. "I will endeavor to be more discreet in future."

"It's just as well you got it over with." Ankh started walking and waved for him to follow. "We're getting ready to leave now."

"Heading for the core again?" Doc asked as he fell in step behind Ankh.

"That's where it's all going down. That's where you're going to work your magic." He swirled his hands in the air with a flourish.

"Then, by all means, let us away," Doc said. "I, for one, cannot wait to see how exactly I am going to work that magic."

"You'll find out." Ankh laughed. "But not until we get there."

"Surely a little clue would not be out of order at this juncture. I think I've more than proved my loyalty and trustworthiness by now."

"Relax." Ankh reached back and patted Doc's arm. "You'll thank me when this is all over. Trust me."

"Oh, of course." Doc smiled and patted his coat over the hidden pouch where he'd stowed the razor blade. "That goes without saying."

Chapter Twenty-Six

"As much as I love you guys," Dr. Hammersmith said, waving around the butt of the joint he'd just smoked, "please do me a huge favor and go."

Ryan was having a hard time being patient with the difficult doctor, who was being both evasive and rude. "I just asked why Union thought you were dead."

"Everyone," Union stated. "Everyone thinks he is dead."

"Exactly." Ryan nodded. "Why is that?"

"Because!" Hammersmith rolled his eyes with exasperation. "I *made* them think that!"

"Impossible." Union scowled. "People saw it happen. They saw you die in that explosion."

Hammersmith sucked on the roach, making its tip flare red. He inhaled deeply, held the smoke for a moment, then laughed it out with his snicker-wheeze. "If that's what they saw, then I guess I must be dead right now. In which case, this is one shitty afterlife."

"If you're already dead, then I guess it won't matter if I use this on you." Union pointed the Heckler & Koch at him. "Bullets ought to go right through a ghost like you."

"That's right." Hammersmith nodded and laughed some more. The marijuana seemed to be kicking in, from what Ryan could see. "Go ahead and fire a few rounds through my ectoplasm for shits and giggles."

Ryan looked at Union, proving he could deliver as icy a stare as she could any day of the week. The message got through to her; her expression was one of disgust, but she lowered the H&K as he'd intended.

"Listen." Ryan leaned on the edge of the table where Krysty still lay unconscious. Whatever Hammersmith had given her, it seemed to be working; she was breathing evenly, and her pulse was getting stronger, which was more than enough reason to be patient with the difficult man. "We just want to understand the situation. You trusted us enough to let us in here, so why not fill us in?"

"I would." Hammersmith cupped his hands around his mouth and whispered conspiratorially, "But then I'd have to kill you."

As the doctor cracked up at his joke, Ryan shook his head and folded his arms across his chest. Maybe he would have to wait until the weed ran its course for Hammersmith to give him a serious answer.

Or maybe someone else would have more luck. "Enough of this horseshit." Mildred stomped over and stood before Hammersmith with her fists planted firmly on her hips. "Did you fake your damn death or what, dipshit?"

Hammersmith snicker-wheezed harder than ever for a moment, then shifted gears. Gaping up at her with his puffy, bloodshot eyes, he stopped laughing and reached out with a thick-fingered hand toward her face. "I love it when you call me that, honey—"

Before he could finish the sentence, she swatted his hand away. "Answer the question!" she snapped.

On the other side of the room, J.B. took a subtle step forward, ready in case she needed backup. As for Ryan, he was thinking about intervening, but then Hammersmith did the unexpected.

He answered the question. "Yes, I did fake my death." He shrugged. "It was the only way to stop those assholes from using me."

"Using you to do what?" Mildred asked.

"Make the Shift even worse than it already is." Hammersmith relit the roach and had another toke, then put it out in an ashtray on the counter. "Which is really saying something, right?"

"But the Shift is your handiwork!" said Union, who sounded more like high-strung Carrie than icy Taryn at the moment. "You created it!"

Hammersmith looked at her as if she was a complete moron. "You think I wanted it to come out this way?" He let out a laugh that was more of a seal-bark than a snicker-wheeze. "I thought I was making a paradise. Instead, I ended up with a king-size shithole."

Union's eyes got huge, and she stammered, "But I... But you..."

"And you wanna know what the worst part of it is?" Hammersmith opened a cupboard under the counter, pulled out a bottle of predark vodka and unscrewed the cap. "Those shifters just love it!" He threw back a swig and wiped his mouth on his dirty lab coat sleeve. "Hell on Earth is their idea of heaven." Another swig from the bottle. "And they want to make it even more of a nightmare. In fact, they want to weaponize it."

Ryan's eyebrows went up at that one. "Weaponize?"

"And the shittiest part of it all?" Hammersmith drank from the bottle again—a big gulp instead of a swig. "They're halfway there, thanks to me."

"Halfway there?" Ryan repeated.

"I put the wheels in motion before I left." Hammersmith guzzled more vodka. "And the shifters aren't all morons. I can think of at least one of them who could take the program the rest of the way without me, sooner or later."

"What happens when the program's done?" J.B. asked. "What will they be able to do with it?"

"Make all hell break loose," Hammersmith said. "Bring about unlimited pain and suffering. That's all you really need to know." With that, he clunked the bottle on the counter. "I suggest you follow my plan and get the hell outta Dodge before then."

"Not leave till rescue friend," Jak said. "Going to core."

Hammersmith smirked and shook his head. "That's the one place you don't want to be when the shit hits the fan, Casper."

"Handling shit not problem," Jak said.

"You've never encountered shit like this before," Hammersmith said. "Take my word for it."

"So you're saying the shifters are going to make all hell break loose because of something you started? They're going to cause a world of hurt because of your invention?" Mildred stared at him with narrowed eyes. "Sounds to me as though you ought to be running to the core instead of away from it."

Hammersmith laughed and chugged more vodka. "Why the hell would I do something like that?"

"Because you want to stop the destruction before it starts?" Mildred suggested. "Because you have a conscience, maybe?"

"Did I say I have a conscience?" Hammersmith drank again and snicker-wheezed his amusement. "I just want to get the hell away from this place before the crazy starts, *capisce*?"

"Or you could man up and take responsibility for your role in this," Mildred said. "Maybe you could do something about it, since you're the one who set it in motion."

"Look, honeybunch," Hammersmith said. "If you're looking for someone to man up, you've come to the wrong misanthrope. I suggest you take your misplaced faith elsewhere."

"But we could work together," Mildred stated. "Pool our knowledge and resources."

Just then, Union interrupted. "Don't waste your breath." This time, she had an auburn braid and sounded like Rhonda. "I've seen this prick in action. He doesn't believe in cleaning up the messes he makes."

"Listen to her. She's right." Hammersmith nodded and hiked a thumb in Union's direction. "I'm a total piece of shit, and she knows it."

"But you live in a place of constant change." This time, it was Krysty doing the talking. Sometime during the conversation, she'd awakened from her deep sleep. "Perhaps there is no better place for you to forge a new beginning and make up for the mistakes of your past."

Hammersmith held off on the sarcasm and seemed to consider her words, but only for a moment. "I'm starting to regret saving your ass, you know that?"

With a snort, he stomped across the lab and disappeared through a door, which he slammed shut behind him.

"That guy sure has issues," Ricky said.

"You think so?" Mildred asked as she moved to examine Krysty. "But I have to admit, he's no slouch in the medical-treatment department. Our girl here is alive only because of him."

Ryan held Krysty's hand and smiled down at her. He'd moved in close as soon as she'd started talking. "We're lucky we found him."

"All right, then." Ricky turned to Union. "Mebbe you can fill us in. What's all this about a 'shared history'?"

"I'd rather not talk about it," Union said coldly.

"But whatever happened between you might be important in helping us find Doc," J.B. told her.

"It's none of your business," Union snapped. "And it won't make any difference in finding your friend."

At that, Ryan looked up from Krysty. "We'll be the

judges of that, Union." His voice was even and numbingly cold, laced with threat and conviction.

As Ryan watched, Union's face shifted from aloof to openly hostile, then to the most surprising expression yet: a big, serene smile. "I was his human guinea pig," she said, her voice sunny…sunnier than it should have been, given the words she was saying. "A volunteer guinea pig, actually. He tested the Shift technology on me, to make sure it wasn't harmful to humans."

Ryan nodded slowly, putting two and two together. "You said you've been broken ever since you lived in the core. Hammersmith's tech is what broke you, isn't it?"

"We thought exposure to it was safe. I had no idea what it might do to me." Union, whose braid had turned brown, scrunched up her nose, raised her hands with palms toward the ceiling and nodded energetically. "In the end, it made me what I am today."

"But you got away," J.B. said.

Union nodded again. "I didn't fake my own death, but I slipped away from the core. Or should I say 'we'?" She tapped the side of her head. "Four women in one body, remember?" Her smile widened.

"And you're the fourth, I take it?" Mildred asked. "What's your name?"

"Dulcet." Union fluttered her fingers in a friendly wave. "Great to meet you!"

"What happened after you escaped from the core?" J.B. asked.

"We ran for the border of the Shift," Union said. "We thought the farther we got from the core, the less fragmented we'd be." She shrugged. "But it didn't work that way. The four of us didn't reintegrate into one personality. If anything, we became more divided."

"So you came back?" Ricky asked.

Union nodded. "We thought mebbe we could fix ourselves by returning to the core instead of running away from it. Mebbe we could find a way to fix our broken mind."

"Now here you are," Ryan said. "With the man who caused your condition in the first place. The man you thought was dead."

"Second-chance revenge," Jak said. "Take out one who ruined life."

"Or mebbe he can help you," Krysty suggested. "Mebbe he can help you heal."

"That would be great, wouldn't it?" Union beamed and gave her platinum blonde ponytail a toss, then sank into a scowl. "If he was a decent human being instead of a total selfish bastard."

Snarling at the door through which Hammersmith had gone, Union spun on her heel and stormed toward the hatch that led outside. Without another word or a look back at the team, she threw the hatch open so hard it slammed against the wall, then bolted through the opening and let it crash shut behind her.

"So." J.B. cleared his throat. "Now what?"

"Can't tell which crazier," Jak said. "Doctor or Union."

"Beats me." Ryan, who was still holding on tight to Krysty's hand, shook his head. "But one thing's clear. We need to get them to cooperate."

"Good luck with that," Mildred said sarcastically.

"If the shifters are taking Doc to the core, we need to get there, and we need to infiltrate the place," Ryan said. "If Hammersmith and Union both help us with that, we'll increase our chances of extracting Doc in one piece."

"Seem like tall order," Jak stated.

"We'll figure it out," Ryan replied. "Mebbe they just need a little time to cool off."

"Sure," Mildred said. "Or maybe Union never comes back."

"She'll be back." Krysty sat up on the examination table

and swung her legs over the side. "There's a reason she's stayed with us so far, I think. As for Dr. Hammersmith…" She boosted herself down off the table and stood for a moment, gaining her equilibrium. "I'll handle him."

Chapter Twenty-Seven

Doc was two hours out of the ville of Struggle, marching with Exo and his troops as always, when he first got the funny feeling.

"Doc." Ankh, who was once more glued to his side, looked at the old man with mild concern. "Are you well? You look a little green around the gills, as they say."

Doc frowned. The feeling had started in the back of his head and was quite unfamiliar—not that he intended to give Ankh any information about it. The less his shifter babysitter knew about his situation, the better. "No, no. I'm fine. But thank you for asking. Your concern is much appreciated."

Ankh stared a moment longer, then shrugged. "You are welcome, of course. Please don't hesitate to let me know if the time comes when you do feel less than good."

"Certainly." Doc smiled, but his distraction over the strange feeling was great. As he walked on across the sand, surrounded by Exo's forces, the back of his head fizzed as if someone had pumped carbonated soda into it.

Doc tried to shake it off and kept walking, looking as trouble-free as he could. But then the feeling grew stronger and spread around the sides and top of his head, as well.

"By the way," Ankh said. "Why do they say 'green around the gills,' if norms don't have gills?"

"Actually, norms do have gills during certain stages of fetal development in the womb." As Doc said it, the fizzing sensation moved into his eyes. His vision began to blur.

"Is that so?" Ankh chuckled. "And here I thought perhaps it was only a figure of speech."

Doc managed to get out one forced chuckle, and that was all. He was too busy trying to keep his eyes focused and steady in spite of the fizzing and agitation going on inside them.

Then, suddenly, everything seemed to flicker and turn bright yellow. The fizzing became an audible crackling sound, and a wave of warmth flowed down from his head to his toes.

Doc took a few more steps, and then the warmth intensified, as if he were moving closer to a fire. Another few steps, and the heat surged and changed, becoming a blaze of pure white light.

Overwhelmed, Doc stopped in his tracks. For a moment, he felt as if his body had burned away, leaving his soul wavering in the flood of light like a single frond of grass in a mighty, rushing river.

Then the shell of his body seemed to resolidify around him, encasing his bright white essence and cutting it off from the powerful tide washing over that particular time and place.

"Doc?" Ankh's voice was like a distant echo at first, but then it shot closer as Doc returned from his experience. "Are you sure you're all right?" He reached for the old man's arm.

Doc brushed him off. "Of course I am." It wasn't easy after what had just happened, but he managed not to tremble and kept his voice from shaking. "Everything is very much all right, I assure you."

Just then, one of the shifters shouted, drawing Ankh's attention away from Doc.

"Excellent." Ankh nodded. "Our sensitives just picked up the first trace of an impending change to the landscape."

Doc made it a point to act indifferent, but the news

caught his interest in a big way. It could have been no more than coincidental timing that the sensitives picked up traces of a Shift change just as Doc experienced his funny feeling. Or it could mean something altogether different and more staggering.

Ankh chatted with other shifters for a moment, then turned back to Doc. "They think a new shortcut is about to open up. A kind of underground chute we can slide through for miles."

Doc raised his eyebrows. "Intriguing," he said, but all he kept thinking was that perhaps he felt the phenomenon approaching.

"Get yourself ready." Ankh strapped the Winchester longblaster to his back and checked the rest of his gear. "If this does turn out to be a slideway, things will move pretty fast. You don't want to be left behind."

Doc looked down and patted his pockets, but he didn't have any gear to check, unless he counted the razor blade. That left him free to focus on what mattered most at the moment, which was the accuracy of his funny feeling.

Because if he really was making a connection to the Shift, he'd been given a truly game-changing ability.

"Here it comes!" Ankh extended his arms in front of him and closed his eyes. He slowly turned from Doc, facing the ground where the old man had sensed the flow of energy.

It was then that Doc had a resurgence of the feeling, a second flood of fizzing, crackling warmth. It bathed him, feeling shocking and soothing all at once, reminding him of the electrical muscle treatments the whitecoats had occasionally given him during his captivity in the past.

Suddenly, an image appeared before his mind's eye— hazy and fluttering like a reflection on the surface of an agitated pond. He saw darkness in the middle, surrounded by a ring of lighter hue. A tunnel?

It was still hard to make out, but it could have been the very "slideway" the shifters had predicted.

Just then, Doc felt a force pulling on him while another force pushed him away at the same time. There was a flash of light, a roar of misplaced air—and then a hole appeared in the earth, perfectly round, with a diameter of ten feet.

Doc stared at it in wonder. The hole was on the exact spot he'd been traversing when the funny feeling had swept over him.

"By the Three Kennedys!" he muttered.

He would not have thought it possible, given his minimal exposure to the Shift, to achieve some kind of sensitivity to its transformations. Could it have something to do with his proximity to the core? Or the amount of time he'd been spending around the shifters?

Even as he asked himself these questions, he realized another question was far more important. For he suddenly had much more than a razor blade with which to approach his future.

The question that mattered most was, what could he do with it?

"Come along, William." Ankh gestured for Doc to approach the hole in the ground. Shifters were already hopping into it, letting out howls of delight as they slid away along its polished interior. "Just think of it as a big chute and tuck in your arms and hands. Stay as streamlined as you can and let yourself zip through it."

Doc nodded, distracted by the many scenarios playing out in his head. For the first time since being abducted by the shifters, he was daring to let himself feel something that might get him through his ordeal.

He was daring to feel hope.

Chapter Twenty-Eight

Hammersmith told Krysty to leave him alone seven times before he finally opened the door to his office. "What's your problem?" he snapped.

"I'm breaking out in a rash from all those stings." Krysty scratched her left arm with a vengeance. "And I need to get my friend back from the shifters."

"Tough break," Hammersmith said. "I'm not in the friend-saving business. Or the friend-having business."

"Mebbe not." Krysty shrugged as she glided past him into the darkened room. "But are you in the payback business?"

Hammersmith snorted and slammed the door shut. "I don't give a fuck about payback. I just want out of this place before those mutie assholes turn up the gas."

"You're full of shit," Krysty said as she plopped down in the only chair in the room—a black-and-chrome swivel chair in front of a bank of computer and video monitors. "If you wanted out so bad, you'd be long gone by now."

"You're talking out of your ass, lady," Hammersmith said. "Maybe I gave you too many of the good drugs when I had you on the table."

"You faked your death and went underground before Union got away," Krysty said, slowly turning back and forth in the swivel chair. "You've been hanging around awhile now, haven't you?"

Hammersmith shrugged. "I just needed to shut down some equipment and pack a few things."

"Right." Krysty smirked at how transparent he was. "Then, why does all the equipment in this place still seem to be running?"

"It's on autopilot," Hammersmith said dismissively. "I've already switched off the hardcore stuff to keep it from falling into those little pricks' hands."

"Okay." Krysty folded her arms over her chest and tapped her chin with an index finger. "So you're telling me that if you had a chance for revenge against the shifters, you wouldn't take it?"

Hammersmith scowled. "I didn't say that."

Krysty narrowed her eyes and stared at him for a moment, still turning back and forth in the chair. "Here's the thing about my friends and me, Dr. H. We're really good at fighting our enemies."

"Not so good fighting animals in the Devil's Slaughterhouse, though," Hammersmith commented. "From what I could see."

"So we had a little trouble with the piranha-wasps and the invisible monsters. So what? We still fought them off and killed them, didn't we? And we'll do the same thing to those muties in the core."

Hammersmith frowned. "You don't seem much like coldhearts to me."

"You can kill without being a coldheart," Krysty said. "Just like you can be a genius without being a complete asshole."

"I wouldn't know," Hammersmith replied.

"Let me ask you a question. How many other fighters do you have lined up to take down the shifters and stop your tech from tearing apart the Shift?"

Hammersmith didn't answer. He just leaned against the wall and watched her with his beady, close-set eyes.

"And how many of those fighters will work for nothing," Krysty added, "while freeing one of their own from captivity?"

"Who cares?" Hammersmith stuffed his hands in his pants pockets and jingled something that sounded like coins. "I'm not recruiting for the job."

"It doesn't matter." Krysty got up from the chair and stepped toward him. Chin up, back straight, shoulders squared, she didn't look like someone who'd been in a coma just a short time ago. "We're going anyway, with or without you."

"Good riddance." Hammersmith jingled his change with increased agitation. "The sooner, the better."

"However..." Krysty took a step closer and raised an index finger between them. "If you came along, we'd have a better chance of finding our friend. Your knowledge of the core would help us find who we're looking for much faster. And your expertise would make it easier to shut down the tech they're using to weaponize, as you call it, the Shift. You built it after all."

Hammersmith nodded slowly as if considering what she'd said, then raised a finger of his own: the middle finger of his left hand. "Forget it. I've got bigger fish to fry."

"You just don't want to face what you've done," Krysty said. "The mistakes you made that have empowered the shifters."

"Fuck them," Hammersmith. "And you, too."

"Mebbe you're a coward, too. Mebbe, for all your attitude, you're a scared little boy."

He remained silent, staring at Krysty.

"Or mebbe there's something else." Frowning, she stepped closer to him, tipping her head to one side. "Something you're not telling us about. Something that keeps you away from the core."

Hammersmith shook his head, looking thoroughly disgusted. "Do you mind?" He gestured at the door.

Krysty took one more step toward him. "So what are you going to do after we leave? Run as far as you can from the core and the Shift? From the destruction you've made possible?" She took one more step closer. "But what happens if it follows you? What happens then?" She smiled grimly. "Because that's what mistakes do, Dr. Hammersmith. They follow you all your life, until you deal with them."

"Wow." Hammersmith nodded. "Thank you." He pretended to wipe tears from his eyes. "You've really turned me around, you know? You've helped me see the light."

Taking Krysty's arm, he guided her to the door. Krysty knew full well what was coming next, but she let him pull her along anyway. Resisting would not have done any good.

"Go ahead out and get your friends ready." Hammersmith pushed the door open and shooed her through it. "I'm so looking forward to working with them to make amends for my mistakes."

As soon as Krysty had cleared the doorway, Hammersmith shut the door. That left Krysty back in the main lab, face-to-face with the rest of her team.

"Well?" Mildred asked. "How did it go?"

"Hammersmith help?" Jak said.

"He refuses, but don't worry." Krysty grinned. "It's just temporary."

"You sweet-talked him?" Ryan asked.

Still smiling, Krysty shook her head. "I didn't need to. He was already convinced."

"Could've fooled me," J.B. told her.

"Deep down, he wants to make things right," Krysty said. "Though he's bound to do everything wrong in the process."

"Sound like liability," Jak commented.

"As long as he's more of an asset, I want him to come with us," Ryan told them.

"You sure about that?" J.B. asked. "He's got some mouth on him."

"I said I wanted him along." Ryan grinned. "I didn't say I'd never give him a fat lip."

Chapter Twenty-Nine

Doc hurtled through pitch-darkness at a ridiculously high rate of speed, rocketing along the contours of the smooth-walled chute. He had zero control of his course.

He heard shifters sluicing around him, their bodies whisking past like pucks on ice. Some of them called out gleefully as they flew by in the dark—a reaction that Doc couldn't quite match. Being propelled without any control or vision through an underground speedway wasn't really his idea of fun.

Doc couldn't help marveling in the back of his mind—even as the front spun with panic—at the structure of the tube. The interior surface seemed to be frictionless, or nearly so; how else could it race them along without the application of additional thrust?

The forces at work in the core had to be truly mind-boggling to be able to create something like this, and to do it so quickly. Controlling those forces, as Doc was expected to do when he got to the core, seemed as if it would be utterly impossible.

Doc continued to rocket forward, swooping through the track like a runaway train, and then he felt it: the familiar fizzing in the back of his head, the funny feeling that had presaged the opening of the slideway.

And as soon as he felt it, his panic multiplied a thousandfold. His heart, which was already hammering like a ticker tape machine on overdrive, flew into a hyperkinetic tattoo fit to blow up the organ in his chest.

The implications of that feeling were terrible. If it signaled another impending change, and that change affected the underground chute, the consequences could be fatal for Doc.

Still, he continued his mad slalom through the dark, swooping up one side of the tube and then the other. How much farther did he have to travel until he reached the other end? No light was visible up ahead, not even a reflection on a polished wall around the next bend.

Had the shifters sensed the approaching change, too? None of them was calling out gleefully anymore. The only sound was the swooshing of their bodies as they flashed through the blackness, rocketing toward whatever fate awaited them.

Meanwhile, the fizzing in the back of Doc's head grew stronger and moved around to the sides and top of his skull. For the first time since entering the chute, he wished he could speed up. The faster he got to the other end, the greater his chance of survival.

The fizzing moved into his eyes next, and his vision suddenly turned yellow. That told him, based on his first experience with the "funny feeling," that it wouldn't be long until the Shift's next change.

Doc thought he felt the chute vibrate around him, but that could have been his imagination. Was that a flicker of light up ahead? He couldn't tell, now that his vision was a wash of bright yellow.

The fizzing in his head turned to crackling, and a familiar wave of warmth flooded his body. Maybe this was it, the end of the line for him at last.

The thought of it was not entirely unpleasant. A surge of relief flowed through him at the notion that he might at last escape the hellish Deathlands. He might be only moments away from the afterlife, in fact.

How long had it been since he'd last seen his wife and

children outside his own memory, dreams or hallucinations? How many seeming eternities had he endured without the loved ones who'd once formed the bedrock of his existence?

And yet, he'd been part of some dark and violent doings in his years in the Deathlands. What if his soul was soiled, no longer fit to join his family in heaven?

He would find out soon enough, it seemed. As he continued to rush onward, the heat in his body banked into a roaring fire. Every nerve screamed out that the change was about to strike; whatever form it would take, it was only seconds away. And all he could do was swoop forward and wait for the outcome.

Doc could see nothing but a field of featureless yellow, but he closed his eyes anyway. He hoped against hope that the next time he opened them, he would see his beloved Emily smiling back at him.

Head filled with crackling, body burning with heat, he rushed along a straightaway, then slid through a tight curve. He remembered what was coming next—a blaze of white light...

Before it could flare around him, Doc found himself shooting out of the tube, flying like a bullet from a barrel through open, empty space.

He came down in a soft, dry dune, landing feetfirst on his back at the end of his flight. His momentum drove him in up to his waist, leaving him half-buried and coughing up puffs of fine sand. It was then, as he opened his eyes, that the blaze of white light he'd been expecting burst to life.

The light quickly faded but left him blinded for a moment. Still coughing, he blinked away the pulsating spots left behind in his eyes, eventually glimpsing bright blue sky between them.

Then he glimpsed a familiar face smiling down at him—only it wasn't the face he'd hoped for during his race through the chute. It wasn't the face of a member of his family.

Clearly he was nowhere near heaven.

"Here we are." It was Ankh, who looked perfectly calm and collected, not at all as if he'd just ridden at lightning speed through an underground slideway. "End of the ride." Smiling, he reached down.

Doc took his hand and let Ankh help him sit up. "Has everyone else arrived, as well?" Doc asked the question carefully, not wanting Ankh to know the real reason for his concern: that some of the shifters might have been lost in the wave of transformation while still in the tube. The less Ankh knew about Doc's new ability to sense changes in the Shift, the better.

"Every last one of them," Ankh replied. "They all got through just in time, before the slideway turned into that." He gestured at something behind Doc.

The old man turned to see what was back there and couldn't suppress a gasp. The exit of the slideway, which had to have been a hole in the ground just like the entrance, was nowhere to be seen.

In its place, a tower of glittering ebony crystal rose at least fifty feet in the air. There was no sign of a slideway hole in the ground at its base, which extended in a graceful, sloping mantle for dozens of feet on each side of its vertical axis.

"Beautiful." Doc slowly stood and turned to face the tower. "Is it made of onyx, I wonder?"

"Who cares?" Ankh asked. "It will be no less beautiful for whatever it's made of."

Doc kept staring upward, transfixed. He could hardly believe the tower had come into being on its own, and so quickly. Frankly, he thought, it was miraculous, one of the most beautiful things he'd seen in all his time in the Deathlands.

And that was really saying something—but not because the Deathlands were full of beautiful things. It was more because the Deathlands had so little beauty compared with his home and home era. Sometimes, in fact, he thought there was no beauty at all in the blasted, blighted ruins that had once been a great nation.

Yet here was proof to the contrary. The crystal spire twinkled in the late-afternoon sunlight, every dark facet dancing with bright sparks.

If he'd been a few seconds later getting out of the slideway, this thing would have killed him. But now it took his breath away with its simple beauty and splendor. He wanted to run his hands over its smooth facets, feeling what he imagined to be its cool, gem-like surface. He felt as if he could gaze at it all day, drinking in the details of its grandeur.

Instead, he was snapped out of his reverie by the shrill, abrasive voice of Exo.

"We made some good time there, didn't we?" For once, there was no candy stick in his mouth. Had he lost it in the slideway? "We covered about five miles, according to the navigators."

"Five miles north." Ankh raised his eyebrows. "That means we're nearly there."

"The core?" Doc asked.

Exo nodded excitedly and rubbed his hands together. "Our destiny is imminent. Your time to shine is almost upon you, William Hammersmith, the part of your life they will write songs about in ages to come."

"Ah, yes." Doc nodded with feigned enthusiasm. "Everything has been leading up to this, hasn't it?"

"Yes, it has, my friend." Exo swaggered over and punched him in the upper arm hard enough to hurt, as usual. "I envy you, being a chosen conduit for power and a witness to greatness."

Doc bowed a little. "Truly, it is an honor beyond imagining." He had to fight to keep the sarcasm out of his voice.

"Meanwhile, the forces of Struggle now roar ever closer to your malevolent abductors. Soon enough, those monsters will be slaughtered."

"An outcome much to be desired." The urge to slash Exo with the razor blade welled up within Doc's heart. He might have given it a try if he'd thought he could have finished the deed.

"The outlanders' location is known to us, thanks to a faithful friend in the enemy camp," Exo said. "The battle will most likely ensue at dawn tomorrow, and conclude very shortly thereafter."

"Wonderful!" Ankh said. "Such heroes, wouldn't you agree, William?" He cast an encouraging look in Doc's direction.

"Our brave fighting men and women are to be commended." Doc nodded, hoping his words had been sufficiently convincing, though he hadn't said anything against his own people.

"Excellent!" Exo lunged as if he was going to lash out, and Doc flinched, but the move was just a feint. Laughing, Exo quickly danced back from Doc. "Now come on! Quit standing around! The sooner we start marching, the sooner we reach the core!"

He feinted at Doc again, then hurried away to rally his men for the march.

As soon as Exo left, Doc relaxed. "So we are almost there."

"Uh-huh." Ankh nodded. "Which means you and I need to have a talk about the future. About how this is all going to play out when we get to the core."

"Good. I have been wondering."

"We'll make it work, don't worry. Trust me, the two of us can't fail."

"I like the way you think." Even as Doc said it, he patted the pocket where he was keeping the razor blade from Struggle. Between the blade and his newfound ability to sense changes in the Shift, he didn't feel as if he was empty-handed anymore. That was a good thing, since Ryan and the others were nowhere in sight, leaving Doc to his own devices.

If he wanted a rescue, he would have to engineer it himself. At another time in his life in the Deathlands, he would have viewed this as an impossible proposition, one he would have refused. But somewhere along the road since his abduction by the shifters, he had made a decision. If no one was coming for him, or coming in time, he would take it upon himself to do everything he could to win his own freedom. He wasn't about to surrender and let mad Exo destroy him, not without a fight.

Come what may, he was going to have to become his own Ryan Cawdor.

Chapter Thirty

Jak knew he was taking a risk when he stepped outside, but he was desperate for some fresh air. Walking through the Devil's Slaughterhouse at night was dangerous, but he wasn't the kind of person who liked being cooped up for too long.

He and the others had already been in Hammersmith's lab for hours. They'd decided to stay the night there—camping on the floor with their bedrolls—but had agreed to leave first thing in the morning, with or without Hammersmith.

Morning wasn't soon enough for Jak to take a walk, though. He needed to feel the wind on his skin, see the moonlight, hear the crickets and night birds. It was possible, in the Slaughterhouse, that those crickets might have laser-beam eyes, and the birds might emit acid sprays from their beaks, but Jak wasn't worried. As always, he was confident in his ability to handle any threat, and the risk was worth it. Getting out for a while would keep him sane; plus, it wouldn't hurt to do a little surveillance.

And he had another reason for being out there, too. He wanted to see if Union was anywhere nearby, after being away from the group for hours.

Had she left for good? Jak thought it was possible. It had been a long time since she'd stormed out after revealing her history with Hammersmith. She'd been iffy about working with the group from the beginning; maybe having Hammersmith thrown into the mix had been the last straw.

Or not. As Jak walked around the base of the next hill, he spotted Union's unmistakably lithe form gliding toward him.

"Look what cat drag in." Jak smiled as she approached. "Gone long time."

"I needed some time alone. I'm sure you can appreciate that."

Taryn was running Union just then; the black braid confirmed it. But Jak wasn't sorry he was facing the ice-maiden personality. "Yeah, appreciate." In fact, she was his favorite of the four. "Better now?"

"I'm not sure." Union frowned. "No worse anyway."

Jak nodded. "Where been?"

"I don't know." Her frown deepened. "Why do you care?"

"Curious." Jak shrugged. "Taking walk myself, wonder what see or avoid."

"There's nothing. Just wasteland for miles. The mutie creatures must all be asleep or elsewhere or something."

"So." Jak narrowed his ruby eyes and stared at her. "Coming back Hammersmith's place? Turning in?"

"I don't want to, but yes." There was resignation in her voice. "There's no place safer to bed down, that's for sure. As long as that son of a bitch keeps his distance."

"Not need worry 'bout him," Jak said. "Rest of us have back."

"Is that so?" She looked and sounded suspicious. "We barely know one another."

"Part of team now. Like family. Take care of you."

Union's braid turned auburn, and she sneered. "You're full of shit, Jack Sprat. Just trying to sweet-talk us into letting you in our pants."

"Tell like it is. Not alone anymore."

She stared at him for a moment, but he couldn't tell if

that was a good thing. Her expression was unreadable—eyes steady, brow creased slightly, jaw set, head tipped forward—but the braid was what caught his attention.

It was striped with all four colors now: black, auburn, white and brown. What could that mean, if it was more than a trick of the moonlight? That all four personalities were acting in concert?

"We are never alone." When she spoke, her voice sounded different, deeper, darker. "We are four women in one body, remember?"

Jak watched and listened, mesmerized. It was then, as if on cue, that the first of the fireflies appeared.

They drifted in lazy looping swirls, blinking as they gathered nearby—but they were no kind of ordinary fireflies. Each bug had multiple nodes on its body, illuminating in sequence, and the nodes were different colors, all the colors of the spectrum.

Jak focused on a single mutant firefly as it swirled around him. Its lights winked as if signaling a secret code: red, yellow, green, purple, red. Another firefly glided after it, lighting up in the opposite order: red, purple, green, yellow, red.

"Look." Jak grinned as he watched yet another firefly drift past. "Cool, huh?"

Union folded her arms over her chest and looked unimpressed. "They will probably shock you to death or impregnate your brain or something."

Jak brushed a hand through the air, stirring fireflies like stardust. "Who say everything deadly?"

In spite of herself, Union's eyes lit on one of the twinkling bugs as it floated past her face. "Don't be fooled. These are probably lures for some monstrous carnivore about to pounce on us."

"Not think so." Jak caught one of the bugs and held it loosely in his fist, watching the multicolored light blinking between his fingers. "Just pretty." He released it so it flew lazily in her direction.

"Pretty can mean trouble," Union cautioned him. "And there's enough trouble in life that you shouldn't go looking for more."

"Then miss all fun." Jak grinned and caught another bug, then held it out to her on the palm of his hand. "All excitement."

Union scowled as if she'd had a sudden urge to hit him. For a moment, Jak thought she might clap her hand down on his, smashing the firefly between them.

Instead, she slid two fingertips over his palm, pushing them up to the nose of the insect. Still blinking in multicolored code, the firefly crawled onto her fingers and perched there, antennae twitching in her direction.

"Not relax much, do you?" Jak asked.

Gazing at the bug, Union shook her head slowly. "That's a recipe for extinction in the Deathlands."

"Going die anyway. Might as well enjoy ride."

Union brought the firefly closer to her face. "I don't think I know how to do that. Not really."

"Need right people." Jak shrugged. "Mebbe finally found."

Union blew gently on her fingertips, and the firefly extended its wings and took off. It fluttered in a circle in front of her, flashing blue, white, red, yellow, blue, and then it drifted over to swim a lazy loop around Jak's head before zigzagging off into the moonlit night.

Chuckling, Jak watched it go, then turned back to Union. Before he could say another word, she lunged at him—but not with the intention of doing him harm.

Instead, she grabbed his head in her hands, lowered her head and kissed him.

Jak was stunned, but not for long. He quickly lost himself in her long, languorous kiss, enjoying the pressure and movement of her lips on his.

When she finally pulled back, her face was flushed, and her gray eyes were sparkling. She stayed close, just inches away, and kept holding his head in her long-fingered hands. "That...that was..." For once, she seemed to be at a loss for words.

"Wonderful." Jak grinned. "About time let self go."

"Only part of me," she told him. "The others don't all agree that I should have done it."

Jak realized her braid had gone all black again. She had to have switched from whatever unified front she'd erected back to Taryn, the original ice maiden.

"Tell others give me little time," Jak said. "I'll win them over, you'll see."

Suddenly, Union shifted again. Auburn braid, snarky attitude...Rhonda. "If you think you've got what it takes, bring it on, white boy."

"Okay." This time, Jak took the initiative, standing on his tiptoes, pushing forward to claim another kiss. Now that the door had been opened, he was only too happy to make contact again.

It was different this time, though, rougher—probably because Rhonda was dominant. Though Jak had started this round as the aggressor, Rhonda quickly took over and locked him in a hungry, tight embrace.

This kiss lasted longer than the first and was equally enjoyable in a different way. Then it suddenly changed, becoming jittery and erratic, a series of quick, birdlike pecks on his lips and cheeks. She blew little puffs of warm air into his ears, making him squirm with delight; her caresses roamed his body with restless grace, sparking little fireworks of intense sensation wherever they lighted.

"I shouldn't have done that," she said in a nervous voice when she pulled back. Her white braid gave her away:

Carrie, the crazy one. "I feel so guilty. This was wrong… but it felt…"

"Shh." Jak reached up to touch the side of her face. "Will be all right." How strange it was to speak to the same woman as if she were separate people in one body…and yet, it was becoming easier for him all the time.

"I don't know why, but I believe you." Her eyes half closed as she turned her face to kiss his hand. "I want to believe you."

"Not hurt you." Jak shook his head. "Will protect you." Slowly, he went in for the softest kiss yet, barely touching her lips with his own. Somehow, it was the most perfect kiss yet, this tender contact with a skittish, vulnerable soul.

When he drew back, she stayed frozen with eyes closed and lips slightly parted as if he was still kissing her. Fireflies blinked all the colors of the rainbow around her, their radiance lighting her face like some kind of softly blended stained glass.

As he started in for another kiss, her eyes suddenly popped open, and she giggled. "I hear you're a good kisser. Is that so?" It was brown-braided Dulcet this time.

"You be judge," Jak said, finishing his approach.

Dulcet's kiss was the most sensuous of the four. Her lips flowed like water, melting into his with supple abandon. Grabbing his shoulders, she bent slightly and pressed her body against his, twining her arms around his sides and back, making sure he could feel the curves of her breasts and hips and thighs.

Jak knew instantly where she was heading, and he wanted the same thing. He rolled his hands down her back to cup her bottom, felt it flex when he tightened his grip.

It had been a long time since he'd been with a woman, and Union was beautiful. They'd had a connection from the start, though only now had it come to fruition.

So what if she was damaged and potentially deadly?

The same could be said of him and just about everyone in the Deathlands, couldn't it?

And could there be a more perfect setting than there in the moonlight, with the rainbow fireflies whirling around them?

In the Deathlands, fleeting pleasures were a thing to be seized and treasured. It was a lesson Jak had learned long ago. But he had also learned that pleasures found with a kindred spirit were more satisfying than those taken from an empty heart. And the fact was, he felt as if Union was a kindred spirit.

So he made a decision to keep going if she would have him. Together, at least for a time, they could forget the challenges ahead of them.

It was then, when he was ready to take the next step, that Union suddenly pushed him away. She stared at him with a strange, dark look in her eyes, a look he didn't recognize from the ones he'd seen there before.

Jack frowned. "What problem?"

Union just shook her head slowly. "Not tonight." Her voice sounded different, laced with some kind of foreign accent. "Big day tomorrow. We need to rest up."

"Not understand," Jak said. "I do something wrong?"

She tipped her head to one side and stared at him as if he were a thoroughly uninteresting bug. "I just explained myself. Do I need to draw you a picture?"

Jak didn't answer. Studying her braid, he saw it was striped with all four colors of hair again.

"I'll take that for a no." Union strode past him as if he didn't exist and headed in the direction of Hammersmith's lab.

"So much for mood." Jak watched her go, wondering what the hell had come over her.

Chapter Thirty-One

Early the next morning, Ryan threw open the hatch in the side of the hill, admitting a shaft of bright sunlight into Hammersmith's lab. "Looks good out there," he said. "Let's get a move on."

The rest of his group was busy cinching straps and tightening buckles on backpacks, checking weapons and filling canteens from the lab's water supply. As one, they looked and sounded well rested and ready for action, except for Union, who was sluggish and had circles under her eyes.

Ryan watched as everyone finished getting ready and assembled near the hatch. They moved quickly and efficiently, but he was still getting itchy to leave. They had a long march ahead of them, backtracking out of the Devil's Slaughterhouse. At least they wouldn't have to split up, now that Krysty had recovered from the piranha-wasp attack and no longer needed to be evacuated from the Shift.

"I guess the good doctor won't be joining us," J.B. said, nodding at the door of Hammersmith's office.

The door, which hadn't opened all night, looked as tightly sealed as ever. "I guess you're right." Apparently, Hammersmith wanted nothing further to do with them. Krysty's efforts to talk him into going with them to the core had failed to move him.

"Probably for the best." J.B. headed for the hatch. "Could've been a deadweight situation at best, or a major liability at worst."

"I know you're right." Ryan patted him on the shoulder on his way past. "But we still could've used his help at the core."

"Don't worry." Mildred was next in line for the hatch. "We'll make do."

Ricky came next. "One less civilian to put our asses on the line for." He grinned and nodded reassuringly.

"Or punch 'cause getting on nerves." Jak grinned and followed.

"Not everybody comes around in the end." Krysty paused before stepping through the opening and lightly touched Ryan's arm. "We help the ones who want to be helped."

Ryan nodded. Leave it to Krysty to say the right thing, as always.

And leave it to Union to do the opposite when she marched up to the exit. "Hammersmith must know something you don't," she said coldly. "Mebbe he knows this is a suicide mission."

She didn't wait for Ryan to reply to fold herself through the doorway and step out onto the sandy ground.

Ryan shook his head. "Pain in the ass." He took one last look at Hammersmith's closed door, then turned and left the lab. Suicide mission or not, he was determined to do everything in his power to rescue Doc Tanner from the shifters.

If there was one thing Hammersmith had accomplished during his time with them, it was to make Ryan appreciate the group's own resident eccentric doctor more than ever and recommit himself to getting him back at any cost.

RICKY WIPED SWEAT from his brow with the back of his hand as he marched through the rising morning heat. It was already a lot warmer than the day before, with no end in sight. The skies were crystal clear in all directions, the air hot and still, the sun a pulsating blotch throwing down wave after punishing wave of soul-melting heat.

As temperamental and downright nasty as Hammersmith had been, Ricky found himself wishing he was back in the cool air of the lab. It wouldn't have killed them to stay there one more day…unless maybe it would have. It didn't seem outside the realm of possibility that Hammersmith might have tried to murder them all; that was why someone had stood guard whenever the team had grabbed some shut-eye.

It didn't matter anymore, though. Hammersmith and his lab were getting farther behind the team with each passing moment.

Ricky wiped the sweat from his brow again, then heard a sharp whistle. Looking left, he saw his partner in manning the point of the group's formation, the one person who seemed unaffected by the heat.

Union. She gestured left, indicating a change of course, then veered in that direction without waiting for his acknowledgment.

Annoyed, Ricky followed her lead. Checking behind him, he saw the others do the same.

In the mood to pick Union's brain, Ricky jogged to catch up with her, then matched her pace. "I wonder why we haven't seen any mutated freak-show animals yet today," he said.

Union looked at him sideways with the usual disdain bordering on contempt. "Do you want to see them?"

"No way." Ricky shook his head briskly. "I just wonder if mebbe they're following us covertly, getting ready to ambush us before we can get out of the Slaughterhouse."

"Ambush?" Union sniffed. "They're animals, not marauders."

"Damn tricky animals, if you ask me," Ricky replied.

"So when do we know we've left the Devil's Slaughterhouse anyway?"

"When I say so."

"And how do you know?" Ricky asked.

"I just do." Union quickened her pace, marching out ahead of him.

Ricky accelerated, too, and quickly caught up. "It wouldn't kill you to be friendly, you know," he told her. "We're on the same side here. We might have to save each other's lives."

"Friendly?" She frowned at him. "I thought I was being friendly."

Suddenly, a booming roar burst out of the silence, distant and fast approaching from behind the formation. Back among the marchers, J.B. roared, "Incoming!"

Whirling, Ricky swung up the De Lisle carbine and peered at the segmented horizon that was visible between the scattered hills. He expected to see some kind of monstrous, mutated beast, a final attack from the deranged menagerie of the Devil's Slaughterhouse.

Instead, he spotted the silhouette of a wheeled vehicle, a war wag with a big square nose. The wag hurtled through gaps between hills, its giant tires churning up sand in great swirling clouds.

Friend or foe? That was the big question in Ricky's mind as he watched the wag charge toward the team. Unfortunately, the answer would only come when the wag arrived and started shooting…or didn't.

Heart pounding, Ricky ran through the group to what had been the rear flank. It was now the point, with Ryan and J.B. taking up positions, preparing to mount a defense if it became necessary.

"What are we up against?" Ricky asked.

"Looks like an APC," J.B. replied. "Armored personnel carrier, affiliation unknown."

"Shoot first?" Jak had just darted in beside Ricky with his Colt Python raised and ready. "Questions later?"

"Negative," Ryan snapped. "Wait for my mark!"

The wag continued roaring closer, churning clouds of sand. Sunlight glinted from its tinted black windows, throwing sparks that burned spots in Ricky's eyes.

"Get ready to scatter if we can't turn it off course," Ryan shouted. "We won't have much time to get out of its way."

Glancing over his shoulder, Ricky saw that Krysty and Mildred had formed a second row, staggered so they had clear lines of fire through the gaps in the front rank.

But one member of the group was nowhere to be seen, Ricky realized. "Where's Union?"

"Don't know and don't care right now," Ryan said without looking back. "Bigger fish to fry at the moment."

It was true enough. The wag was bearing down on them fast.

Ricky braced himself, finger on the trigger of the carbine, aiming at one of the wag's huge front tires. The rest of the team did the same beside and behind him, chambering rounds, taking aim and tightening their grips on their weapons.

"Here we go!" Ryan shouted. "Get ready!"

The wag continued to race forward. Sweat ran down Ricky's neck and back as he prepared to take action.

Then, thirty yards out, the wag jolted to a stop. Suddenly, Ricky became less likely to get run over by an APC, though his odds of getting shot at still seemed high.

Like the others in his group, he kept his weapon aimed and ready to fire. He didn't take his eyes off the wag for a second; it had no visible external blasters, but someone could pop out of the vehicle at any time with ordnance in hand.

"Come out of there!" Ryan called. "Reach for the sky!"

As if on cue, the driver's door sprang open. Ricky fully

expected to see the barrel of a blaster or grenade launcher poke out of that cover, aimed in their direction, but for a moment, he saw nothing.

Then he saw the fingers of one hand grip the edge of the door. Another hand caught the door frame, and then a head appeared as the wag's driver boosted himself up from inside the vehicle.

Ricky's eyes shot wide with surprise. The driver was pretty much the last person they expected to see.

"Really?" It was Dr. Hammersmith, shouting back with his usual disgruntled attitude. "Not only do I decide to rejoin your suicide brigade, but I bring along a damn war wag, and this is the shit you give me?"

"For all we knew, you were coming to kill us," Ryan snapped. Ricky noticed he hadn't lowered his blaster yet.

"Why in seven shades of hell would I kill you before you help me reach my objectives?" Hammersmith asked. "There'll be plenty of time for that later!"

"You're assuming we want you to join up with us," Ryan said. "Let me tell you, that's a hell of a big assumption!"

"Then, maybe you ought to just shoot me and take the wag!" Hammersmith replied. "At least then mebbe you'll act as though you've got some balls."

For a moment, Ricky thought Ryan looked as if he wanted to pull the trigger. But then he lowered his Steyr Scout longblaster.

As the rest of the group followed his example, Ryan posed a question. "Who wants to go for a ride with this lunatic?"

"Depends," J.B. said, and then he raised his voice so Hammersmith could hear him. "Is he at least gonna try to act civil?"

"Hell no!" Hammersmith snapped. "I'll probably be crankier, since I'm doing this against my better judgment!"

J.B. looked at Ryan. "Do we have a choice?"

Ryan shook his head. "Those bastards who took Doc are way out ahead of us. Mebbe the wag gives us a chance to catch up."

J.B. scowled and blew out his breath. "Damn. Doc better appreciate this."

"If he's even still alive, he will," Ryan told him, and then he looked around the group. "Anyone not riding?"

No one spoke up or raised a hand.

"What about Union?" Ryan frowned as he looked for her.

"Sign me up," Union said as she strolled out from behind a hill, looking slightly disheveled. "As long as Hammershit stays away from me." Ricky didn't have to see the auburn braid to know Rhonda was in charge.

The real mystery was where Union had been for the past few minutes, but Ricky figured he had zero chance of finding an answer for that one.

"I'll stay clear of you if you stay clear of me," Hammersmith said, then added, "Bitch."

"All right, then." Ryan started for the wag and waved for the others to follow. "Enough pissing around. Let's pile in that thing and get where we're going."

"Hammershit." Jak chuckled and elbowed Ricky. "Good one, huh?"

"And please." Ryan glared at them over his shoulder. "Don't antagonize this dick."

"You just did," shouted Hammersmith, who'd heard every word. "And furthermore, fuck off, all of you!"

Ryan grinned at Jak and Ricky. "Let me take care of the antagonizing for you," he said.

"Good enough," Jak agreed. "Always enjoy watching master work."

"Now saddle up, people!" Ryan shouted. "We've got a bastard load of ground to cover!"

Chapter Thirty-Two

"We are almost at the core, are we not?" Doc asked, though he didn't say how he knew. He didn't tell Ankh that the fizzing feeling in his head had become more or less constant at that point.

"That's right," Ankh told him. "It's less than a mile away now."

"Good, good," Doc said matter-of-factly as he trudged along through the high late-morning heat. The temperature had forced him to take his frock coat off and carry it over his shoulder from a hooked finger. The clothes he'd been wearing underneath were soaked with sweat anyway; he found himself wishing he could take some of those off, too.

Just then, Ankh cleared his throat. "What we talked about earlier." He spoke in a low voice, though he didn't need to. Doc was moving so slowly, he was keeping the two of them well back from the squad of shifters, out of earshot. "Are you clear on your part in the plan?"

"It could not be clearer." Doc nodded. "Though I feel compelled to remind you that I am not any kind of expert on whatever equipment my predecessor might have developed."

"Just follow my lead and keep a clear head, and you'll do fine."

"Good," Doc said, though his head was anything but clear at that moment. Was the rising intensity of the fizzing due to the core's proximity, or another landscape change waiting to happen?

"Remember, once the action starts, things will happen fast," Ankh stated. "But I've got plenty of friends among the troops as well as the core station guards. Exo and his people are outnumbered, and our victory is assured."

Doc thought of saying something about how quickly an assured victory could become the opposite, but then he decided to keep that one to himself. "That is most excellent news, Ankh," he said instead. "Your plan seems to me quite sound indeed."

Suddenly, Doc felt the ground shudder underfoot. Exo, at the front of the ranks, shot a hand in the air, and all the shifter troops immediately stopped in their tracks.

Was another transformation in the making? Was that the source of the fizzing in Doc's head? All he knew for sure was that the earth was shaking, and the shifters were very much on alert.

"What's happening?" Doc asked. "Another change in the Shift?"

"Yes and no," Ankh replied. "You'll see."

Just then, fifty feet away between two big hills, the sandy ground lifted up, revealing a pitch-black gap underneath it.

"What spontaneously generated landform will this be, I wonder?" Doc asked as he watched the slab of ground continue to crank backward.

Ankh looked at him as if he was stupid. "It's not spontaneously generated. It's a hidden door, is what it is."

"Ah. I see." Doc nodded as the slab reached a forty-five-degree angle and stopped. Its underside was mounted with machinery—giant gears and levers that stopped turning and left the great weight propped above its socket in the ground.

"This is it, Doc," Ankh said. "Congratulations on returning to the core after too long away."

Doc was distracted by the entryway before him. He'd

never been there before, but it looked very familiar to him nonetheless.

"Don't worry." Ankh elbowed him in the side. "It's a lot more impressive once you get through the door."

"That's good to know."

"Just remember," Ankh whispered urgently, "Hammersmith has been here many times before, so don't act as if this is your first time seeing the place."

"Understood," Doc replied.

Up ahead, Exo started toward the entrance, signaling with a wave for the other shifters to follow. Ankh and Doc fell in step, moving as quickly toward the opening as the rest of the troops.

"This is a massive complex," Ankh whispered. "Hammersmith was brilliant, creating it as his base and staging ground."

"So it would seem." Doc peered into the gaping dark cavity up ahead, wrestling with the nagging feeling that it was somehow familiar to him. "I take it you've spent a good deal of time here yourself, Ankh?"

"You might say that. I know the place like the back of my hand."

Exo was the first one over the threshold. As soon as he set foot on the ramp leading down from the edge of the entryway, lights flashed to life on the underside of the slab above him.

"Motion sensors," Doc said. Technology like that wasn't common in postdark times; he'd rarely seen it outside caches of predark equipment that had survived the apocalypse for one reason or another.

"Wait till you see what else is in this place," Ankh said. "Exo chose it as the base of his new empire for a reason, you know."

Doc followed him down the ramp on the heels of the troops. The slab lowered back into place behind them, automatically closing the door when the last of the visitors had gone inside.

When Doc descended to the first level with the shifters, he saw there was a wide, short hallway ahead, well lit and ending in a pair of giant blast doors. The layout suggested a shelter of some kind, designed to keep out the extreme force of a nuclear explosion and its aftermath.

Exo walked to an intercom panel set into the wall near the doors. He used the silver lion's head of Doc's sword-stick to tag the button that would connect him to whoever was on the other side.

"I have returned!" Exo shouted into the panel. "And I've brought back our runaway whitecoat and hope for the future."

As soon as he said it, the shifter forces cheered. Every one of them roared with approval, which made Doc wonder how much support Ankh really had. He claimed to have Exo and his people outnumbered, so victory was assured, but those pro-Exo cheers sounded pretty genuine.

"Open the doors!" Exo ordered. "Let's not waste another second in setting my glorious empire in motion!"

Again, every shifter soldier cheered. Blasters were raised and shaken overhead in martial jubilation.

Exo turned from the intercom and faced the crowd. "We shall rule all the Shift and then the lands outside the Shift, as well! A new era is about to begin!"

The troops chanted his name over and over. The sound of all those voices raised to the ceiling filled the corridor with a deafening roar. Doc put his hands over his ears to take the edge off, but it didn't do much good.

It was then that a siren howled, overriding the cheers, and lights along the gray metal walls began to flash. With a boom of separation, the big blast doors began to slide apart.

"This is it." Ankh rubbed his hands together eagerly.

"We're going in. How does it feel to be on the cusp of destiny, my friend?"

Doc didn't answer. He was too busy gazing at what lay behind the opening doors.

His breath caught in his throat as the doors moved farther apart. The hairs on the back of his neck sprang up, but the reaction had nothing to do with what Exo had claimed was history in the making.

At that moment, Doc was much more focused on the past.

"By the Three Kennedys!" he whispered to himself. "This place…"

When the blast doors had parted most of the way, he saw the view beyond them with clarity. He saw crimson-skinned muties gathered in the extension of the hallway, cheering as the doors parted before them.

But Doc wasn't nearly as interested in the new batch of muties as he was in the layout of the place…the walls, the tunnel.

"Ah, yes." Ankh was grinning at him. "I see you are awestruck already, and this is but the entrance to our magnificent complex."

"Awestruck, yes." Doc nodded slowly. Up ahead, the shifter muties from both sides of the blast doors were rushing together, hugging and laughing as they reunited at the threshold. Someone on the other side was playing a musical instrument that sounded like a cross between a guitar and a dying cow, and the happy muties were dancing to the music.

But all Doc could focus on was the blast doors. They meant something to him, something unexpected, something that cast this place in an entirely new light.

"This is where it will all happen," Ankh said. "A new beginning, though not quite the one that Exo expects."

Doc did not reply. His mind was too busy racing, processing the new information about the core and the Shift, considering what it meant to him and his friends. The implications were staggering.

If the core of the Shift was a redoubt, and the shifter muties were in control of it, as they appeared to be, Doc's life had just gotten a good deal more complicated.

Chapter Thirty-Three

"Where did you say you got this wag again?" asked Ryan, who was sitting in the passenger's seat of the APC across from Hammersmith, the driver.

"A hidden garage in my bunker." Hammersmith had to shout to make himself heard over the wag's big engine. "Where'd you think I had it stowed? Up my ass?"

"Before the bunker. Where did you get it originally?" As he spoke, Ryan kept his eyes on the hilly landscape hurtling toward them. Hammersmith drove like a maniac, jolting the big vehicle through a wild pattern of hard rights and harder lefts. The insane driving would get them to their destination fast, though whether they'd all be alive when they got there remained an open question.

"Bought it from a little old lady in Texarkana." Hammersmith said it with a Southern accent. "She only drove it to church on Sundays and bingo on Friday nights."

Ryan didn't have a clue what he was talking about. But it was clear to him and the rest of the companions that Hammersmith was a freezie.

The predark wag was in such pristine shape, someone who didn't know any better might have thought skydark had happened only a few weeks earlier. But, as usual, getting information out of Hammersmith was about as easy as prying it out of Union.

Nevertheless, Ryan kept trying. "Did you use this wag to escape the core?"

"Fuck no." Hammersmith fished a joint out of the pocket of his lab coat. "I faked my own death, remember? Kind of hard to do if you're riding into the sunset in a big war wag."

"Then, how did it end up stowed away in the middle of the Devil's Slaughterhouse?" Ryan asked.

Hammersmith stuck the joint into a corner of his mouth, then produced his butane lighter from another pocket of his coat. "Brought it here a long time ago, before I got involved with those shifters. Thought I might need it someday, and, whoa, what do ya know? I do!"

Ryan held on to the door handle as the wag swooped around a hill and burst onto a broad plain, right behind a galloping herd of large ratlike creatures.

As the wag charged through the middle of the herd, Ryan second-guessed his decision to let Hammersmith choose a route through the middle of the Devil's Slaughterhouse. They were saving a ton of time going that way, he couldn't deny it, but if something went wrong and some freak-of-nature beast got in the way, things could go off the rails fast.

"Be prepared, that's my motto." Hammersmith lit the joint and inhaled deeply. Then he blew out the smoke and coughed. "What's your motto? Make it up as we go along?"

"Pretty much," Ryan said. "That, plus 'Smart-asses get shot first.'"

"Funny stuff there!" Hammersmith had another toke, then released the smoke from his lungs. "You ought to be on a TV sitcom. Oh, wait! There are no sitcoms! And there's no TV, either! Guess you're out of luck."

"How much longer till we get to the core?" Ryan asked.

"Just after sundown, I'm thinking," Hammersmith said. "Though, this is good shit I'm smoking, so that estimate might be a little off."

"Mind if I have a hit?" Ryan reached across the cabin.

Hammersmith hesitated, then gingerly handed him the joint. "Totally primo, guaranteed."

Ryan promptly opened the window and tossed out the joint.

"Hey!" Hammersmith snapped. "That was a real douche bag move!"

"You're stoned enough already," Ryan told him. "Now pay attention to your driving, or you're going out the window next."

BACK IN THE main body of the wag, the rest of the team sat in seats along the walls, bracing themselves against the jarring ride through the bumpy Slaughterhouse.

While the others talked about the next stage of their mission to save Doc, Jak and Union sat silently beside each other in the rearmost seats on the driver's side.

Jak had tried several times to get her talking, with no success. He'd pretty much given up when she finally leaned in close to him and whispered, "I want to kiss you again, but she won't let me."

Jak was surprised to hear from her. "She who?" He wondered which personality he was talking to, but he couldn't tell. Since Union was sitting closest to the door, he couldn't see the color of the braid on her left temple.

"She." Still Union's voice remained a whisper. "I'm not even supposed to be talking to you."

"What I do?" Jak kept his voice to a whisper, as well. "Thought was perfect gentleman."

"Shh." Union put a finger up to her lips. "You need to trust me. I want to save you."

"Save? Who from?"

She shook her head. Her eyes were wide; she looked frightened. "When I give the signal, you must do as I say."

"Why? What going happen?"

Again, she shook her head. "I can't tell you anything else. I've already taken a terrible chance saying this much."

"Need know more."

Union grabbed his hand and squeezed it tight. "Whatever you do, don't say a word to anyone else. Especially anyone else in here." She turned her head fully toward him and tapped the side of it.

Only then did he see that her braid was white. He was dealing with Carrie, the basket case. Of all her personalities, this was the one who had chosen to save him.

But then she let go of his hand and was gone. He saw the change as she leaned back in the seat, her stare turning icy and distant, her braid turning jet-black. Taryn was back.

For a moment, Jak thought of trying to say something to her. But he changed his mind and instead sat back to ponder what Carrie had told him.

If what she'd said was true, the team was in danger. But what was the nature of the danger, and when was it coming for them?

And what did it say that she knew about the threat in advance?

Two hours into the ride, Krysty's head started pounding. She kept it to herself at first; the pain was bearable, nowhere near the brain-splitting agony she'd felt during transformations of the Shift.

But Mildred, who was sitting across from her, soon picked up on it. "Krysty?" She leaned across the cabin with a look of deep concern on her face. "Honey, are you all right?"

Krysty nearly denied it. She was sick of being a liability and didn't want the mission scuttled or delayed because of her.

But she couldn't lie to Mildred. Shaking her head slightly, she leaned forward and spoke as quietly as she could without being drowned out by the noise of the wag. "I think it's starting again. Just the leading edge of it so far."

Mildred nodded. "Okay." She didn't do as Krysty had feared and suggest they turn back. "So maybe we can manage it a little better this time."

"Manage it?"

Mildred held up an index finger, then turned to the driver's seat, which was on the other side of her. "Hey! Hey, Hammertime!"

"What do you want?" he snapped from behind the wheel. "Can't you see I'm trying to drive up here?"

"Screw you!" Mildred looked back at Krysty and winked, then returned her attention to Hammersmith. "Got any more of that sweet leaf up there, buddy boy?"

"Why do you care?"

"Because Krysty's in need of some pain management, and I'm thinking your special stash might just do the trick."

"The last time I shared, the One-Eyed Wonder threw my doobie out the mofo window." Hammersmith glared at Ryan, who studiously ignored him. "Fat chance I'll dip into what stash I've got left just to see you throw it out again!"

"It won't happen," Mildred said. "Swear to God. Krysty feels a head-splitter coming on, and I'm guessing the pot might help her get through it."

Krysty frowned. "You think so? I really don't want that stuff."

Mildred nodded firmly. "I'd bet money on it." She thumped the back of Hammersmith's seat with her fist. "Come on, Dr. H. Otherwise we might have to turn this bucket of bolts around and get her the hell out of here."

Hammersmith's beady eyes jumped to the rearview mirror, sizing up Krysty. He jolted the wheel a few more times, wrenching the wag through an obstacle course of boulders and sinkholes, then pulled a plastic bag full of weed from the pocket of his lab coat. "All right, honeybunch. Just don't waste it," he said as he handed it over his shoulder. "That's almost the last of my supply."

Mildred took the pot, then asked for papers and a lighter, which he also provided. "Where did your supply come from anyway?"

"Got a grow set up in a secret cove not far from the core. You wouldn't believe how much the Shift's transformations enrich the soil around these parts. You get all kinds of wild varietals and effects!"

"But this batch isn't like that, I hope." Mildred held up the bag.

Hammersmith snicker-wheezed. "As if I'd ever share the good shit." His shoulders hopped up and down as he laughed some more.

Mildred put the bag and lighter in her lap, then slipped a rolling paper out of the little box. "Fine with me. Krysty just needs something to smooth out the rough spots." As she said it, the wag hit a big bump, rocking the cabin hard and bouncing the lighter right out of her lap.

Krysty caught it and handed it back. "Thanks, Mildred. I don't think we can afford to turn around because of me."

"Don't worry." Mildred smiled, put the lighter on her lap and proceeded to start packing a joint. "Just let me know if you experience any negative effects."

"Hey!" Hammersmith shouted. "You forgot something!" With that, he reached into a pack on the floor beside his seat and pulled out a plastic bowl with a resealable lid. "You're gonna need these, too!"

Krysty took the bowl, popped open the lid and peered inside at what looked and smelled like two dozen chocolate-chip cookies. "Are these real chocolate chips?" There was a tinge of amazement in her voice.

"Never you mind!" Hammersmith said. "But you're gonna need those when the munchies set in!"

"Where did you get them?" Krysty asked. "They look homemade."

"What do you think I was doing in my office last night?" Hammersmith asked.

"But we didn't smell any cookies baking," Ricky commented.

"How is that possible?" J.B. chimed in.

"Trade secret, dipshits." Hammersmith snicker-wheezed.

"Why won't you tell us?" Ricky asked.

"Because you're dealing with science power, rug rat." Hammersmith whipped around and jabbed a finger at him, sneering. "Get used to it."

Then, cackling like a lunatic, he whipped back around to face forward, pounding the wheel with the heel of his hand as if he was drumming along with a song on the radio.

Chapter Thirty-Four

Doc was in shock as Ankh led him through the underground complex that the shifters called the core. As a repurposed redoubt, the place was very familiar in terms of layout and design. A few times, as Doc rounded a corner or looked into a particular room, he felt a twinge of déjà vu at how much it resembled other redoubts he'd visited.

There were offices, armories and garages, much as there were in other redoubts, as well as barracks, bathrooms, dining halls and an auditorium. When the tour finally ended on the third level down, things got really interesting…and cold. Doc had to pull on his frock coat against the chill.

Doc was led to a nondescript door at the end of a long featureless corridor. Ankh punched a code into a numbered keypad, then the door slid open.

"This is it." Ankh stepped aside and gestured for Doc to enter. "Your laboratory, Dr. Hammersmith. I think you'll find that everything is exactly the way you left it."

Doc knew he should enter the lab warily, but he couldn't restrain his curiosity. He ambled through the door without another word.

Looking around on the other side, he did not at first realize the significance of the place. He was too dumbstruck by the level of the mess that surrounded him on all sides to wrap his head around the obfuscated details.

Cables hung from the ceiling and sprawled across the

floor like enormous tangles of spaghetti. Equipment squatted around the large room in various stages of disassembly, with open panels revealing ruined circuitry, jumbles of wiring, broken probes and scorched and shattered computer monitors.

Ceiling lights flickered, and paper printouts fluttered in the breeze from the open door. Books and notebooks were stacked and spread open on counters, crates and flooring. Not to mention, there were spare parts, hand tools and garbage everywhere, scattered hither and yon with seeming abandon.

Plus, the place reeked of rotten food, urine and what he knew was marijuana. Someone—the real Hammersmith or maybe the shifters—had to have smoked a lot of marijuana in there.

Doc was just about to comment on the smell when the configuration of the room finally got through to him. Frowning, he counted the amber-and-green walls. Armaglass walls.

Six. The room was hexagonal.

"Dear God," he muttered. His gaze fell to the floor, but it was too cluttered for a clear view. He nudged aside a fat cable with the toe of his boot, then also pushed away an open bucket full of screws, nuts, nails, bolts and tacks.

What he saw in the space he'd cleared made his heart beat faster. It took everything he had not to react visibly and clue in Ankh about the importance of what he was looking at.

"Did you find something, William?" Ankh asked from the doorway.

"No, no, not yet," Doc replied, even as he stared down at the silver disks set into the floor. "Just taking a quick mental inventory."

The truth was, though, that the armaglass walls, hexagonal layout and silver disks set into the floor all added up. Finally, he knew what he'd stumbled into, and how it might be connected to the Shift.

If only he knew what to do about it.

Behind him, Ankh walked into the room. "Helpers are available, if you like. Until now, we refrained from touching anything in here in case it was important, but you'll find our people aren't afraid of hard work on behalf of the new empire."

"Fine, fine." Doc made a point of looking away from the disks in the floor. Turning, he folded his arms over his chest and raised his eyebrows at Ankh. "Then, I suppose I ought to get to work, eh? Don't want to keep destiny waiting."

Ankh cocked his head for a moment, as if something seemed wrong, but then he seemed to shake it off and smiled. "Be sure to let us know if you need anything, Doctor. Just tell whichever attendant is assisting you, and he or she will see to it that you get what you need."

"Don't want to hold up the project," Doc said cheerfully, though the truth was, Ankh didn't expect him to work miracles with the equipment. His work in the lab was actually intended to be a delaying tactic, and then a distraction while power was seized from Exo.

But Doc's new secret was this: he might actually be able to use what was in that room to his advantage. He wasn't a whitecoat with mastery of predark tech, but he did know a little about the room. The good Lord knew, he'd used it often enough, along with Ryan and the others.

Because the truth was, he was standing in the middle of a mat-trans chamber, much like the ones that had transmitted the companions all over the Deathlands and beyond.

"Aren't you going to ask what happened in here?" Ankh kicked a metal pipe, sending it clanging into the base of some kind of diagnostic device. "How it all got to be such a wreck?"

Doc looked back at the doorway, making sure no one was lurking and listening in on their conversation. "I assumed it was Hammersmith's doing. My doing, I should say."

"It was his top assistant, actually. Heir to the throne," Ankh said. "There was an accident, and she was badly damaged."

"This is the aftermath of the accident?" Doc asked.

"The aftermath of her temper tantrum when she took off out of here. She was completely out of control, let me tell you."

"So she ran?"

"For a while." Ankh nodded smugly. "But now she's come back to the fold. She wants to make amends for what she's done."

"I see. And how will she do that, I wonder?"

"By infiltrating and betraying your comrades," Ankh said. "She has already set them up for the slaughter."

Chapter Thirty-Five

When the war wag stopped for a bathroom break, not a single soul stayed inside the vehicle. They'd been on the road for four hours by then, and everyone needed to stretch his or her legs.

Fortunately, they were finally out of the Devil's Slaughterhouse, so the fauna promised to be less lethal. And according to Hammersmith, they were less than half an hour from the core, so it was the perfect place to stop.

In fact, everything seemed to be going smoothly. They were making great time, and the wag was holding up. Hammersmith's attitude was still cranky, but his driving had evened out somewhat. And in spite of their proximity to the core, Krysty wasn't having agonizing seizures, just moderate headaches. The pot had really made a difference in her pain level, and it didn't seem to be causing any negative side effects.

But as well as things were going, Jak couldn't relax even a little. Union's warning continued to resonate in his head. Some kind of threat was imminent, one she wanted to save him from, though she'd told him to keep the rest of the team in the dark about it.

Jak's tension over this warning had increased with each passing mile. Of course he had to tell his companions, but he had to do it without Union seeing him. That had been impossible on board the wag, but at least he had a shot at it when Hammersmith stopped for a break.

As casually as he could, Jak split away from Union. He saw Ryan circling a nearby hill and couldn't follow in case she was watching, but then he skirted another hill and doubled back. He caught Ryan just as he was finishing relieving himself and approached with a finger over his lips, warning him to keep quiet.

Ryan scowled as he zipped up his pants.

Jak hurried over and whispered, very aware that he wouldn't have long until Union came hunting for him. "Union said threat on way. Offered save me, said not tell anyone."

"What kind of threat?" Ryan whispered.

Jak shrugged. "Won't talk 'bout now. One personality broke ranks but silent since."

"Okay." Ryan nodded. "We need more information. We need to interrogate her—at least draw out the friendly personality and get more info out of her."

"Draw out? Good luck. Is three against one in that head."

"But one ally is still better than none." Ryan drew his SIG-Sauer. "Let's go round her up."

"What about others?" Jak asked.

Ryan shook his head grimly. "They'll figure out what's happening soon e—"

Suddenly, a great thunderclap of an explosion erupted nearby. Ryan and Jak exchanged a quick look that said it all: there's that threat she was talking about.

Then, without a word, the two men charged around the hill and headed in the direction of the blast, which also happened to be the general vicinity of the wag.

RICKY HAD BEEN walking toward the wag when the artillery shell came down beside it.

Hearing the telltale whistle of the shell, he instinctively turned and ran, but he didn't make it far before impact.

The resulting explosion threw him forward, facedown in the sand, then showered him with shrapnel and debris.

His back and ribs hurt, but at least he was in one piece. He'd been just far enough away, with the wag between him and the explosion, that he hadn't become a fatality.

But that could change fast. Because shells were like cockroaches: if you saw one, more were always close behind. Not to mention whoever had fired the round.

The relative peace of what had been an uneventful drive to the core had just gone out the window.

Listening for more artillery whistles, Ricky scrambled to his feet and quickly assessed the immediate area. The wag lay smoking on its side, the passenger compartment blown open by the shell. Luckily, from what he could see, no one had been blown open with it.

In fact, the other members of the group were sprinting in from behind the nearest hills. Krysty and Mildred ran together, weapons in hand. J.B. charged around another hill with his Mini-Uzi in one hand and his Smith & Wesson scattergun in the other. Hammersmith and Union, however, were nowhere to be seen.

As for Ryan and Jak, they raced from behind a hill on the opposite side of the bombed wag, heads instantly whipping toward the swath of visible horizon up ahead.

Ricky followed their gazes and immediately got the same burst of adrenaline he always got right before a big fight. There in the distance, he saw something he'd seen a few times during his young lifetime, during his time in the bloodstained Deathlands.

It was an army bristling with weapons, every blaster barrel pointed in his direction.

Chapter Thirty-Six

Doc stood in the middle of the wrecked mat-trans chamber and looked around glumly, unable to decide where to begin.

Technically, all he had to do was clean up a little and pretend he was repairing and upgrading equipment according to Exo's bidding. Ankh had told him that was exactly what was expected of him—that he put on a good front long enough for Ankh's plan to come to fruition.

But Doc wanted to do so much more. He was surrounded by devices that, if operating correctly, could enable him to escape. As much as he hated the side effects of travel by mat-trans, he knew it could whisk him away to another location far from the Shift.

The mat-trans could also make escape possible in a less direct way. If tampering with the mat-trans had given the Shift its metamorphic properties, perhaps further tampering would provide some degree of control over the region's transformations, just as Exo hoped. Such control might stir things up enough to give Doc the diversion he needed to break away from the shifters.

There was just one problem with these possibilities: Doc lacked the mastery of the tech that he needed to make them happen.

Stepping over scattered parts and debris, Doc made his way to the control panel set into the wall. Clearly, it had been modified; he could tell that much by comparing what he saw with his memories of other mat-trans control panels. Sections of the panel had been pulled apart, circuit boards reconfigured and rerouted, new dials and switches wired in. A digital readout had been attached above the main panel, and a keyboard had been stuck to the panel's front edge.

It was all, oh, so familiar, yet very different from all the other mat-trans panels he'd seen. If only he understood the purpose of the modifications and how to manipulate them.

Perhaps, it occurred to him, guesswork would be sufficient. Maybe fiddling with these new controls would cause enough mayhem that he could get away without being stopped.

Or it might blow up the mat-trans and kill Doc in the process. That was possible, too.

Doc reached for one of the jury-rigged dials, then hesitated. "Hell's bells." Should he wait and see how Ankh's plan played out instead? Though Doc had zero faith that Ankh was any more benevolent than Exo, perhaps he would at least keep his word to help Doc regain his freedom.

Doc pulled back, realizing it would be better to err on the side of patience, but then, on impulse, he shot out a hand and tweaked a single dial, turning it a few degrees clockwise.

He held his breath, but nothing happened. There was no detectable change in any of the equipment in the room, and the fizzing in the back of his head didn't get any stronger.

Doc turned the dial again, with the same result, then flipped one of the jury-rigged switches. Still, nothing changed.

Next, he pressed a red button in the upper-left corner of the modified keyboard. Again, there was no change in the mat-trans chamber.

At first. After a moment, though, lights in the floor flashed to life. The bright circles they cast were visible around the silver disks—those that weren't completely buried by debris.

At the same time, a shrill squealing erupted throughout the room, so high-pitched and loud that it drove Doc to cover his ears with his hands. Then the digital readout above the control panel lit up, displaying the number 30 in red digits. As Doc watched, the number counted down to 29, 28, 27, 26, 25…

Heart racing, Doc jabbed the red button on the keyboard again, holding it down hard. The countdown, squealing and lights all shut off at once, leaving him surrounded by silent stillness once more.

A moment later, he heard someone clearing his throat from the direction of the doorway.

Turning, Doc saw an unfamiliar face, a crimson-skinned shifter male wearing gray coveralls and an ancient black baseball cap with a yellow letter *P* embroidered above the bill.

"Hello?" Doc attempted a casual smile and tone, as if there'd been no squealing, lights and cryptic countdown a moment ago. "May I help you?"

"Other way around." The mutie's voice was low and raspy. "Ankh sent me. I'm your assistant now."

"I see." Doc nodded. "And your name is…?"

"Fixie," the shifter said. "I fix things."

Doc narrowed his eyes, wondering how much the taciturn mutie had seen and heard before announcing his presence. "And you just got here, I take it?"

"More or less." Fixie shrugged. "Where do you want me to start?"

Doc decided against pressing the issue. Interrogating Fixie about what he'd witnessed might just make matters worse. "That depends. Do you have any experience with the technology in this room?"

Fixie tipped back his baseball cap, then took a long moment and looked around the mat-trans chamber. Finally, he nodded slowly and returned his gaze to Doc. "You might say that. Did some work with the previous Dr. Hammersmith back in the day, until I got fired."

Doc tried not to twitch, though Fixie had just identified him as not being the real Hammersmith. It was obvious, of course, though Doc had tried not to worry much about it; as long as deluded Exo kept calling him Hammersmith, it seemed the other shifters were prepared to accept it.

"How did you get fired?" he asked evenly.

Fixie stared at him for a while as if sizing him up. "Because I tried to talk him out of activating the modified device while it was pulling from an intermittent power source. I warned him it could cause sporadic and unpredictable effects."

Doc was surprised to hear so many words tumble out of Fixie's mouth and further surprised that he seemed to have some technical expertise. "But he ignored you?"

Fixie shrugged. "Too much wacky weed. That or too much ego. Mebbe both."

"Okay." Doc hiked a thumb at the control panel he'd been fiddling with before Fixie's arrival. "Over there. Let us start with that."

Fixie pursed his lips and nodded. "Good choice." Then he gave Doc a funny look out of the corner of his eye. "What should I call you anyway?"

Doc thought for a moment, then smiled. "Theo." It was something no one called him anymore, a name abandoned in the mists of history. Maybe now, as he tried to take charge of his own destiny for a change, was as good a time as any to blow the dust off it. "You can call me Theo."

"All right." Fixie cracked his knuckles. "Sounds good to me. Let's get started, and I'll jump in when you tell me what you want me to do."

"I have a better idea." Doc bowed. "How about if I assist you?"

Fixie thought it over for a moment, then shrugged. "Sure, Theo. Why the heck not?"

Chapter Thirty-Seven

Ryan assessed the oncoming force in one heartbeat and decided on a strategy in the next.

At first glance, he saw one piece of artillery and lots of attackers—hundreds, maybe, judging from the crowd pressing forward at the front line.

So he and his team were drastically outnumbered, but at least there was only one big blaster to contend with. Since the shifters had to reload after each shot, there wouldn't be a constant stream of shells pouring over the battlefield.

The best strategy was instantly clear to him: scatter, and kill from a distance.

Whirling, he shouted in his most commanding voice, "Scatter!" Eye sweeping across the group, he saw everyone but Union and Hammersmith present, already armed and steeling themselves for battle. "Get some elevation! Mow them down as they advance!"

He didn't have to tell anyone twice. Without hesitation, they leaped into action.

Everyone bolted in a different direction, heading for a vantage point in the hills bracketing the battlefield. They would cut down the muties from the heights, then catch whoever got through in a cross fire.

If the artillery didn't blow them to pieces first, that was. Even as Ryan ran for the closest hill, he heard the *poom* of the big blaster, followed by the wail of an incoming shell. The shriek passed overhead and dropped behind him, not far from the overturned wag. The ground shook when it hit, jarring his steps as he raced up the side of the hill.

The blastermen were pretty good. Once Ryan and the others started their sniper fire, it wouldn't take long for the big blaster to sight in on their nests.

Breathing fast, Ryan quickly scaled the hillside. He stopped short of the peak, about fifty feet from the ground, and threw himself down so he was facing the attackers.

Even as he sighted the Steyr Scout longblaster on the front rank of muties, he heard a shot from another blaster crack through the air nearby. He instantly recognized it as the sound of Jak's .357 Colt Python. As he watched the field before him, he saw a big mutie up front take a hit to the left chest and fly over backward into comrades behind him.

"My turn." Ryan aimed at another big mutie up front and squeezed the trigger. The mutie's head exploded in a sudden burst of crimson. "Next."

Even as Ryan swung his longblaster to pick another target, and shots from his teammates boomed from the surrounding hillsides, he realized that the strategy was probably futile. His team of five had ten blasters among them and limited ammo, versus what looked to be hundreds of shifters with what looked like one blaster for every third man. The rest of the muties carried swords or maces or clubs. And then there was the artillery.

Ryan and the others had been up against some lopsided odds in the past and triumphed, but this was an extreme situation. No matter how hard they pressed the shifters, the numbers weren't in their favor. The smartest play would be to flee…

The front rank of the shifters was less than a hundred yards away and fast approaching. They fired at the hills where Ryan and his people were posted, to no avail. Dozens of blasters fired at once from those enemy ranks, but no shot came close to striking any of the snipers.

Meanwhile, Ryan's group kept picking them off, one after another, right down the line. It was a little like shooting at the surf of a rising ocean tide, but no one gave up. No one stopped shooting longer than it took to reload a weapon or sight a new target.

As Ryan cranked off another shot with the Steyr Scout, he heard the familiar boom of the artillery cannon, followed by the screech of a shell in flight. This time, the shell came down on the face of Jak's hill, close enough to rattle Ryan's teeth. Looking over, he saw Jak tumbling down the backside of the bombed hill, but then Jak stopped his fall and clambered back up to his nest.

Too close. As long as the big blaster was in play, Ryan's side would have a very short life span.

But there was no good way to take it out of the game. The enemy's front line was strung across a broad swath of sandy flat; no matter how he cut it, getting to the cannon would require a tooth-and-nail fight through tightly packed mutie infantry.

Ryan knocked down another shifter. J.B.'s M-4000 blew away another to the immediate left of that toppling victim.

The shifters continued to march forward, sending up clouds of blasterfire in the direction of the hills. Through the Scout's sight, he saw the soldiers carried a hodgepodge of weapons, everything from machine blasters to streetsweeper shotguns to semiautomatic handblasters.

The big blaster unleashed another shell that hurtled over the troops, heading straight for one of the hills. Only as the shell whistled down did Ryan realize the hill was Krysty's position.

He saw her looking up, then throwing herself in a wild roll down the hillside. She moved fast, almost a blur, even then only barely getting out of the way in time.

The shell hit just above her former position, blowing apart a chunk of hillside that would have included Krysty if she hadn't escaped. As it was, the blast kicked her off the hill midway down, sending her flying.

Ryan's heart raced, but she was beyond his help. Fortunately, she was athletic and recovered from the piranha-wasp attack. As he watched, she twisted and rolled in midair, tucking in her head and elbows and knees. She came down in the sand in a series of fast somersaults that bled off the momentum of her fall, bringing her to a gradual stop. When she uncurled and got to her feet, she looked undamaged. Ryan let out the deep breath he'd been holding ever since the shell had first hit.

Again, he ran the possibilities for disabling the big blaster. If the shelling continued, his group might not have to worry about the attackers after all; the artillery might kill them first.

Just moments after Ryan went back to sniping the shifters, he heard another boom from the cannon, then the signature whistle of a shell.

Looking up, he saw where it was headed. Clear as day, the shell traced an arc through the blue-green sky, passing gracefully over the horde of murderous muties.

Zeroing in on the very hill that Ryan currently occupied.

Chapter Thirty-Eight

"Hand me those wire cutters," Fixie said from inside a crawl space in the wall of the mat-trans chamber.

Doc grabbed a rusty pair of wire cutters from a battered metal toolbox on the floor. "Here they come." He pushed them into the crawl space as far as he could; Fixie, who was on all fours, contorted himself to reach back and get them.

"Thanks, Theo. I'll need the pliers next."

"Coming right up." Doc liked Fixie and didn't mind playing second fiddle to him. Of the shifters he'd been spending time with, only Fixie had a remotely genuine personality.

"So are you sure about this?" Fixie asked from the crawl space. "You really want to fix this device and hand it over to Exo or Ankh?"

Were the questions a test? Doc couldn't be sure they weren't, though he had a gut feeling that Fixie was trustworthy. "Do you really think you can fix it? That you can finish Hammersmith's work?"

"What if I do?" Fixie asked. "Would that be in the best interest of the people of the Shift?"

Doc pushed the pliers into the crawl space. "I do not think we have much choice, do we?"

Fixie chuckled. "Let's just say I know a lot more about this gear than they think I do." He reached back for the pliers. "Though it's true that our old friend Union really did a number on the place."

"Union?"

"Hammersmith's number one assistant who trashed the joint," Fixie replied. "I've been repairing it on the sly ever since, in dribs and drabs from detailed plans that Hammersmith drafted."

"But Ankh said nothing in here had been touched since Hammersmith left."

"He doesn't know everything that goes on, though he likes to act as though he does." Something clanked in the crawl space, and Fixie cursed softly. "I've been sneaking in here for months, setting things to rights."

"So you can hand control over to Exo or Ankh?" Doc asked.

"So I can make this gear work the way Dr. Hammersmith intended. He created the Shift, you know, but he never meant to." Fixie backed out of the crawl space, then stood and dusted himself off. "He wanted to turn the area into a Garden of Eden."

"And that's what you want, too?"

Fixie shrugged and dropped the pliers and wire cutters into his toolbox. "It wouldn't hurt, would it?" He smiled and reached for a screwdriver. "It would sure beat what we've got now."

Doc frowned. "You really think you can do it?"

"Do I understand everything Hammersmith set up here? Heck no." Fixie swept the screwdriver in a circle, encompassing the room. "But can I get everything running again, and implement the changes mapped out in his plans? Pretty sure, yeah."

"Then what?" Doc asked.

"Transform the Shift into paradise," Fixie said. "Then destroy this equipment so no other idiot can get in here and ruin it."

Doc nodded slowly. "If you can finish without Exo or Ankh interfering."

"Good thing there are two of us in the picture now." Fixie winked, then turned and headed across the cluttered room.

"If they do not get us before you finish, they will get us after," Doc said. "Unless you have an escape plan of some kind."

"Not yet. Though if we didn't have all this torn apart, we'd be fine. This used to be a matter-transfer system."

Doc knew all too well about the mat-trans, though he decided to keep playing his cards close to his vest. And he didn't want to tip his hand by asking Fixie how he knew what it was.

"I had heard rumors about some sort of matter-transfer device but doubted its existence."

"If it was still in one piece, we could supposedly just zap our way out of here," Fixie said. "But we need to use it to make paradise instead."

"Right." Though Doc didn't understand exactly how Hammersmith had converted the mat-trans to transform the local landscape, it did seem logical that it worked. Mat-trans tech juggled matter and energy, turning one into the other and back again. If it could reconstruct a human body from a beam of particles, why not use it to convert other matter into different forms, as well?

"If only we had some kind of weapons." As Doc looked around the room, he took in the scattered tools and piles of junk. "Perhaps we could convert some of the contents of this chamber to that purpose."

"Mebbe," Fixie said, "but I think we ought to focus on getting this equipment up and running." He went to a panel in the wall at eye level and loosened the screws in the corners. "First priority is solving the power-flow problem."

Doc approached and watched over his shoulder. "You said the power source is intermittent?"

Fixie nodded as he pulled the panel off the wall.

"There's a nuclear reactor that powers this whole complex, but there's a problem with the core. I haven't figured out how to fix it, so I've been hooking this room up to a different source—a special high-yield nuclear battery backup. Once I switch over, we should have a steady, dedicated power flow to the mat-trans."

"This will be up and running then?" Doc asked.

"I didn't say that." Fixie used the tip of the screwdriver to nudge apart some colorful wires in the space where the panel had been. "We've got a bigger problem, actually. The transmitter."

"What about it?"

"It's failing, too. Exo's people have been trying to 'fix' it, but they're clueless. We need to undo what they've done, which is the tricky part."

"Why is it tricky?" Doc asked.

Fixie looked back at him. "Because it's under armed guard."

"But we have a mandate to repair the equipment, don't we?"

"*This* equipment." Fixie pointed at the floor. "But the transmitter's handled by a separate team. Less possibility for one person to take control of all the components that way, I guess."

Doc nodded. Though his tendency, in past adventures, had been to let others take the lead, his attitude had shifted in recent days. He'd begun thinking in a more proactive way.

Reaching down, he patted the razor blade in his coat pocket. "I suppose we'll have to prove them wrong about that," he said calmly.

Chapter Thirty-Nine

Ryan didn't hesitate. As the shell from the shifters' big blaster soared toward his roost, he scrambled down the back side of the hill as fast as he could.

Holding tight to his longblaster, he descended the sandy slope in leaps and bounds, mentally bracing himself for the impact. It came within seconds, when he was three-quarters of the way to the bottom.

The shell burst against the opposite face of the hill with enough force to kick his legs out from under him. Amid a shower of debris, he slid and tumbled the next thirty feet to the base of the hill, coming down on his back and shoulders.

Wincing at the painful landing, Ryan threw himself over to get his hands and knees under him. He quickly boosted himself into a runner's crouch, then got all the way to a standing position.

As far as he could tell, his back and shoulders were the worst of his injuries. Nothing was broken, and he'd managed to hold on to his weapons and ammo.

It wasn't a bad result, but he couldn't afford to waste time counting his blessings. He needed a tactical status, and he needed it now.

Adrenaline burning in his bloodstream like a bomb's lit fuse, Ryan charged around the base of the hill for a look at the battlefield. What he saw was about what he expected: the shifter front line advancing from fifty yards away, firing more or less indiscriminately at the surrounding hilltops.

In the few seconds that he was standing there, some of the frontline shifters spotted him and swung their weapons to shoot in his direction. Ryan immediately flung himself back behind the curve of the hill, planning to clamber back up to regain some altitude.

Instead, he found himself being struck in the middle of his back with the butt of a longblaster.

Ryan pitched forward and whipped around, getting a look at the person who'd attacked him. He fully expected to see a shifter there, a sneaky point man who'd run ahead of the oncoming attackers and gotten behind him.

But that wasn't at all what Ryan saw. Instead of a shifter, a six-foot-four woman with platinum blonde hair glared back at him. Union.

He wasn't completely shocked, though, after what Jak had told him she'd said. She'd pretended to be an ally—a frigid one, to be sure—but now the mask was off, and she was moving in for the kill.

Without a word, she stormed forward and lashed around the butt of her Heckler & Koch assault weapon, aiming for his head. Ryan ducked just in time, and the stock whipped past above him.

Spinning the automatic longblaster back, Union caught the barrel in one hand and the grip in the other. But before she could squeeze off any close-proximity shots at Ryan, he charged and tackled her backward, taking her all the way to the ground.

Ryan landed on top of her and latched on to the longblaster, jamming it lengthwise against her throat. He pressed it down with all his weight, hoping to black her out, but she used the ground under her as leverage and threw him off with one sudden twist.

As Ryan rolled one way, she rolled the other, coming up facing him with the H&K pointing in his direction. Ryan kept rolling, making it down into a dip in the sand just as she squeezed off a shot that narrowly missed.

Breathing deeply, Ryan waited until just after her second shot, then launched himself to his feet and sprinted for the closest hill. Legs pumping, he barely outran her next shot, diving behind the hill as if he was slicing into deep water there.

"Hey, One-Eye!" she shouted in a taunting voice with a heavy foreign accent. "You forgot your longblaster, big fella! What're you going to do without that?"

She was right; he'd dropped the Scout in the ambush. But it made no difference to him. He still had the 9 mm SIG-Sauer and all the deadly odds and ends he needed, including his fists and feet. And now that he recognized that accent and realized what her nationality was, he was more motivated than ever to hammer her down hard. Because not only had she betrayed his team from within, but she was part of the nation that had brought the Deathlands into being in the first place.

"I am coming for you, One-Eye." Her accent was Russian. "When I am done, I will wear your balls around my neck, on either side of that one eye you have left."

Ryan drew the SIG-Sauer, checked the magazine, flicked off the safety and started around the hill, then doubled back when he heard her footfalls coming around the same side. He darted halfway back to the spot where she'd originally surprised him, wondering if she was coming up behind him or doubling back herself.

Then, following his gut instinct, he sprang up the hillside instead of staying at ground level. He quickly climbed twelve feet up the base and flung himself on his belly with the SIG pointing downward.

Seconds later, he saw Union creeping along below,

crouching and peering ahead for some trace of him. She would be an easy shot, though he wasn't going for the kill; he still needed answers regarding her betrayal, her true motivation and whomever else she might be working with.

Before he could squeeze the trigger, though, she saw something on the ground—a footprint?—and swung up the H&K and blasted a round up the hillside. Fortunately, she wasn't as quick a shot as she needed to be, and the round went wide by a foot.

Ryan responded by putting a 9 mm slug square in her left shoulder. The impact spun her back, and she followed it around the curve of the hillside. Looking down, he saw her blood trail speckled in the sand, but she was otherwise out of sight.

He wasted no time leaping to his feet after that. Now that she knew where he was, altitude was no longer his friend.

He skirted the brim of the hill, following the blood trail below until he ran out of trail. Somehow, she'd stanched the bleeding enough to take it out of the equation, at least long enough to confuse him.

Then, where the hell was she?

Ryan continued to ease along the brim, keeping the SIG up and ready for quick action. A little farther, and he started to wonder if she was nearby at all, if perhaps she'd given up the hunt and gone in search of a medic.

Just then, something caught his eye: a single red spot on the sandy hillside up ahead. Blood.

Somehow, she'd gotten the higher ground.

Turning to look up the hill, he saw her sprawled six feet above him, grinning behind the sights of the H&K. The barrel of the longblaster was pointing right at him, and she started to squeeze the trigger.

Chapter Forty

Doc and Fixie huddled together at the end of the ventilation shaft, watching the shifters at work on the other side of the grate in front of them.

"Ready, Theo?" Fixie whispered.

"Yes." The two of them had followed a convoluted path through the duct work of the redoubt, staying well hidden all the way from the mat-trans chamber to their destination: what Fixie said was the transmitter vault. Now they faced the prospect of taking on the three shifters who were working there—none of them visibly armed, but potentially dangerous nonetheless.

"Okay, then." Fixie squirmed around so that he was sitting back with his feet against the grate. He kept his weapon—a red-handled fire ax—beside him on the sheet-metal floor of the duct. "Once this opens, we need to move fast. We need to take them out of action—boom, boom, boom."

"Right." Doc shivered nervously and battled the butterflies in his stomach.

"Here goes." Fixie drew back his knees, getting ready to kick out the grate.

Doc gripped the monkey wrench he'd brought with sweaty hands. Was he ready to use it on the shifters? His freedom, and the future of the entire Shift, depended on it, yet he still had his doubts. It wasn't so easy, attacking someone who was simply doing a job, who hadn't acted with malice directly against him.

But the result of their actions was the same, he reminded himself. Malice committed under orders from another was still malice, wasn't it?

"On three. One." Fixie pulled his knees back farther. "Two." A little farther. "Three!" Suddenly, he thrust his feet forward, kicking the grate free of the surrounding duct.

The metal grate clanged to the concrete floor, and Fixie scrambled out after it. Behind him, Doc took a deep breath and followed, clutching the handle of the monkey wrench.

The three shifter workers instantly abandoned what they were doing and looked toward the duct. One ran toward the new arrivals without hesitation; another tossed aside the clipboard he was holding and ran to grab a length of metal pipe from the floor. The third shifter turned tail and sprinted for the door, which evened the odds.

Except for one problem. If he ran to get help, Doc and Fixie would be in trouble.

Doc did the math for a split second, then abandoned Fixie to the two fighters and went after the runner.

Instantly, Doc regretted not having a gun. The vault was huge, and the runner had a big lead on him; Doc sprinted as fast as he could, but he still couldn't catch up. Any second now, the shifter would be out the nearest door, and Doc might lose him.

Though perhaps the weapon at hand might be sufficient. Closing to within twenty feet of the runner, Doc hauled back the monkey wrench as if it was a medieval war hammer. Then he swung it forward with all his might and released it, aiming at the runner's back.

The big wrench soared forward and came in lower than Doc had expected, but it still hit the target. The makeshift weapon crashed into the backs of the runner's knees, colliding just hard enough to jolt his stride out of sync. He tripped over his own feet and flew forward, floundering as the floor raced toward him.

Doc retrieved the monkey wrench from the floor and charged up to stand over the shifter. But when he got to that position, he found himself at a loss as to what to do next. The little mutie cowered with his hands over his head; he didn't seem to possess a single drop of military-style aggression.

Doc's first thought had been to knock him unconscious with the wrench, but he couldn't get himself to do it. It would be too easy to injure the mutie fatally with the big, heavy wrench.

Hearing a cry from across the vault, he turned and saw Fixie facing off with the other two shifters, swinging the fire ax at one and missing by inches. The shifters kept circling at a safe distance, armed only with metal pipes but looking as if they had the upper hand.

Doc needed to join that fight, though he still had the runner to contend with. Thinking fast, he ran and grabbed a spool of cable from nearby, then brought it back to bind the shifter's hands and feet.

When he had the shifter secured, Doc retrieved the wrench and bolted over to help Fixie. He had to hope the runner wouldn't break free, though he hadn't had time to test his bonds properly.

As Doc ran up on the standoff in progress, one of the shifters immediately broke away to attack him. The shifter wielded a three-foot length of iron pipe over his head like a Cro-Magnon with a club, ready to cave in his enemy's skull.

But when he heaved the pipe down, Doc checked the swing with the monkey wrench. The two bludgeons crashed together with a loud clank, stopping inches from Doc's forehead.

Grunting, Doc struggled to push off the pipe with the length of the wrench. He clenched his teeth and strained every muscle in his arms and shoulders, causing a chain reaction of pain to light up his back.

Hand-to-hand combat was not his strong suit, and the mutie was much younger than he, but Doc held his own. He couldn't quite drive back the pipe, but he kept it from pushing in closer.

Remembering a move that Ricky had tried to teach him, he slid the pipe over, away from his head, then suddenly released the pressure and sidestepped. The shifter dropped hard, all the way to the floor, as Doc yanked the wrench out of his path.

As the shifter went down, Doc hurried out of his reach. At that exact moment, Fixie bolted past him with the fire ax clutched in both hands.

As Doc watched, Fixie swung the ax back from his side. For an instant, Doc feared his ally might have a fatal blow in mind for the shifter.

But Fixie used only the flat of the blade, not the sharp edge, smacking the shifter hard in the chest as he tried to crawl to his feet. The blow knocked the mutie down on his back, where he thrashed like a beetle trying to flip itself onto its legs.

Then Fixie followed up with a glancing kick to the side of the shifter's head. After that, the shifter went limp on the floor.

"Thanks for the assist." Fixie grinned. "You handle yourself pretty good in a fight."

I do? Doc caught himself before he said it. "Same to you," he said instead.

"Let's get these guys tied up." Fixie looked over his shoulder at the third shifter, who lay unconscious on the floor some thirty feet away. "Then we'll do the work we came here to do."

"Is that the transmitter?" Doc pointed at a huge apparatus in the middle of the room—what looked like a giant cannon swaddled in cables and studded with nodes and antennae. It was not at all what he'd expected.

"The one and only." Fixie headed for a reel of cable on the floor by the wall. "It fires the modified mat-trans beams that reshape the terrain of the Shift."

"I see." Doc frowned at the apparatus, which was mounted on a swivel base and pointed up at a forty-five-degree angle. "So if we blew up this one device, it would instantly stabilize the Shift?"

Fixie scowled at him. "I guess it would, but we won't. We're here to restore Dr. Hammersmith's vision, remember?"

"Of course." Even as Doc said it, he wondered how he might best destroy the transmitter. Ending the transformations and associated side effects might be the best thing he could possibly do for the people of the Shift and his own friends.

And now might be the only chance he would have to do it.

"Help me tie up these two." Fixie rushed past him with a reel of cable in each hand.

Doc took one more look at the transmitter apparatus. The tip of the device glowed with a pulsing blue light that struck one ring of polished glass lenses mounted in the ceiling. Doc guessed the lens had to focus the beam through channels of some kind, leading it to the surface and angling it toward its targets.

"Come on," Fixie snapped as he wrapped cable around the ankles of one of the unconscious shifters. "I need help here."

"All right, yes." Doc nodded and walked over to assist him. "Let us get this done."

Chapter Forty-One

Ryan was dead meat and he knew it.

Then, suddenly, there was a thunderous boom and a powerful shock wave ripped through the hill, jarring Union just as she pulled the trigger.

Her shot went wide in a big way. Ryan, who'd managed to stay on his feet through the blast, charged up the hillside before she could fire again.

He grabbed the H&K by the barrel and tore it away from her, hurling it off into space. But the lack of a weapon didn't keep Union from fighting back. She lunged at him like a panther, catching him at the knees and sweeping his legs out from under him.

Ryan came down on top of her, and she flung herself backward so he was pinned beneath her weight. He used the position to his advantage, snaking an arm around her neck and clamping it tight.

Teeth clenched, he cinched the choke hold tighter. Union strained to roll to one side to break the pressure, but Ryan used his own weight to hold her in place.

She tried to maneuver a booted foot to kick him in his crotch, but the move was impossible. Union pushed up and slammed herself down on him, trying to hurt something, but then the choke hold finally took effect. The pressure of his arm cut off the blood flow to her brain, and her thrashing struggles diminished.

Union went limp. Ryan waited a moment afterward to

make sure she was out before letting go of her and rolling her body aside.

Then he got to his feet and jogged around the hill to see where the artillery had hit this time. It didn't take long; there was now a smoking crater midway between his hill and Jak's.

As Ryan took in the damage, he heard a loud whoosh from the opposite side of his hill and scrambled to get there. He arrived just in time to see a small guided missile race from below and soar out over the battlefield, leaving a trail of curdled gray smoke.

In a heartbeat, the missile flashed over the heads of the approaching muties, zooming unerringly toward a single huge target behind enemy lines.

As Ryan watched, the missile hit, and the big blaster exploded. Even before the smoke cleared, he could see that the barrel of the weapon had been destroyed.

As the army of attackers turned to see what had happened to their biggest asset, Ryan ran a little farther and saw the source of the missile. Below, between his hill and the next one over, stood a man with a portable rocket launcher braced on his left shoulder.

Instantly, Ryan recognized him. Dr. Hammersmith was front and center, and he was loaded for bear.

Ryan grinned and shook his head. Thanks to the pot-smoking whitecoat, the biggest threat on the field was out of action. The sniper nests were secure for the moment and still running hot; he could hear the crackle of shots being fired up and down the line by his companions.

Now, if only that mutie army wasn't quite so big. Whittling it down a few heads at a time with sniper fire wasn't shrinking it fast enough.

Fortunately, Hammersmith had the right idea. After taking a moment to reload, he fired the rocket launcher directly into the approaching front line. Muties blew apart in the blast, sending body parts churning into the air and leaving a nice gaping hole in the middle of the line.

Keep it up, Doc, Ryan thought. Even as the thought crossed his mind, he chastised himself. That man with the rocket launcher might call himself a doctor, but he would never be Doc.

As bullets from the muties below hissed past him, Hammersmith fired another rocket. This one opened an even bigger hole in the front line, scattering twice as many muties as it blew them to pieces.

Ryan saw fresh confusion in the ranks as the battle's momentum shifted. Some of the shifters turned and fled, unable to take the heat now that the enemy had a big blaster of their own.

But not all of them retreated. A large contingent moved up to fill the gaps, focusing their fire on the man with the rocket launcher.

To his credit—or the credit of the drugs in his system—Hammersmith stood his ground and calmly reloaded. But he wasn't bulletproof, and Ryan knew he wouldn't last long.

Running around and down the hill, Ryan retrieved Union's H&K from the ground where it had fallen. Charging back up the slope, he found his Scout longblaster and grabbed it, then made his way back around to the hillside above Hammersmith.

Picking a spot with good visibility of the approaching force, Ryan hunkered down with the longblasters and went to work. Cranking off round after round from the H&K's drum magazine, he knocked down key shooters who were going after Hammersmith. The heads of determined shifters popped like balloons along the new front line; apparently, the H&K's magazine was currently loaded with explosive rounds.

Meanwhile, Krysty picked up on what he was doing

and joined the action from the next hill. Her shooting was almost the equal of his own as she did her part to shield Hammersmith. The snipers gave Hammersmith time to fire another rocket at the crowd, turning a slew of muties into blown-apart fragments and fluids. This time, the slaughter gave more of the shifters pause; again, a group of retaliators moved forward, stomping on their comrades' remains in their push to the front line, but there were only half as many as there had been last time. And the slow leak of retreating fighters from the rear echelon had become a steady pour.

Ryan kept shooting, but he knew what the end of a battle looked like. The tide had turned, and there would be no further reversals.

All that was left was the cleanup—speeding the enemy soldiers' retreat until they'd all abandoned the field of battle. Then Ryan could turn to the next problem on his list, the one he'd stepped away from long enough to give Hammersmith the cover fire he needed.

Union.

Chapter Forty-Two

"Hand me that circuit board," Fixie said. "I'm almost done with this thing."

Doc did as he was asked, handing over the circuit board in question to Fixie, who was half-buried in an access hatch at the base of the transmitter.

"Thanks." The circuit board quickly disappeared inside the access hatch, just as numerous tools and parts had done over the past half hour. Fixie had done most of his work inside that hatch, which he said contained the heart of the transmitter's control system.

Though, for all Doc knew, it could just as easily have been the core of some doomsday device that Fixie was nursing back to health. He seemed trustworthy, but anything was possible, and Doc was on guard.

"There, that did it." Fixie popped out of the hatch and handed several tools to Doc. "The transmitter has been restored to the operational state that Dr. Hammersmith intended. Once we connect the mat-trans system to the nuclear batteries and throw the switch, everything will finally be running perfectly."

"The nuclear batteries?" Doc repeated. "I take it that is our next order of business."

"Yes, and we need to get to there fast." Fixie boosted himself out of the hatch and planted his feet on the floor. "People will start noticing things soon, if they haven't already. Like the fact that we're not where we're supposed to be, for example."

"Are there regular check-ins with the people manning this facility?" Doc looked across the room to where the three workers were bound and tied to iron cleats mounted on the wall.

"I'm sure there are." Fixie gathered up his gear in a hurry. "All the more reason for us to get moving."

Doc gathered up the rest of the gear and headed for the ventilation duct, but Fixie stopped him with a loud whistle. Turning, Doc saw him gesturing toward a closed door on the far end of the vault.

"This way," Fixie said.

"Are there no guards?" Doc asked.

Fixie shook his head. "I don't think most people even know that the batteries exist."

Doc looked back at the duct opening. "Maybe it would not hurt to be on the safe side anyway."

"Go that way if you want, but I'm taking the hallway, Theo." Fixie laughed and headed for the door.

Doc still worried they might come across trouble that way, but he followed Fixie. Splitting up didn't seem smart at that stage, and besides, he had no idea how to find the nuclear batteries via the duct work on his own.

Luckily, Fixie was right. No guards or workers awaited them at their destination.

After a short trip down the corridor, Fixie opened the door on a much smaller room, at most, a fourth of the size of the transmitter vault.

The room was brightly lit and lined along three walls with various monitors, displays and control panels. The fourth wall looked like heavy armaglass, but it was completely transparent and without color. On the other side of the armaglass, Doc saw a water-filled space. Opaque gray cubes the size of refrigerators occupied the area, suspended from long metal racks and wired together with cables and conduits that hung in sagging loops like vines in a jungle.

"The batteries are underwater?" Doc asked.

"For cooling purposes." Fixie immediately marched over to a panel on the wall and went to work, fiddling with knobs and dials. "The batteries produce far less heat than the reactor, but the heat they do generate has to be controlled and dispersed. Otherwise, big problems."

"I see." Doc walked the perimeter of the control room, stopping at the window wall to place his palm against the glass. The surface was warm to the touch.

"This shouldn't take long." Fixie finished tweaking the panel he was working on and moved to another. "I've already done most of the work to make the changeover possible. The transmitter takes an enormous amount of energy, but the batteries are more than up to the task. We just have to adjust a few things, disconnect the reactor feed and switch to the battery feed. Then it's smooth sailing after that."

"Smooth sailing." Doc pulled his hand away from the glass. "The fulfillment of the true Dr. Hammersmith's dream. But why?"

"Why?" Fixie looked at him and frowned.

"He fired you, didn't he? Because you tried to help perfect his system. So why do you have any interest in his dream?"

"Why not?" Fixie shrugged and went back to work. "It's a good dream. Making the Shift a better place is a *very* good dream, if you ask me."

Doc thought for a moment. He had questioned Fixie's sincerity, but maybe there was no reason to doubt him. "It does seem like a most worthwhile goal," he said. "I only hope we both live to see it come to fruition."

"Have faith, like I do," Fixie said. "We'll figure out an escape route, or one will present itself. We're doing good work, and we'll be rewarded for it."

"Faith? I had a great deal of it once. Not so much anymore." Doc gazed at the rising bubbles behind the arma-glass wall and remembered going to church in the days before his travels through time. It had filled a void inside him, one that had been empty since his arrival in the Deathlands. "I do not object to it on principle, though. I must admit, I would like to think it has a bearing on our destinies."

"Then, I'm feeling better already about our chances." Fixie grinned and extended a hand. "Now, how about giving me the needle-nose pliers so we can wrap this up?"

Chapter Forty-Three

"So tell us," Ryan ordered. "Tell us everything."

Union, who sat on the ground with her hands and feet bound securely, just glared up at him. She glared at all of them in turn—the team members she'd betrayed, who stood in judgment in a semicircle in front of her now that the battle with the shifter army was over. The muties had fled toward the core, leaving behind their dead and the scattered pieces of their shattered artillery…also leaving behind Ryan's team, which had nearly been shattered by Union.

"Why do it?" Jak's voice bore an extra layer of tension. Of all of them, he took her betrayal the most personally. "Why lead into mutie trap?"

Union turned toward him, then winced as the movement set off pain in the bullet wound in her shoulder, which Mildred had bandaged. "Why lead into mutie trap?" She repeated his words mockingly, in a heavy Russian accent, then shook her head and laughed. "Albino moron."

Jak scowled. He was furious at what she'd done, yet also deeply hurt, though he kept up as stoic a front as he could for her benefit. "You traitor from start?"

"What kind of question is that?" Union laughed again. "I fed you to the wolves. Of course I was 'traitor from start.'"

"What about other women in head?" Jak asked.

Union sneered up at him. The braid that hung from her left temple was striped with all the colors that signaled the presence of her alter egos. "I swear, your English is worse than mine. Would it kill you to use a fucking article or conjunction once in a while?"

"What about other women?" Jak grabbed her by the shoulders and shook her. "Where Carrie, Dulcet, Rhonda, Taryn?"

Union laughed, ignoring the pain of her wound. "There's just me in here now, boy."

Jak shook her again, harder, as she continued to laugh, and that was when Ryan stepped in. He grabbed Jak's wrist and shook his head once. Jak got the message and let her go, taking a step back. As angry as he was, he trusted Ryan, as always, to do what was best for all of them.

"What makes you so great?" Ryan asked. "Because this is the first I've heard anything about you, lady."

"It will soon be the last. This battle was just a warm-up."

Ryan gazed into her eyes a moment, then turned to Dr. Hammersmith. "What do you know about this Russian bitch anyway?"

"Nothing." Hammersmith shook his head and raised his hands, palms up. "I never met her before in my life, I swear."

"Maybe she's some kind of dormant subpersonality," Mildred suggested. "A kind of override routine implanted during brainwashing."

"Or maybe you don't know what the fuck you're talking about, capitalist bitch," Union snapped.

Mildred ignored her. "It's also possible the other personalities were strictly camouflage."

"No," Hammersmith said insistently. "I know those women. They exist."

"Make it past tense, dumbass," Union said. "They're long gone, you idiot pothead."

"Perhaps they only merged," Mildred stated. "Some kind of trigger event might have set the process in motion."

"Does it matter why she did it?" Ricky asked.

"It does if there are parts of her worth saving," Krysty told him.

"There aren't." Union spit in her direction, not quite hitting her, and laughed. "There is only one Wicked Witch of the East in here, hungry to eat your eyeballs."

"Called what?" J.B. adjusted his fedora. "What's the wicked witch's name?"

"It isn't Union. That's all I'll say."

"But don't you want us to know who finally took us down?" J.B. asked. "Don't you want us to die with your name on our lips, cursing you for what you've done?"

Union thought for a long moment, then said the name slowly, like a purring cat, "Sasha. My name is Sasha."

"So what's coming next, Sasha?" Ryan asked. "You said the fight with the shifters was just a warm-up, so what's next?"

"You'll find out soon enough." Sasha laughed loudly, as if she'd just been told a hilarious joke.

"Where will it happen?" Ryan probed. "When will it happen?"

"You won't find out until it's too late," Sasha said. "But what I *will* tell you is what comes after. The new beginning that will leave you people in the dust."

"What new beginning?" Krysty asked.

"A collective intelligence. All minds in the Shift joined together by the power of his machine." She sneered at Hammersmith.

Mildred turned her gaze on the man, as well. "Is that even possible?"

"Of course not!" Hammersmith snapped.

"Oh, but it is." Sasha grinned and raised her eyebrows. "And I have made certain of this."

"What are you talking about?" Hammersmith frowned, looking confused.

"Such was my mission all along, when I served as your assistant," Sasha said. "Using your device to bind together many minds, using my own to seed the process."

"I don't understand," Hammersmith told her.

"My mind does not contain multiple personalities. Rather, it represents the integration of actual separate minds from multiple human beings. I have a collective intelligence, and I intend to use it to spark a much larger network of minds—one that encompasses the Shift. And eventually, beyond it."

"Assuming you could even do such a thing, why would you?" Mildred asked.

Sasha looked at her with an expression of grim amusement. "I was cryogenically preserved, awaiting reactivation, then freed, dear Mildred. My home country, like yours, long ago lost the greatest war of all time and ceased to be. But thanks to me, my country will achieve the ultimate victory!

"I will create a true collective in the heart of what was once America—a collective intelligence that will give birth to a new Soviet Union. And none of you will be able to stop it!"

"WHAT A STORY," J.B. said later, as he and Ryan salvaged gear from the ruined war wag. "An awakened Russian freezie out to build a collective intelligence that brings the USSR back to life in the heart of the old US of A." He gave Ryan a sidelong look. "You believe her?"

Ryan shrugged. "I just wish we knew more about whatever surprises are waiting for us at the core."

"You and me both." They hadn't been able to get anything else out of Sasha after her revelation about the plan to create a beachhead for a viral Soviet collective intelligence. Though she'd told them about her true nature and goals, she'd kept her cards close to the vest when it came to information they could actually use. "So it's business as usual, I guess? Headfirst into the shit with next to nothing in the way of knowing what awaits us?"

"And come out on top anyway? Pretty much, J.B."

J.B. fished a box of shotgun shells from the rubble and tossed it into his backpack. "I don't suppose ol' Hammersmith has any more rockets for that launcher of his squirreled away in here, does he?"

Ryan shook his head. "I was surprised he came up with the last ones."

"I'm just glad he's turned out to be an asset. Not that I ever had any doubts."

"Me, neither, what with all the dope smoking and crazy talk." Ryan found a bag full of grens and lifted it clear of the wreckage. "I just hope he can get us over the finish line, especially if there's some kind of game-changer waiting for us."

J.B. slapped him on the back. "What fun would life be without a curveball now and then? Or every five minutes, as the case may be in the Deathlands."

"Give it up, Jak," Ricky said. "She's a lost cause."

Jak should have been prepping for the next stage of the mission—the march to the core—and he knew it, but he couldn't break away from watching Union.

The traitor still sat on the ground with her wrists and ankles bound, staring into space. She hadn't said a word in more than a half hour, and she didn't look inclined to speak anytime soon.

Jak had nothing to gain from watching her. He wasn't even on guard duty; that was Ricky's job. But he couldn't stay away.

How could he have been so wrong about the connection between them? It didn't seem possible. Jak's instincts were usually solid when it came to the opposite sex, and his instincts had picked up on an attraction.

Nevertheless, he'd heard her confession with his own ears. She was a Soviet freezie who hated them all and craved the fulfillment of a plan. She'd left no room for misinterpretation.

"Come on." Ricky nodded toward the war wag, where Ryan and J.B. were still working. "Go help those guys. Shake it off."

"Already shook," Jak replied. "Just hoping silence breaks."

"Promise?"

"Promise."

"All right, good." Ricky still looked concerned but managed half a smile. "So can you hold down the fort for a minute while I go take a leak?"

"Consider held." Jack winked one ruby eye.

"I'll be right back," Ricky said, then wandered off behind a nearby hill.

Almost as soon as he left, Union turned her gaze on Jak and started talking. "I'm still in here," she said softly.

Jak frowned. "Who talking?" he asked, though he noticed that her braid was Carrie white.

"You know who! Now, listen, before *she* comes back." She leaned forward and dropped her voice, though the woman she was trying to keep in the dark was inside her head. "Don't trust her, Jak! She lies."

"About what?"

"Us!" Carrie-Union snapped. "Who we are. Why she's doing all this. Don't believe her!"

"Should believe you instead?" Jak snorted. "Believe any of you?"

"Yes!" Carrie-Union hissed. "You can trust me! I want to help you!"

"Want help?" Jak asked. "Tell what Russian knows. What danger coming?"

"I don't know." Carrie choked out a sob. "She doesn't show the rest of us everything! She keeps us locked away whenever she's driving, and we're blind and deaf and trapped."

"How you get out?" Jak asked.

"I fought my way out, because I love you. And no matter what you say or do, I will never give up on you!"

Jak stared at her, feeling the urge, against all common sense, to believe her. Maybe his instincts hadn't been so wrong after all; maybe the woman who had feelings for him was still in there, fighting to get free.

Or not. Suddenly, a wicked sneer spread across her face. She tipped her head to one side and oozed out a single word in a heavy Russian accent.

"Sucker."

Then she broke down in hysterical laughter, just as Ricky returned from his bathroom break.

"Not so quiet anymore, huh?" Ricky asked. "So what got her making noise again?"

"Told her joke."

Ricky looked at Union, who was still laughing uproariously. "Must've been hilarious."

"She didn't get." Jak shrugged. "Didn't know joke on her."

Again, Ricky watched Union as she continued to crack up. "Are you sure about that?"

Jak met Union's gaze for an instant. Did he see a flicker of Carrie or any of the others in her eyes? Did it even matter anymore?

"What can say? Some people, everything just big joke." With that, Jak shook his head and walked off in the direction of the wag to get ready for what was to come.

Chapter Forty-Four

Doc and Fixie had been back in the mat-trans chamber for less than five minutes when the door flew open and Exo stormed into the room.

"Hello, children!" Instead of a candy stick, Exo had what looked like a strip of leathery black jerky in a corner of his mouth. "You've been naughty, haven't you?"

Doc froze, wondering if Exo knew what he and Fixie had been up to for the past few hours. Had he come to punish them for their unauthorized foray to the transmitter and their efforts to restore Hammersmith's dream?

"Well?" Exo pulled the jerky strip from his mouth and flapped it at each of the men in turn. "Who's been the naughty one? Dr. Hammersmith, or his lovely assistant?"

"Neither." Fixie smiled and spread his arms. "We've both been working hard and keeping our noses clean."

"That's too bad." Exo looked deeply disappointed. "I was going to give the naughtiest one a treat!" He held up the jerky. "A hunk of the *last* naughty one to get my attention." He waved the jerky in the air, then brought it down and bit off the end of it with savage gusto.

Doc went on smiling but recoiled inside. Cannibalism. It never got old in the Deathlands.

Exo strolled the perimeter of the chamber, looking around at the parts and pieces in various states of repair. "So can we have this ready by tomorrow?"

"Of course!" Fixie saluted with a flourish. "We were just saying that was when we'd be ready, weren't we, Dr. H.?"

Doc met Fixie's gaze, which told him all he needed to know. Play along. "Yes, yes. No later than tomorrow."

"I can't wait!" Exo twirled Doc's swordstick like a majorette's baton. "Tomorrow, the Shift will be mine! And after that, the sky's the limit!"

"Actually," Fixie said, "we'll need a little more time for the sky."

Exo whipped around and glared Fixie, shaking the point of the swordstick at him. For a moment, Doc thought he was going to go ballistic and punish Fixie for his egregious comment.

But instead, Exo's glare turned into a grin. "A *little* more?" He laughed. "So be it! But I expect the stars to be part of the package."

"Done and done." Fixie dusted off his hands and took a bow.

Exo hurried over and gave him a long hug. Then he turned to Doc, reaching out as if he was going to hug him, too.

Instead, as usual, he took a swing at him. The blow was an uppercut pumped deep into Doc's belly, blasting the breath right out of him.

Exo bit off another hank of jerky, then threw the remaining piece on the floor between Doc and Fixie. "Here, fight over that for your dinner." Laughing, he strutted out the door, twirling Doc's swordstick at his side. "No time for a sit-down meal today! You can feast all you want tomorrow, after my empire has come to pass."

As Doc watched him go, his hand patted the razor blade in his pocket. He wanted to fish it out and put it to use so badly, just to finish off that mutie monster.

But he knew the time wasn't right.

"Don't worry about him," Fixie said after Exo had gone. "He'll be out of the picture before you know it."

Doc frowned as the pain from the punch in his gut

began to subside. "What do you know about his brain damage?" he asked.

"From the fever, you mean?"

"I suppose." Doc shrugged. "Ankh told me that Exo had experienced some form of brain damage and hasn't been the same since."

"You might say that." Fixie nodded. "Everything in the Shift is subject to transformation, including diseases. Exo and Ankh caught one of the worst of them and nearly died. Only Ankh came out of it with his mind intact. Exo's mind was twisted, many of his memories lost or altered. That's why he thinks you're Hammersmith, and he doesn't remember the truth about Ankh."

"Truth? What truth?"

"Ankh is family," Fixie replied. "Ankh is Exo's younger brother." With that, he trotted across the chamber and opened a panel in the floor. "Hey, I could use a hand over here."

Doc heard him but didn't move. He was too busy processing what Fixie had just told him. "But…but Ankh is plotting to overthrow him."

"Wouldn't you?" Fixie grabbed a voltage meter and sat on the edge of the open floor panel. "He is one cruel, crazy son of a bitch. The sucker punch he gave you is nothing compared to the atrocities he's committed since his mind went."

"Then, why hasn't anyone overthrown him until now?"

"Better the devil you know, right?" Fixie nodded knowingly and eased himself down into the opening in the floor. "Until now."

"Exactly." Fixie raised his voice to be heard from under the flooring. "Things are finally about to change around here. Only they won't change the way Ankh thinks they will. When it's all over, he'll be finished, too."

"And who'll be in charge then? You?"

"Not me." Fixie laughed. "No one will be in charge."

"You are referring to a state of anarchy?" Doc asked.

"We're making a paradise here," Fixie said. "Who needs tyrants in paradise?"

Doc couldn't argue with his logic, though history provided far too many examples to the contrary. "So when will the device truly be ready? Tomorrow must be an overly optimistic deadline, but…"

"No, it's not." Fixie popped up from the hole in the floor, shaking his head. "If anything, it's overly conservative. Not that I was going to tell him that."

Doc frowned. "You can get it done sooner?"

"You better believe it, Theo. We'll have the system online within the hour, barring unforeseen failures. I told you, I've been working on this for a while now."

"Dribs and drabs, you said."

Fixie shrugged. "I might have been playing it down a little, now that you mention it."

Chapter Forty-Five

Krysty reluctantly smoked another of Hammersmith's joints, but the pounding in her head kept getting worse.

The reason seemed pretty clear. She and the rest of the team, and their prisoner, were hiking the last few miles to the core. The landscape-warping and animal-mutating forces emanated from there. According to Hammersmith, the core represented the greatest concentration of those forces in the Shift. So it was to be expected that they would break through whatever relief she had found in Hammersmith's drug.

But the fact remained that she had to work through the pain, no matter how bad it got. They were too close to finding Doc, if he was still alive, for her to hobble the team in any way and jeopardize the rescue.

Thinking back to her earlier seizures, which had occurred much farther from the core, she dreaded the onset of more pain at that level. To ward it off, she tried placing herself in a meditative kind of state, focusing on peaceful thoughts and maintaining an even keel in all ways.

It helped, at least, that Ryan was by her side. His presence always calmed her in even the most extreme situations.

His arm brushed against her now and then as they walked, just enough to remind her that he was there. That he would do everything in his power to keep her from suffering, no matter what it cost him.

"Not far now," said Hammersmith, who was guiding

the group, walking in front between Jak and Ricky. "Everybody keep alert from here on out."

"Thought you said way back," Jak stated. "Keep us off radar."

"We are, Casper," Hammersmith snapped. "But you never know when one of those mutie bastards might happen to be out having a smoke or taking a piss when you least expect it, do you?"

"Jumpy?" Jak asked. "Nervous 'bout going home?"

"Not a bit, you pasty-faced bastard."

"Not worry. We got back." Jak chuckled. "Sides and front different story."

"Up yours," Hammersmith snarled.

Krysty managed a small smile in spite of the rising pain in her head. A little friction wasn't a bad thing on the way to a fight; it helped take the edge off, took their minds off the danger just enough.

It was better to focus on Hammersmith's trash talk than the real wild card in their midst: Union. Taking her with them had the potential to blow up in their faces. It was impossible to predict what she might do at the core, which crazy or malicious whim her split personalities might decide to indulge.

J.B. and Mildred had eyes and blasters on Union at all times. Her hands were bound behind her back, and her mouth was gagged. But Krysty wouldn't bet jack that she wasn't still a threat. If an opportunity presented itself, Krysty couldn't imagine that Union would pass it up.

Suddenly, Hammersmith slowed his pace, gesturing for everyone to do the same. The group eased along a winding path through a maze of small hills, casting long shadows from the almost-setting sun.

They emerged in an open space, a broad, sandy flat centered on two big hills some fifty yards away.

"This is it," Hammersmith announced. "Welcome to the core."

"Not see anything," Jak said. "Core invisible?"

"Underground." Hammersmith pointed an index finger downward. "It's inside an old military base that survived skydark. My old stomping grounds."

Immediately, Krysty realized he had to be referring to a redoubt. She looked over at Ryan, who kept his poker face firmly in place but met her gaze with the same instantaneous understanding.

"How get in?" Jak asked. "Underground bases not have back doors."

"This one does." Hammersmith pointed at a spot near the base of the closest hill. "I put it there myself a while ago, in case I needed a way in. Be fucking prepared, that's my motto."

"Motto sound familiar," Jak said sarcastically.

"I've got another motto just for you," Hammersmith said, and then he gave Jak the finger.

Jak laughed. "Better watch. Might cut off for souvenir."

"Bite me." Hammersmith then headed for the two nearby hills.

Jak and Ricky, both grinning, fell in step on opposite sides of him. Ryan and Krysty were next in line, but when they started forward, Krysty faltered.

"You okay?" Ryan looked at her with concern.

Krysty nodded. "I'm fine, I'm good." She gestured at the men ahead of them. "Let's go get Doc."

"Tell me if you need a rest."

"I will." Krysty flashed her best "all's well" smile, though Ryan probably knew all wasn't well. She'd faltered because of a bolt of pain in her head, the biggest one so far that day. She forced it down with all her strength, determined not to burden the group, but she knew it wouldn't be the last.

And she wasn't sure she'd be the kind of asset the team needed her to be once the last of the drugs wore off and the flashes of pain came stronger than ever. But Doc needed her, and she wouldn't give up until he was safe…if she was physically able.

"Come on," she said, and then she started forward again, this time without faltering. Meanwhile, the pounding in her head grew ominously more intense.

J.B. JABBED THE barrel of his Mini-Uzi in the small of Union's back, but she wouldn't walk forward.

At first, he thought she might be making some kind of play to get herself free, but when she turned her head, giving him a look at the side of her face, he changed his opinion.

Union actually looked scared. Her eyes were wide with panic, her lips quivering slightly.

J.B. jabbed her again. "Get moving!"

But she just stood there. Up to that point, she'd marched the whole way with erect defiance, as if the bonds were a badge of honor. Now she looked terrified of going the rest of the way.

Mildred, the other half of Union's escort, poked her with the barrel of the ZKR revolver. "What's the problem?"

Union shook her head emphatically. She couldn't speak with her mouth gagged, but her body language told the story.

Whichever personality was in charge at that moment, she didn't want to get any closer to the core.

Briefly, J.B. considered peeling off her gag to find out exactly what the problem was, but there were too many ways for that scenario to go sideways. Besides, they didn't have time to waste; the rest of the group was already up ahead, crossing the flat.

"Just go." J.B. jabbed her harder with the Mini-Uzi. "It's not as if you're going in alone."

Still, she resisted. The fear on her face blossomed, expanding like a mushroom cloud.

They had to catch up to the others, or the mission could fall apart.

"Walk. *Now*." J.B. raised the blaster and pressed the barrel against the back of Union's head. "Or I pull the trigger and leave you here to rot."

He had no intention of killing her in cold blood. Her braid was white, which told him an innocent personality—Carrie—was in the driver's seat. But he needed her to believe him.

"Dead serious, girl." J.B. pressed the barrel tighter against her skull. "Get moving or die."

Union shivered violently, then suddenly stopped and stiffened. When she turned to look back at him, the fear in her eyes had been replaced by ice, and her braid had changed to black.

Taryn was back in the saddle, as frigid and defiant as ever. She needed no further encouragement to start walking; she spun on her heel and followed the footsteps of Ryan and the others without hesitation.

J.B. shared a look with Mildred, and they both shook their heads. Then they hurried to catch up with Union before her next unpredictable move.

HAMMERSMITH LED THE group to the base of the nearest hill, then circled behind it. Halfway around the hill, he stopped and kicked sand off something on the ground.

As the sand cleared, Ricky saw there was a round metal hatch at their feet—an actual predark manhole cover cast from iron. The middle of the Sandhills was no place for such an object, so Ricky guessed it had to have been repurposed from somewhere else…maybe within the redoubt.

"Somebody give me a pry bar." Hammersmith reached out a hand and snapped his fingers impatiently. When no one gave him what he wanted right away, he sneered at the team. "You mean to tell me none of you bastards has a pry bar?"

Ricky shrugged. "Doc's swordstick might have worked."

Hammersmith shook his head. "How'd I ever let myself get mixed up with you morons?" He hunkered down, squatting by the cover, and fluttered his fingers overhead. "How about loaning me a rifle, then?"

Ryan handed him Union's Heckler & Koch. "Safety's on."

Hammersmith scowled. "Really?" He jammed the barrel of the blaster in a groove along the rim of the cover, then got to his feet and leaned on the weapon. "We're about to find out." Grunting, he pried at the cover, pressing the longblaster ever downward until the metal disk finally rose from its cradle.

Ricky and Jak rushed over and lifted it the rest of the way clear, dropping it in the sand beside what was now an open hole in the ground. Then everyone crowded forward.

Ricky saw that a ladder led down the uncovered shaft into pitch-blackness. Whatever waited down below, he couldn't see it.

"This is it, guys." Hammersmith lowered himself into the pipe, stepping on the first rung of the ladder. "The secret entrance, such as it is."

As they all adjusted their packs and weapons to fit through the access shaft, Ricky looked at Union, anticipating a problem right before Mildred mentioned it.

"She can't get down the ladder unless we untie her," Mildred said.

"Do it," Ryan told her. "Hurry up."

Mildred untied Union while J.B. kept his Mini-Uzi

trained on her. The second her hands were free, Union reached up and whipped the gag out of her mouth.

"Hey!" J.B. snapped.

"Deal with it, asshole." Union tossed the gag over her shoulder and headed for the hole with her usual imperious stride.

Ricky made sure he entered the shaft in front of her, and he noticed Jak pushing in behind her. If Union tried something on the way down, she'd have both of them to contend with, not just Hammersmith.

She entered the shaft after Ricky as if she was the one in charge. Her boots clomped quickly on the rungs above his head, making him feel as if they'd stomp on his head if he climbed down any slower.

"Careful!" Hammersmith's voice came from not too far below. "There's a little jump at the bottom, and we're almost there."

Shortly after he said it, Ricky heard Hammersmith's feet land on solid ground a little ways down. Ricky slowed his descent, and sure enough, he ran out of ladder after another half-dozen rungs.

Jumping off, Ricky landed as Hammersmith had done. Just as he touched down, Hammersmith fired up a battery-powered lantern that lit the surrounding space.

Looking around, Ricky saw he was standing in a square, dirt-walled room, no bigger than fifteen feet on each side. Other than the ladder and lantern, the room was empty; a single doorway was cut in the wall opposite the ladder, framing a rectangle of absolute darkness.

As the others came down after Ricky, the room quickly filled. The whole group was now crowded in a confined space underground, too close for any kind of comfort.

"Everyone follow me." Lantern in hand, Hammersmith headed for the doorway. "The access point for the core facility is—"

Suddenly, Krysty cried out. As everyone looked her way, she fell back against the dirt wall, clutching her head.

"It's coming!" Her face contorted, she thrashed back and forth. "The biggest one yet!"

As she said it, Ricky felt a faint tremor underfoot. The tremor quickly became a strong rumbling, sending dirt trickling down from above.

Ricky wasn't claustrophobic, but a frightening image suddenly seized his imagination. What if the walls collapsed, burying him and the others underground?

Krysty's cries seemed to give weight to the image. "We've got to get out of here! It's coming! It's coming!"

Chapter Forty-Six

The fizzing in the back of Doc's head went off the charts just before the ground started shaking.

All this because Fixie had flipped the master switch on the equipment in the mat-trans chamber. As promised, he'd gotten Hammersmith's system ready for activation within the hour. There had been no unexpected failures, and he'd brought everything online in short order.

But whatever the system was doing to fulfill its programming, Doc's head had reacted badly. The fizzing, which had been strong since he'd arrived at the core, shifted into high gear and pushed into his eyes.

By the time the earth started moving, the fizzing had turned to crackling. The noise was so loud that Doc couldn't quite tell if it was still inside his head or part of the quake.

Groaning from the surge of noise and feeling, Doc doubled over in the middle of the room. Then he stayed that way, planting his hands on his knees and taking slow, deep breaths against the tide.

The whole time, Fixie was too caught up in fine-tuning the system to notice Doc's reaction. "The nuclear batteries are working! The power flow is steady!" He ran from console to console along the room's periphery, adjusting controls and seemingly taking no notice of the earthquake in progress.

Doc's body flooded with heat from head to toe. The

sequence of physical responses was familiar from before, when he'd first tuned in to impending changes in the Shift, but they seemed faster and more intense this time. That fit with what Fixie said the system would do, converting the entire region into some kind of Garden of Eden. It made sense that Doc's reaction to such a major transformation would be extreme.

That, however, didn't make it any easier to handle, and the quake itself didn't help, either. The tremors got so strong, they nearly knocked Doc over. He stumbled forward and caught himself on a stepladder under an open ceiling panel, barely staying erect as his body flared internally with what felt like blazing white light.

"Fixie!" Doc had to shout to be heard over the loud rumbling of the quake. "Is this what is supposed to be happening?"

"This and worse!" Fixie shouted. "It'll take a lot of tectonic activity to reshape the entire Shift!"

An especially strong tremor rocked the chamber, and Doc braced himself on the stepladder. "What if you bring down this entire facility?"

"What if?" Fixie spun dials and laughed. "More like when! The forces we're unleashing will be especially strong here, at the epicenter."

Clenching his teeth, Doc wrapped his arms around the ladder and rode out the waves that were buffeting him from within and without. He felt completely disoriented on every level, overwhelmed with fever and motion sickness.

Lights flashed from control panels and displays around the room, bathing him in flickering rainbows. The ground shook harder, as if trying to shake him loose from his anchor. He hated to think how bad it would get, if this was just the beginning.

"Sorry, but I cannot help you anymore." Doc swung

himself around to the other side of the ladder, closest to the door. "I need to...need to go..."

"Anywhere you go within the Shift will be the same," Fixie said. "Nothing but upheaval now. You're as safe here as anywhere for the time being."

Doc cried out as the white light burned like a nova inside him. His gorge rose, and he felt as if he was going to throw up at any moment.

Gathering all his will and strength, he let go of the ladder and aimed himself at the door. He had to do something, had to get out, in spite of what Fixie had said.

Doc stumbled across the floor as it bucked underfoot. He nearly fell once, then twice, but managed to stay upright and cross the distance to the door.

When he had almost reached the exit, however, the quake suddenly surged. The fiercest tremors yet rocked the mat-trans chamber, sending him toppling forward, completely out of control.

Before he could hit the floor, however, someone darted through the doorway and caught him. The save was just in the nick of time; Doc had missed hitting the floor face-first by inches.

As his rescuer lifted him by the shoulders, Doc finally got a look at his face...and instantly wished he hadn't. The first thing that caught his eye was the red-and-white-striped candy stick hanging from the corner of a crimson-faced sneer.

"Dear, sweet Hammersmith." Exo's high-pitched voice cut right through the crackling in Doc's head and the rumbling in the room. "What the *fuck* have you gotten yourself into now?"

Doc recoiled from Exo's rancid breath as it gusted in his face. "We were just... We were..." He dug deep for the smart thing to say and came up empty. "It is fixed."

"Good boy, good boy." Exo shook Doc like a rag doll.

"Now, if you don't mind, I've got to go kill that guy over there." With that, he tossed Doc aside, slamming him into the wall, and marched toward Fixie with purposeful steps, unaffected by the lurching of the earthquake.

Chapter Forty-Seven

When the tremors started, sending dirt trickling into the shaft, Krysty sounded the alarm with her cries. "We've got to get out of here! It's coming! It's coming!"

In those first seconds of distraction, Union made her move. With a sudden burst of energy, she charged for the open doorway in the dirt wall, bowling over Hammersmith and slipping away before anyone could lay a hand on her or get off a shot in her direction.

Without hesitation, Jak bolted after her. The others were still processing what had just happened when he sprinted through the doorway.

Fortunately, his night vision was excellent. Even without a portable light of any kind, he could still glimpse Union's fleeing form in the darkness up ahead.

His hearing wasn't bad, either, which also helped. Even as the darkness thickened further from the shaft leading down from the surface, he could hear her running footsteps on the packed dirt floor in the distance. The rumbling of the quake didn't block them from his sensitive ears.

He homed in on those footsteps as if they were beacons and raced after her, determined to stop her from doing whatever it was she meant to do.

"UNION'S GONE, AND Jak went after her!" Mildred had to shout to make herself heard over the rumbling in the shaft.

"At least they're headed in the right direction," Hammersmith said as J.B. helped him to his feet. "We need to follow them."

"So there's an earthquake, and we're going deeper underground?" J.B. asked.

"Unless you'd rather waltz in the front door?" Hammersmith switched on the lantern, then dropped it in the next big tremor. "Son of a bitch!" He quickly snatched the lantern up again but had to shake it twice before the bulb relit. "We need to go!"

Ryan leaned close to Krysty, who was moaning from the pain in her head. "Can you keep going?"

She met his eyes and nodded forcefully. "Hell yes."

"Come on!" Lantern in hand, Hammersmith darted through the doorway. As he entered, clumps of dirt fell down from the shaft above.

Mildred realized that if the quakes kept up, that entrance might soon be blocked. But what alternative was there?

Ryan and Krysty plunged into the opening after Hammersmith. J.B. gestured for Mildred to go next. "After you."

Dirt continued to fall. "Let's do it." Mildred swallowed hard, then nodded once and ran into the darkness, hoping she hadn't seen daylight for the last time in her life.

EXO YANKED THE swordstick from a loop on his belt as he stormed across the mat-trans chamber. Fixie, still consumed by his work on the control panels, didn't even hear or see him coming.

"Fixie, watch out!" Even as Doc raised the alarm, he knew it was too late. He scrambled to his feet as he called out, only to fall back down when the next tremor kicked in.

Fixie turned just in time to see the silver lion's-head top of Doc's swordstick hurtle straight at his head. He tried to block the blow, but his arms made it only halfway before the silver lion's head smashed down on the middle of his skull.

"No!" Doc grabbed a length of pipe from the floor and used it to help himself up. He intended to use it further to give Exo a taste of his own medicine.

But the earthquake and the white light raging within him were throwing him off his game. He weaved drunkenly over the heaving floor, stopping at every large solid object to steady himself and rest.

Unfortunately, Exo did not share his unsteadiness. In the time it took Doc to get halfway across the room, Exo whacked Fixie three more times with the cane—once more on the head, then once on the chest and once on the back as he went down.

"How *dare* you operate this sacred technology without my permission?" Exo snarled. "This is my weapon, not your toy!"

"Stop it!" Doc roared. "He was only testing the device! It's all yours!"

"Test this!" Exo clubbed Fixie harder than ever on the back of the neck, then giggled like a lunatic. "Whoops!" Pulling back the swordstick, he held up the silver lion's head, which was drenched in blood. "I guess you failed, little bitch!"

"No!" Doc hauled back the pipe and let it fly. It struck Exo on his left shoulder and bounced off, clattering to the floor.

Exo didn't even acknowledge the hit. Instead, he swung up the swordstick for another strike, giggling the entire time. "Don't worry, Hammersmith!" He lashed the cane downward, thumping the heavy head in the meat of Fixie's side. "I'll clear aside this deadwood so you can get to work again!"

Suddenly, a blastershot exploded in the room. The shot

was meant for Exo but went wide, punching into a control panel on the wall instead.

Doc whirled to see Ankh standing inside the doorway, aiming his Winchester longblaster at the man who was supposed to be his leader.

"Ankh?" Doc said.

"Son of a bitch." Ankh shook his head, looking disgusted, somehow holding perfectly steady in spite of the latest round of tremors. "I can't trust you people to do anything, can I?"

Chapter Forty-Eight

Jak followed Union through a labyrinth of dark tunnels, using the sound of her footsteps on the packed earth as a guiding signal.

She swooped around one turn after another, staying always just far enough ahead that he couldn't catch up. Nailing her with a throwing knife or a shot from the Colt Python wasn't an option, either; getting a bead in the darkness, with the continued quakes and so many twists and turns along the route, would be next to impossible.

So Jak just kept running and hoping for a break. Maybe the tunnel would open up soon into a well-lit area, and he would have a better chance of stopping her with a blade or gunshot.

But when he got his wish and followed her through a door into a big, bright space, he had no more luck bringing her down. The room they emerged in was full of shifters, a whole mob of them standing stiffly, staring in the direction of the opposite corner from the door Jak and Union had come through.

So much for getting a clear shot with a throwing knife or a round from the Python. There were too many bodies in the way.

Union sprinted through the crowd as if it wasn't there. The shifters made no effort to stop her, nor did they try to obstruct Jak when he waded through them.

But when Union reached the other side of the room, she

whipped around and shouted at the top of her lungs for all the muties to hear. "Stop the intruder! Stop the intruder!" She jabbed a finger at Jak. "He has brought destruction down upon the Children of the Shift!"

All eyes turned to Jak, who kept heading for the side of the room where Union had landed. He felt the spreading tension all around him, fanning out over the assembled muties like poison gas.

Then, before he could reach the wall where Union was waiting, she opened a door and slipped through. Just as she left the room, the first of the shifters to lift a hand against Jak made his move, stepping in front of him with shoulders squared and arms folded across his chest.

"You're not going anywhere." The shifter slowly shook his head. "Except hell."

"Been there." Jak grinned and took a step toward him, accessing a throwing blade in the sleeve of his jacket. "Not all cracked up to be."

"DID YOU JUST shoot at me?" Exo shook the swordstick in Ankh's direction.

"Of course not." Ankh raised the Winchester and aimed it at Exo. "Whatever gave you that idea?"

Just as Ankh pulled the trigger, Exo leaped behind a welding unit a few feet away. The bullet pinged off the unit's metal case, missing the true target hunkered down behind it.

"What the fuck?" Exo howled. "You work for me."

"Absolutely." Ankh cranked the action on the longblaster, ejecting the spent cartridges, and loaded fresh ones. "I wouldn't have it any other way. What about you, Dr. H.?"

Doc, who'd ducked behind a tool cart that only partially concealed his form, called out over the continued clamor of the quake, "Likewise, of course."

"Fixie's *your* man, Ankh!" Exo said. "Yet he activated devices that it is only my right to operate!"

"Terrible. Just terrible." Ankh swung up the Winchester and kept it aimed at the welding unit. "He must be reprimanded most severely."

"I've already beaten him to death. What else could we possible do to him?"

Ankh started walking toward Exo's position. "Don't worry, brother, we'll think of something."

Was Fixie dead? Peering out from behind the cart, Doc spotted his inert form on the floor under the control panel where he'd been working. His body was drenched in blood, though it was impossible to tell from a distance if he was definitely dead.

Doc's own future looked pretty bleak, given the circumstances. Whichever of the shifters survived, Doc thought his own chances of survival were poor. He'd doublecrossed them both by working with Fixie to switch on the device; once one was killed, it wouldn't take long for the other to murder Doc for his betrayal.

If the earthquakes and the blazing heat and light inside him didn't kill him first.

Even as Ankh continued his advance, Doc's internal torment kicked into its highest gear yet. The white light flared stronger than ever, pressing against the restraints of his flesh as if it might blow him apart from within. The crackling noise in his head reached a deafening peak, drowning out the next exchange between Ankh and Exo.

Through tightly slitted eyes, Doc saw Ankh fire another round at the welding unit, then Exo fire back with Doc's LeMat. But he barely heard the blasterfire through the crackling roar filling his skull.

Then, suddenly, the forces at work inside him rose in a tidal surge that seemed to wash away his physical form.

He felt like a single, flickering candle flame whipping in a strong wind, barely keeping from being extinguished.

Seconds later, his body seemed to recrystallize around that single flame. The sounds and sensations of the outside world reasserted themselves, beginning with another pair of blastershots.

This time, Exo's latest round found a home in Ankh's belly, doubling him over. As for Ankh's round, it punched into the heart of Fixie's main control panel, sending sparks and shrapnel in all directions.

But none of that was Doc's most immediate concern. The focus of his attention was a nearby section of the floor of the mat-trans chamber, to which he felt unmistakably drawn. Now that the sequence of "funny feelings" had run its course—from fizzing to crackling, from bodilessness to resolidifying—the attraction of that one spot could mean only one thing.

As he watched, the metal and plastic plating of that part of the floor buckled and broke. Cracks turned to fissures, fissures turned to gaps, and gaps widened into holes...all of which joined together in one big crater.

As Doc stared into that gaping pit, a vision of a winding tunnel leaped into his mind, a chute etched in yellow neon light. It took only a heartbeat for him to realize it was a diagram, a map of where the new hole in the ground led.

And the final destination, when he saw it, was reason enough for him to consider jumping into the maw of that newly formed chute. According to the map, the opposite end of the tunnel opened onto the outside world, aboveground and away from the buried redoubt.

At the sound of another shot, Doc looked away from the crater and saw Ankh take a second slug in the belly. He toppled backward to the floor, and Exo immediately marched toward him with the .44 raised, looking ready to finish him off.

With Ankh gutshot and Exo distracted, Doc realized he had a moment to run for the crater if he so chose. If the map in his head was right, the chute connecting to that crater would send him out of the line of fire, away from the worst insanity.

And the fact was, he instinctively believed in that map. Under the influence of the Shift, he'd been gradually tuning in to the region's changing topography; now, perhaps because of his extended exposure to the core, his Shift sense had fully evolved. He believed he was experiencing what the shifters experienced when they communed with the transformations of the Shift, right down to the detailed diagram in his head.

Given those possibilities, he could think of no good reason not to take a leap of faith. It might be his only chance, his absolute last chance, to get to freedom.

Taking a deep breath, Doc got to his feet. Watching as Exo stood over Ankh and gloated, he tried to brace himself against the quakes and prepare to make a run for it.

But as soon as he took his first steps toward the crater, the ground shook more roughly than ever. Doc stumbled once, then twice, barely staying upright…then found himself with both feet off the floor as it seemed to drop out from under him.

But he didn't go down. The floor lurched back up, and he regained his footing, then propelled himself with three quick steps to the crater's edge.

He hesitated, on the verge of doing something he and his teammates would once have considered so completely un-Doc-like. Taking courageous leaps into the unknown was something that his companions would do. As much as he felt like a changed man since his abduction, as clear as the map in his head seemed to be, this was still a pretty big risk for the old man.

But watching Exo pump three more rounds into Ankh

helped move things along. Doc took another step closer to the edge of the pit, preparing to jump.

The darkness beckoned. Would it lead him to freedom or extinction?

The floor rocked, nearly throwing him in. Doc spread his arms wide and steadied himself, which was the exact instant when Exo looked back at him.

Their eyes met through the sparks and smoke. Exo sneered, and Doc knew instantly that the mutie would kill him if given the chance.

The floor heaved, but it didn't manage to hurl Doc into the pit. When he jumped feetfirst off the rim and shunted down into the blackness, he did so of his own accord, taking a chance that he knew he never would have taken just a few days earlier if given the opportunity.

Chapter Forty-Nine

Ryan pushed through the doorway leading out of the tunnel right after Hammersmith. He found himself standing in a big, bright chamber, blinking at the aftermath of a major knife fight.

"Fuckin' A." Hammersmith let out a long whistle at the carnage around them. "Somebody kicked some serious ass in here."

Krysty and the rest of the companions hurried into the room, eager to get out of the dark tunnel. The whole time they'd been in there, the earth had never stopped shaking, and the dirt had never stopped falling around them, suggesting a collapse was imminent.

Stepping over bloody bodies, Ryan found a victim who was still alive and conscious, a shifter male with a knife wound in his upper chest and a severely dislocated left arm.

"Was it an albino who did this?" Ryan asked sternly.

The shifter nodded. "The woman said he was an enemy of the Children of the Shift and had to be stopped."

"And you believed her?" Ryan asked.

The shifter tried to shrug, then winced and gave up on it. "She is well-known here. We heard she'd returned to the fold after betraying our holy mission."

"I wouldn't bet the farm on it." Ryan spun, found the exit and headed straight for it, calling to the team in his wake, "Let's go!"

The floor shook as the others rushed after him. They

all knew they had their work cut out for them, catching up to Jak and Union before everything went south. Rescuing Doc was the top priority, but they didn't want to lose anyone else along the way.

Ryan waited in the hall outside the exit long enough for Hammersmith to join him. "Which way?"

Hammersmith swung left without hesitation. "This way." The floor rocked, bouncing him off a wall, but he didn't miss more than a step. And he didn't waste time whining about it. "Look alive, bitches!" he shouted to the people behind him. "We're almost there!"

MOMENTS AFTER DOC started his long slide through the dark chute out of the mat-trans chamber, he heard the high-pitched voice behind him.

"Wait for me, Hammersmith!" It was Exo, calling from a distance. "I need to teach you a very important lesson, my friend!"

Suddenly, Doc's ride through the chute took a darker turn. Exo's voice was staying with him, keeping pace— that meant he was riding along after Doc, not calling from the mouth of the tunnel.

And that meant Exo would catch up to Doc at the end of the chute. The man who'd just brutally killed his own brother, Ankh, in cold blood would pop out of the chute right behind Doc.

The old man had escaped the mat-trans chamber but hadn't gotten away from Exo at all. And this time, there would be no one else to distract the insane mutie leader from taking out his frustrations on Doc.

JAK DIDN'T HAVE any trouble finding the mat-trans chamber, thanks to the trail of mutie bodies strewed through the corridors. He was moments behind Union, thanks to her dirty trick of pitting a mob of shifters against him, but the bodies of the muties who'd gotten in her way were like bread crumbs.

By the time he ran through the doorway into what appeared to be a large mat-trans chamber, Union was already hard at work wrecking the place.

She didn't see him at first as she swung a crowbar into a control panel, shattering glass displays and plastic control surfaces. That gave Jak a chance to quickly size up the room, taking in the crater and the two mutie bodies sprawled on the floor. One had been gutshot, the other bludgeoned. Had Union killed them? Had she grabbed a blaster from a shifter in the corridor, then shot her way into the room?

The big question on his mind, though, was why was she demolishing the equipment?

She was in midswing when she finally saw him. "Grab something to smash with!" she shouted over the firecracker snapping of blown circuits and the rumbling of earthquake tremors. "Give me a hand!" Her Russian accent was gone as she called out to him.

Jak stepped closer, weaving through debris and bobbing as a spike from the latest quake shook his footing. "Why smashing?" he shouted back at her. "What about triggering collective intelligence, bringing back Soviet Union?"

"That's right." She grinned at him. "I did say I was going to do that, didn't I?" Then she spun and swung the crowbar into the control panel again, kicking off the loudest crackling and the biggest sparks yet.

Jak stepped closer, keeping a knife palmed in one hand and the other hand near the butt of his holstered .357 blaster. "What 'bout multiple personality problem? Also said wanted machines fix that."

"Is that what I said?" She swung the crowbar again, smashing more controls. "And you believed me?"

Another quake struck, and Jak teetered. "Not understand. If not doing those things, what want? Why smash?"

"What do I want?" She was wild-eyed when she looked his way again. For the first time since he'd met her, the braid that hung from her left temple had turned bright purple. "I want to destroy the whole damned Shift and everyone living in it!"

Chapter Fifty

Just as Ryan and his team rounded the corner, a squad of shifters burst into the hallway, charging straight at them.

Then, when they spotted Ryan's group, the onrushing muties thundered to a halt. They stood in the middle of the corridor, sizing up Ryan and his people with narrow-eyed stares of suspicion, just as Ryan's team did the same thing to them.

Sensing an opportunity, Ryan addressed the man he thought was the leader of the muties. "We don't want a fight," he said evenly. "We're not your enemies."

The corridor shook with another quake as the mutie leader thought it over. His men's eyes flicked alternately between him and Ryan, watching for a sign from either one.

"Are you the ones causing these quakes?" the mutie leader asked finally. "Destroying the balance of the Shift?"

"Absolutely not." Ryan shook his head. "We're only here to find a friend of ours."

"Did *she* cause the quakes?" asked another mutie, perhaps the leader's second in command.

"It's a *he*," Ryan replied. "And I don't see any possible way he could have done that."

"Liar!" shouted the second in command. "Norms *always* bring destruction!"

"Enough!" The shifter leader snapped an arm stiffly upward. "We don't want a fight, either. We just want to get out of here." He stepped to one side and gestured for the other shifters to do the same. "You go your way, and we'll go ours."

The rest of the muties followed the leader's example and made room. Ryan nodded and started forward, with his team close behind.

But midway down the corridor, the second in command leaped from the ranks and charged at Krysty.

Before the attacker had taken his third step toward her, a blastershot boomed in the corridor, and a round punched through his skull. The impact jerked him sideways, then he dropped to the floor in a bloody heap.

All eyes flashed to the shooter, Ryan, as he calmly lowered his handblaster. "Thought we had an agreement," he said slowly.

"We do," the leader stated firmly. "Let's go," he told his people, and they headed down the corridor.

Some moved more slowly than others, white-knuckling weapons and giving Ryan's group the stink eye, but no one crossed the line laid down by the second in command's corpse.

"Assholes," Hammersmith muttered as the two groups slipped past each other.

"Less talking, more walking," Ryan urged, though his idea of walking, as he hurried down the corridor, was more like a full-tilt run.

DOC KNEW HE was near the end of the chute, but he wasn't sure what to do when he got there.

Exo was somewhere behind him, coming up fast. His voice seemed a little bit closer every time Doc heard it.

That meant Doc wouldn't have time to do much of anything when he left the chute. No sooner would his feet hit the ground than Exo's would do the same...at which point, all bets would be off. The maniac shifter had already beaten him repeatedly in casual meetings with no provocation; Doc could only imagine what he would do to him now, when Doc had tried to escape him.

Exo's nonthreatening comments didn't offer any clues. "Looking forward to having a chat when we get out of this," he called through the chute. "We've really got our work cut out for us, Doctor H." Somehow, the lack of blatant threats was more frightening than if he'd just come out and screamed a litany of terrible things he was going to do to Doc.

Suddenly, the old man swooped around a bend and saw a circle of sunlight in the distance. Heart pounding, he raced inexorably toward that circle, even as he knew from the map in his head that it represented the final exit.

The chute angled upward, and Doc's momentum carried him toward the light. He would be outside in seconds.

Jaws clenched, muscles tensed, he tried to get ready, tried to prepare himself for the prospect of fighting for his life against the lunatic mutie.

JAK SCOWLED AS Union hauled off and bashed another control panel with the crowbar. "Why destroy Shift and everyone? Not make sense."

"Not if your sisters weren't murdered by the locals, it doesn't." Again, Union wrenched back the crowbar and smashed it into the console. A storm of sparks erupted in her face, forcing her back a step.

"Sisters?" Jak thought about taking her down before she did more damage. He knew he could, with the weapons in his hands, but then he wouldn't hear her story. He wouldn't get the answers he wanted more than anything, to explain why a woman who'd seemed to care for him could have been lying to him from the start.

"Four of them," Union added. "All whitecoats, specializing in treating animals with the energies of the Shift. They developed hybrid creatures and turned them loose in a wilderness area, hoping to evolve life-forms that could clean up the ruined ecosystem of the Deathlands. That one area became their outdoor laboratory."

"Devil's Slaughterhouse." Jak nodded as the pieces fell together in his mind. "Sisters made beasts that attacked us there."

"And they were murdered for it. The locals executed them when some of the Slaughterhouse creatures attacked a ville and killed some people." Her face contorted with rage, she let the crowbar fly again, shattering a computer monitor. "My sisters were trying to help, and they were murdered for it."

"Wait." Jak leaned against a welding unit as the latest quake nearly rocked him off his feet. "Four sisters, you said?"

"Yes!" Again, she hammered the console with the crowbar. "Four!"

Jak knew that what he was about to say was true before he said it. "One was named…Taryn?"

Union swung the crowbar without answering.

"And the others," Jak said. "Names Rhonda…Dulcet… Carrie?"

"Yes!"

Finally, Jak felt as if he was getting the picture. The four women in one body—they were all dead sisters, or at least echoes of their personalities. But one question still remained about those women and that body.

"If four sisters in there, who talking now? Not sound like Sasha."

"Because there *is* no Sasha," Union snapped. "Sasha was just a lie to hide our real reason for being here."

"Then, who talking now?"

"The lucky sister! The one who survived!" As she said it, the quake rumbled and crashed like thunder. "The one who will help the others get revenge for their deaths!"

Chapter Fifty-One

Doc popped out of the end of the chute, propelled by the momentum of his ride, and landed on his butt on the sandy ground. Driven by the thought of Exo popping out next, he quickly got to his feet, taking in his surroundings as he did so.

He was somewhere outside the redoubt, looking up at one of the rounded hills that stood on each side of it. The sun was down, and gray twilight was settling over the rumbling land.

Nowhere did he see an abandoned weapon or something that could be used as one. The only thing he had to fight with was the razor blade in his pocket.

As for hiding places, there was nothing within a hundred yards. His best bet was to run for the hills bracketing the redoubt, though he knew, even as he started running in that direction, that he could never get there in time. He could never outrun a bullet from his own LeMat .44 revolver, which Exo would certainly be carrying when he emerged from the chute.

But running was still the only strategy that made any kind of sense to Doc, so he threw himself into it with every bit of energy he had. Legs churning furiously, he charged across the sand toward the nearest hill, listening all the while for sounds of Exo behind him.

He finally heard them when he'd gotten a third of the way to his destination: the sounds of running footsteps and a high-pitched voice. "Dr. H.! Wait for me! I need to show you something!"

For an instant, Doc wondered if maybe he'd been wrong about Exo's intent. Was it possible Exo didn't want to kill him? Would Doc have been better off staying back at the exit of the chute to meet him instead of running away?

His answer came in the form of a blaster and a .44 slug whizzing past his right ear.

"Come on!" Exo hollered. "I just want to talk, my friend!"

Just as he said it, Doc heard the crack of a second shot and another whizzing slug—this time sailing past his left ear. And a thought flitted through his mind—what if the third shot was the charm?

JAK WAITED UNTIL the worst of the quake had tapered off, then eased around the welding unit, taking care not to step on the body of the shifter on the floor behind it. "How kill everyone?" he shouted. "Equipment haywire, but will wrecking destroy Shift and kill everyone?"

Union laughed and twirled the crowbar. "Fuck no!" Turning, she jammed the end of the crowbar in the crack between two nondescript panels in the wall. "Wrecking the equipment is just for kicks! It has nothing to do with destroying the Shift!" With that, she pried the panels apart, pulling one loose from the wall.

One mighty heave, and the loose panel came free and went flying to the floor. In the rectangular space exposed by its absence, Jak glimpsed something glinting in the flashing light of the malfunctioning mat-trans controls around it.

"Now, *this*..." Union reached in and wrapped her hand around whatever was stored there. "This is that big danger I told you about earlier. The big surprise. The one that everything else was just a warm-up for."

Jak watched, spellbound, as she pulled out the object and held it up for him to see. From where he was standing, it looked like a silver cone, six inches long, studded with circuitry and multicolored crystals.

He knew he should attack at that instant, put her down hard and snatch whatever it was from her grasp—but he waited. He felt compelled to know more, to hear her tell it, as if that might somehow explain what she'd put him through. As if that might somehow make it all make sense.

"What that?" Another strong quake knocked him around but didn't knock him over. "Why big danger?"

"I'll tell you this much." She grinned as she turned the object around in her hand. "This won't kill everyone living in the Shift, but it will summon something that can."

Jak frowned. "What talking 'bout?"

"You'll see." Union slid the cone into the hip pocket of her jumpsuit. "Briefly, at least. You won't live longer than that, I'm afraid."

He got the feeling that she was about to make a move, and he steeled himself to do the same. "Don't do it," he said. "Why kill innocents with guilty?"

"Everyone's guilty if they're part of this sick society."

"Not children," Jak said. "Not babies."

She shrugged. "Collateral damage happens. Tough shit."

"Just kill everyone? You, too?"

"I guess so."

"No!" Jak felt an irrational wave of emotion rise within him. "Carrie, Taryn, Dulcet, Rhonda not deserve to die! I want them live."

"They're already dead! Long dead!"

"Still alive in you!" Jak said. "Good still inside!"

"Gullible moron." Union laughed cruelly, then stopped. A change came over her face, as the wickedness seemed to drain out of her features. Her eyes widened, her mouth opened, her look softened. In the beat of a heart, she went from dark and secretive to bright and revealing. Her voice, when she spoke, was familiar—upbeat and sweet. "Jak, wait. You're right! You're so right about us!"

And her braid was brown.

"Dulcet." Was it possible? Had Jak gotten through to her? "Good hearing voice." He'd never stopped believing she and the others were still in there, no matter what Union had told him.

"Oh, Jak! We've missed you!" Suddenly, her expression changed again, becoming less open, more timid. "It's true! We have!" Her braid was white now—Carrie.

The ground shook as Jak took a step toward her, searching her eyes. He thought he saw Carrie looking back at him, thought he felt her familiar presence.

Then her face shifted again, becoming rougher, more sardonic. Her braid turned auburn. "You pasty son of a bitch!" It was Rhonda. "I knew you were too pigheaded to give up on us!"

She changed one more time, then, turning frigid and distant with a jet-black braid.

"Taryn," Jak said.

"Yes." She nodded once. "And no."

Then, in that one instant when he'd dropped his guard the tiniest bit, she suddenly lashed up the crowbar and hurled it at his head.

Jak had been half expecting something and leaped to one side, but the crowbar still struck his left shoulder. It threw him just enough off balance that the latest quake brought him down.

Even as he hit the floor, Union charged past him. Twisting, he saw her dive headfirst into the pit in the middle of the chamber and disappear. Her black boots were the last trace he saw of her.

It was then, as he scrambled to his feet, that he heard

another familiar voice over the rumbling of the quake and the crackling of the ruined lab.

"Holy shit!" It was Hammersmith, glaring in the doorway. "What did you motherfuckers do to my lab?"

Chapter Fifty-Two

The latest in a long line of earthquakes saved Doc's life as he ran from Exo.

Just as the mutie fired the third shot from Doc's LeMat, the ground shook violently, throwing Doc off his feet. He came down hard on his right side, crying out in pain, but at least he missed taking the bullet that soared past above him. No question: the round would have struck him if he'd still been upright.

Unfortunately, the fall that saved him also left him at Exo's mercy. Doc wasn't fast enough to leap up and keep running before Exo could get to him.

Wincing, the old man pushed himself to a sitting position, but that was as far as he got. Suddenly, Exo trotted up in front of him, grinning and pointing the revolver at Doc's face.

"Wow, finally!" Exo was panting from the run. "What does a guy have to do to have a talk with you anyway?"

Doc was much more winded than the shifter. "What do you…want to…talk about?" He had to force himself to act as if he wasn't worried about the revolver in Exo's hand.

"My device, for starters," Exo said. "You need to get back there and fix it for me, Hammersmith."

Doc nodded as if he had every intention of doing just that. "Right." Playing along with the brain-damaged lunatic had to be the better plan…if any plan was better in these circumstances.

There was another quake as Exo shook the LeMat at him. "My empire is crumbling from within! We need to save it!"

"Of course." Doc slid a hand in the pocket of his coat and found the razor blade. He pinched it tightly between his thumb and forefinger, trying to gather the courage to use it.

Could he bring himself to try to slash Exo's throat? Did he have the slightest chance of success against the insane and murderous shifter?

Sweating from the run and the stress of what he was considering, Doc got to his knees. "Ankh and Fixie forced me to help them," he lied, fighting to stop the rampant shivers rippling through his body. "I ran away because I was afraid you would not understand."

"I understand perfectly." Keeping the LeMat in one hand, Exo reached down with his free hand to help Doc to his feet. "I know exactly what happened."

"Thank you." Doc saw his moment present itself, as both Exo's hands were full, and his bare throat beckoned. "You were always so good to me."

"We need to hurry, Hammersmith," Exo said. "Time is running out."

Doc nodded. "It is." Slowly, he started to pull his hand with the razor blade out of his pocket.

As RYAN AND the rest of the group pushed into the mat-trans chamber behind Hammersmith, Jak rushed over to the gaping maw of the pit. Gazing into it, he saw only darkness, but he knew Union was down there somewhere.

"Oh, my God," Mildred said. "This big room is a mat-trans chamber. Of course!"

"Did that bitch do this?" Hammersmith still sounded furious. "Did Union tear this place apart?"

Standing on the edge of the pit, Jak waved for the others to join him. "Come on! Need go now!" He jabbed a finger at the pit.

"Go where, Jak?" Ryan asked. "Where does that lead?"

"Not know, but she went this way!"

"We're not here for her!" Ryan shouted over the loudest rumbling yet. "We're here to rescue Doc!"

"Mebbe Doc there, too." Again, Jak pointed at the pit.

"You see him go in?" J.B. asked.

Jak shook his head. "Big fight before got here. Two dead muties." He gestured at the bodies of Ankh and Fixie on the floor. "Mebbe happen before Union got here, too. Mebbe Doc involved, got away." Something caught his eye then, and he walked to the opposite edge of the pit. Bending, he picked up a long black object discarded there amid a jumble of wires and broken glass. "Look."

Ryan marched over and took the item from Jak's hand. "He was here, all right." Ryan held the object up for the others to see. "It's the sheath of his swordstick."

"Which could have been left here by someone else," J.B. pointed out.

"Gut says Doc there." Jak motioned at the pit once more. "I go that way, too. You go somewhere else if want."

With that, he nodded once at Ryan—goodbye—and leaped into the darkness on the trail of Union and, hopefully, Doc.

Chapter Fifty-Three

Doc slid the razor blade out of his pocket and tried to psych himself up enough to use it. If he slashed Exo with it and failed to kill him, it would be a death sentence…though, truth to tell, Doc might be a dead man soon anyway, given Exo's volatile nature.

Swallowing hard, Doc tensed, about to sweep the blade up and across Exo's throat.

Then, suddenly, he heard a thunderous clamor from the direction of the redoubt like the roar of a hundred lions…

Exo's head snapped around at the noise. "What is that?"

Doc's head did the same. "Dear God." And, suddenly, he forgot what he'd been planning to do with the razor blade and dropped it on the ground.

One of the rounded hills beside the redoubt had been gouged open from within. A giant red creature—about twenty feet tall—was tearing its way out of the hill with huge scarlet claws, digging to freedom in a thrashing, roaring frenzy.

"Some kind of monstrosity," Doc said in a hushed, awestruck voice. "A mutation, perhaps induced by Hammersmi… by my experiments with matter transformation."

"Who's that down there?" Exo pointed at a human figure on the ground, not far from the base of the hill. "That thing will stomp her into goo if she doesn't get her ass the hell out of there!"

"What's she doing?" Squinting, Doc saw the woman

raise an object to her mouth. He thought she was blowing into it, playing it like an instrument while looking up at the creature.

Meanwhile, the creature forced one giant leg out of the hole in the hill. When its vast red foot came down in a powerful stomp, the ground shook even harder than it was already shaking from the current quake.

"Wait a minute." Exo, looking mesmerized, took two steps forward. "I know that woman. It's her."

"Her, who?" Doc asked.

Without further explanation, Exo started to run toward the woman and the monster.

Doc felt no compunction to join him, however...at least until he saw someone else emerge from the chute, leap up and run in the same direction as Exo.

Even from a distance, even in the dimming grayness of twilight, he instantly recognized the new arrival. The lean physique and long white hair were unmistakable; the face, as white as the moon rising in the sky, could belong to only one person.

"Jak!" Doc's heart soared. His albino companion, whom he hadn't seen for days, was a sight so welcome that Doc felt as if he might explode from pure joy on the spot.

Suddenly, the old man had a good reason to get closer to the creature after all...but not too close. For he hadn't seen a friend in what seemed like ages.

And wherever Jak happened to be, Ryan and the rest of the companions couldn't be too far behind.

RYAN FLASHED THROUGH the darkness of the chute, hoping he was doing the right thing.

Following Jak into the pit had seemed to make sense a few moments earlier, especially after the sheath of Doc's swordstick had turned up. But the one-eyed man kept wondering if he and the others should have stayed in the mat-trans chamber…if maybe they were heading farther from Doc rather than closer.

Only Hammersmith had stayed behind, determined to set the out-of-control equipment to rights and stop the disruptions attacking the core. Ryan had given him Union's Heckler & Koch longblaster to defend himself, then locked and jammed the door to the chamber before leaping into the chute with the others.

But what if he was leading them in the wrong direction? And what if Doc paid the ultimate price for that mistake?

Just as these questions haunted him on his ride through the blackness, Ryan forced them back and committed himself to whatever lay ahead. Difficult decisions—and fatal mistakes—were part and parcel of daily life in the Deathlands.

Ryan knew it was more important to hold on tight to his weapons than his doubts. Doubts had never saved him from boarding the last train west.

As JAK RAN toward Union, he couldn't help staring up at the giant creature bursting out of the hill. The beast was enormous, and it was unlike any creature he'd ever seen before. From where he stood, it looked as if it was composed of a multitude of crimson-skinned mutie bodies and body parts jammed together in one monstrous form—hundreds of heads and upper torsos sticking out, mangled and contorted.

Were those muties even dead? As Jak watched, they flailed and writhed. Their mouths worked, and their eyes rolled and blinked. If they were dead, were they somehow animated by the force binding the creature together? If they were alive, were they aware of their imprisonment, struggling to break free?

Whatever those poor muties were or weren't thinking, one thing seemed clear to him: Union was calling their tune. She stood thirty yards away from Jak, playing the silver cone she'd retrieved from the mat-trans chamber as if it was some kind of trumpet. It blinked and flashed as she held it to her mouth and aimed it up at the creature. Union had said it would summon something that could kill everyone living in the Shift, and the creature certainly looked as if it fit that description.

Had she created the device or stolen it? At the moment, none of that mattered. Jak just kept racing toward her over the rumbling ground, determined to stop her and the monstrosity she was controlling at any cost. He would do the same for the mutie who was also running toward her, if he got in the way.

Chapter Fifty-Four

At the sound of approaching footsteps, Union lowered the device and turned. There, in the flesh, was someone from the top of her shit list. Exo.

Life was good. She wouldn't have to chase him down, because he was coming right to her.

"Union!" Exo's high-pitched screech cut right through the creature's latest roar and the rumbling of the quake. "What have you brought me? What *is* that thing?"

Union flashed him her brightest smile and gestured with the controller at the creature. "I call him Fido." She laughed. "He's a girl's best friend."

"Amazing!" Exo stopped beside her and reached for the device. "Let *me* try!"

"Hold on." She pulled the controller away from him and brought it to her lips. "Let me show you something first."

Pointing the device at the creature, she blew into the mouthpiece gently and flickered her fingers over the jeweled control studs along its surface. No sound came out that she could hear, but the beast—like a dog with a higher range of hearing—picked up on the signal right away.

The great monstrosity was completely free of the hill now, towering above her on two massive legs. As the signal played, it stared down at her with bright yellow eyes that blazed like twin suns in a misshapen reptilian face.

Carefully, Union padded away from Exo as she played.

It wasn't hard to put some space between them, as he was entranced by the creature looming above him.

All she had to do was play the final notes for her pet to complete the demonstration. But first, she lowered the device once more to speak.

"By the way, I know you were the one," she said.

Exo frowned as if he'd only just remembered she was there. "The one what? What are you talking about?"

"The one who turned the shifters against my sisters years ago," Union said. "The one who put the wheels in motion that got them killed."

Suddenly, she was no longer a distraction to Exo. He locked eyes with her, giving her his full attention, and opened his mouth to speak.

But before a single word could emerge, she played the controller again. The silent signal went out, and the creature roared its rage.

Then it raised one mighty foot and brought it down suddenly. Exo didn't even try to get out from under it.

He just screamed as the leviathan's weight came down on top of him, the mass of mutie flesh crushing the life out of him.

Union lowered the device. Walking over to that enormous crushing foot, she patted it and smiled.

"Good boy," she said. "Such a good boy."

When the foot finally lifted to take a step, she could see Exo's flesh had been absorbed into it. His flattened face gaped out from the bottom of the foot, his eyes blinking in mindless terror.

Doc couldn't run fast enough to catch up to Jak. He stopped to recover, even as Jak kept charging toward the woman and her monster.

It was then, as Doc bent over and panted for breath, that he saw the creature trample Exo. Just like that, the shifter who'd abducted him, put him through all kinds of craziness and beaten him repeatedly was gone.

Doc even felt a brief stab of regret that he hadn't followed through with slashing Exo's throat when he'd had the chance.

But the regret was quickly replaced by a different feeling altogether. This one didn't have anything to do with Exo's death, in fact.

It started with a fizzing in the back of his head, a familiar sensation he identified immediately. It meant the transformational power of the Shift was building again, about to unleash another change in the landscape.

And Doc, once again, would have a front-row seat for whatever was coming.

RYAN POPPED OUT of the chute and quickly hopped to his feet, making way for the others who were close behind him.

Heartbeats later, the rest of his companions zoomed out in short order. Each one got out of the way fast, so only a minor pileup happened between the last two.

Even as J.B. and Mildred untangled themselves, Ryan took in the bizarre scene in front of him: the giant creature roaring to the heavens; Union playing her device like a musical instrument; Jak running across the sand toward them both.

"Gaia." Krysty was standing beside him now, sharing the view. Her voice was strained—she was clearly still in great pain, but she was forcing herself through it. "What is that abomination?"

"What's it made of?" Ricky asked, taking up position on Ryan's opposite side. Leaning forward, he squinted at the great beast, then whistled softly. "Holy crap, are those people?"

"Some kind of amalgamation." Mildred finally joined

them, dusting herself off. "A colony creature? Or maybe it just uses discarded organic matter to create a kind of shell, like a hermit crab."

"The real question," J.B. said, "is how do we stop it?"

"Jak has the right idea." Ryan unslung the Steyr Scout and made sure it was ready for action. "We go after the bitch who's calling its tune."

AS THE MONSTER roared, Jak kept his eyes and mind fixed on a single target: Union. It was either that or take on the creature single-handedly, and Union was probably the key to stopping it anyway.

Now, if he could just avoid getting stepped on by the monster like the shifter who'd just gotten crushed...

In spite of all the noise from the beast and the earthquakes, Union still heard Jak approaching. She spun to face him, holding a blaster—Doc's LeMat .44, which the shifter had to have dropped when he got stomped.

Without a word, she cracked off a shot. Jak instantly judged the trajectory and leaped upward, spinning above the path of the bullet.

The second his feet touched the ground again, he hurled one of his leaf-bladed throwing knives with his usual deadly accuracy. Union bobbed fast to one side, firing another round—but the knife still caught her under the collarbone, and her round went wide.

Jak's second blade went in just as smoothly, flashing into the middle of her abdomen. Anticipating another round from the .44, Jak dived and rolled after making that second tag. Sure enough, Union unloaded three rounds in his direction...but he rolled so fast that none of them even nicked him.

Springing up out of his roll, he saw her use the controller even as she pulled the trigger on the .44 again. No rounds fired, as the blaster was empty, but the controller delivered. The creature swung around and dropped a three-fingered fist as if it was a giant sledgehammer, aiming directly at Jak.

As fast as he could, Jak sprinted away from that dropping fist. When it came down, it barely missed him, and the impact threw him off his feet. He heard a chorus of screams and groans as it lifted away, and he had a terrible realization: the bodies making up the creature's enormous frame were alive. The beings that had been absorbed into that monster were aware of everything, and they were suffering.

Even as Jak vaulted to his feet, he knew those terrible cries would stay with him long after that day. He also knew, beyond a shadow of a doubt, that he had to find a way to take that thing down and give those poor people some measure of peace.

"Jak, wait!" Union said it in Carrie's voice, skittish and full of sincerity. "Stop running! That thing only reacts to movement! You'll be safe if you stand in one place!"

But Jak never stopped moving, which was a good thing. No sooner had the words left Union's lips than the creature swung its fist back after Jak like a gigantic pendulum. It would have smashed Jak to a pulp if he'd done what she'd told him to do.

Then the creature surprised him, sweeping its fist around in an unexpected loop that intersected his zigzag path. The side of the fist only brushed him, but that was enough to pitch him several yards. Jak came down hard, feeling the jarring impact in every bone. His head swam, and he barely managed to stay conscious.

But he found himself wishing he'd blacked out after all. He was still on his back, staring upward, expecting to see the creature's fist or foot plummet toward him…when, instead, he saw Union step into his field of vision.

"Poor Jak." She had Doc's sword, which had to also

have fallen free when the shifter was crushed—and was waving it over her head. "We had a real thing together, didn't we? A real connection."

Teeth clenched, Jak struggled to slip a blade from one of his sleeves, but the spring-loaded scabbards were jammed from the fall. He was going to have to pull from one of his pockets, meaning he'd have to move faster to beat her to the draw.

"Don't worry, I'll always remember you fondly." She said it in Carrie's voice, then switched to Dulcet's. "That kiss will always leave us wanting more."

Jak tensed, ready to grab for a knife, hoping he could outrace the sword in her hand.

Her next words were Rhonda's. "Say good-night, dumbass." Then Taryn's. "For a man, you weren't a complete waste of flesh."

She shook the sword overhead. Jak knew she was ready to strike.

This time, when she spoke, it was as Sasha. "*Da svidaniya*, comrade shithead."

Then, finally, she used the voice from the mat-trans chamber, that of the "true" Union personality that had overridden all the rest. "Notice, I didn't whistle for Fido to take care of this. Some things a girl just has to do for herself."

She stopped shaking the sword and grinned down at him. "Consider this a breakup, Jak."

Chapter Fifty-Five

Just as Union was about to slash Jak with Doc's sword and Jak was about to hurl a knife at her neck, a blastershot rang out over the earthquake's rumble and the creature's roar.

Suddenly, a bullet punched through Union's forehead, leaving a perfect red hole. The back of her head wasn't quite so neat; it exploded, blowing out a shower of blood and bone and brain.

The sword fell from her hand, but she somehow managed to stay on her feet. She teetered there a moment more, until Jak swung around on the ground and kicked her legs out from under her.

Then she collapsed in a heap like the dead meat she was.

Jak knew who'd fired the shot before he looked behind him. Even amid the cacophony in progress, he'd recognized the distinctive sound of Ryan's Steyr Scout letting one fly.

"You okay, Jak?" Ryan asked as he and the rest of the crew ran toward him.

"Not need help." Jak shot to his feet and waved dismissively.

"Whatever," Ryan said as he charged up beside him. "You're welcome."

"So what now?" Ricky yelled, bounding over with the others. "How do we stop that thing?" He pointed up at the creature.

"Who says we have to?" J.B. asked. "Mebbe it's somebody else's problem."

Jak narrowed his eyes. "I say have to." He kept thinking about the poor people screaming and moaning on the monster's body. "Put them out of misery." He jabbed a finger in the creature's direction.

"He's right," said Krysty, who was still grimacing from whatever the core was doing to her. "Plus, who knows how much death and destruction that beast will cause if allowed to roam free?"

"So where's that control device of hers?" Ryan bent over Union's body, poking at her jumpsuit with the barrel of his longblaster.

Jak hunkered down and dug into Union's hip pocket, where she'd kept it before. "Here." He pulled out the silver cone and held it up. "But what do with it?"

Ryan took it and turned it over in his hands. "It looked as if she was blowing into it. Playing it like an instrument."

Mildred reached for the device and examined it closely. "So how do we figure out how to operate it? Trial and error?"

"What other way is there?" J.B. asked.

"Apparently, he's come up with one." Ryan gestured at a distant figure running over the sand toward the creature.

Everyone in the group turned and looked at the same time. All eyes and mouths fell wide-open at once as they realized what they were seeing. Whom they were seeing.

"Dark night! Is that—?"

"It is." Mildred nodded fiercely. "It sure as shit is."

"Doc!" Ricky grinned. "It's Doc!"

"Yeah," Ryan said. "And he's going to get himself killed!"

Doc was filled with blazing white light as he ran toward the roaring behemoth.

The fizzing in the back of his head had gone through the usual stages, moving into his eyes and out through his body, making everything he saw turn yellow, then becoming a loud crackling, followed by waves of warmth...and finally the white light, pointing the way to the next transformation of the Shift.

With the certainty of a shifter mutie, he knew exactly where the next major change was going to strike. When he looked there, at that piece of ground some fifty yards due south, he knew exactly what it was going to become. He saw a map, a cross-section in his mind, and he knew without a doubt that it was accurate.

He also knew it would be the perfect answer to the problem of the rampaging creature. He just had to get it to go there without getting stomped to death in the process.

When Doc got to within twenty yards of the monster, he stopped and called out to it, "Hey! Hey, you, big fellow!" He jumped up and down, waving his arms and trying to attract its attention.

Even as he did it, going against his nature in courting danger, he couldn't help marveling in the back of his mind. If someone had told him, back before the abduction, that he would someday be doing what he was doing, he probably would have laughed at them.

But now there he was, alone and unarmed, facing off against a monster many times his own size.

"Hey! Look here! I am down here!" When the creature completely ignored him, Doc ran in circles in front of it, shouting louder. "Hey, you!"

The creature raised one mammoth foot and brought it down. Doc scrambled out of the way, and the creature took another step forward without looking down at him.

"Hey!" Doc darted back out in front of the monster, still waving and calling to no avail. The behemoth was still ignoring him.

Then, suddenly, it wasn't so oblivious anymore. Blasterfire erupted from nearby, and the monster roared in outrage as a wave of bullets pelted it.

Looking in the direction of the shooting, Doc felt a burst of relief and hope. Running toward him with guns blazing were the friends he hadn't seen in days, his traveling companions in the Deathlands.

They were racing to help him. Their timing couldn't have been any better.

But there still wasn't any time to waste. He knew from the way the white light was surging that the transformation he expected was about to occur. "Come on!" he shouted, waving for them to follow him. "Drive it this way! This way!"

He didn't have to tell them twice. The team peppered the creature with rounds, blowing apart a host of the mutie bodies bound to its enormous form. But instead of moving away from the blasterfire, the monstrosity lumbered toward it.

"Around the other side!" Doc shouted, though he didn't need to say it. His teammates already had the right idea.

Splitting up, they sprinted around the creature, ducking and weaving to avoid its stomping feet and swinging fists. Doc went with them, staying focused on the goal.

Once the team had circled to the other side of the beast, Ryan gave the order to fire, and they all cut loose. Instantly, the creature swung around, enraged by the weapons fire, and unleashed its loudest roar yet. Then it thundered toward them, punishing the ground with its gargantuan footsteps.

Ryan and the others ran and fired, ran and fired, drawing the beast ever onward. It was a deadly game, to say the least; one slip or misstep and any of them could be instantly crushed by a monstrous footfall plunging from above.

But soon they didn't have much farther to go, or much

longer to shoot. Their destination, where the transformation foreseen by Doc was about to occur, was less than twenty yards away.

"Almost there!" Doc shouted. "Keep going!"

Up ahead, his Shift-attuned eyes saw the site of the change as a glowing circular area, approximately a hundred feet in diameter. The white light inside him, stoked to new heights, told him the place was nearly ready to transform.

The trick now would be to get the creature onto the target and get Doc's friends far enough away from it that they wouldn't share its fate.

"Come on! Come on!" Compelled by the urgency of the impending change, Doc ran those last twenty yards as fast as he could. Then he crossed the threshold, and his feet were pumping over what he saw as glowing sand, carrying him toward the center of the target.

Looking back, he saw his companions racing toward him, followed by the raging monstrosity. They kept running and shooting, pulling it toward the target like a bull toward a bullfighter's red cape.

When Doc reached the middle of the target, he stopped and faced his friends. "Right here! Bring it right here and then scatter!"

Then, as Ryan and the others crossed the boundary of the target zone and rushed toward him, Doc ran for the far side. He didn't stop until he reached the edge, and then he spun to watch what happened next.

Ryan and his team drew the creature farther, ever farther—halfway to the center, then farther still. Together, they kept up a constant barrage of blasterfire; if anyone needed to reload, the others filled the gap for their companion.

As Doc watched from the edge, the white light flared within him. Just like before, he felt as if it burned away his body, leaving his essence shivering like a single blade of grass in a flood, like a single candle flame in a windstorm.

He hung there a moment, feeling formless, thoughtless, weightless, watching as his friends finally drew the leviathan to the dead center of the target zone. Just as he'd asked, they quickly scattered, fanning out around the creature, peppering it with continuous blasterfire.

Attacked from all directions, the creature couldn't make its mind up which way to turn next. It roared in what sounded like bestial frustration, thrashing its enormous head at the silver disk of the full moon.

Suddenly, Doc felt as if his body had coalesced around him once more. His focus sharpened, his strength intensified, his thoughts clarified. He knew, as always happened at this stage, that the transformation would happen at any instant. He could feel it percolating under the surface; he could see it coiling and building, getting ready to blow.

"Go!" he roared at the top of his lungs. "Everyone run! Get out of there now!"

Casting back intermittent fire to keep the creature confused, Ryan and the others ran from the center of the target zone in every direction. The creature thrashed and roared and shrieked behind them, staying put, just as Doc had hoped.

And then it didn't. Suddenly, it started stomping after J.B., perhaps because his Mini-Uzi laid down the most fire.

"Run, J.B.! Faster!" Doc shouted, fists clenched in suspense. "Go! Go! Go!"

J.B. stopped shooting and leaned into his run, pouring on every bit of speed he could summon. Arms and legs pumping, he charged toward the edge of the target zone, racing to freedom.

At the same time, the creature stomped after him, roaring for his blood. And Doc could see the energies of the

Shift roiling under the sand, about to reshape the landscape according to the neon map in his head.

Doc's heart thundered in his chest as he watched. "Please. Oh, please." He said it softly, like a prayer. "Please do not let me lose one of them now, after I have finally gotten them back."

J.B. kept running, and the creature kept chasing him. The target zone tensed, building up to whatever was coming next.

All around the zone, the other members of the team made it to safety. Only J.B. remained within the perimeter marked by Doc's Shift-sensitized vision.

"Please," Doc whispered. "Please let him live."

Suddenly, the target zone transformed. A blast of light consumed the area, so bright it blinded Doc.

He heard the creature roar, releasing a deafening howl. He heard a sound like the tinkling of glass amplified a thousandfold. And then the roar was cut off and only the glassy tinkling remained.

By the time that sound faded, too, Doc finally regained his eyesight. The whiteness that had drowned out everything else in his range of vision drifted away like dissipating fog.

It was then he was able to see what had become of the creature. It yet remained within the target zone, but it was sealed away from the outside world, locked inside the base of a pyramid of glittering crystal. The monster had been contained, and probably killed.

The pyramid blocked Doc from seeing what had happened to J.B., though. Frantic, Doc ran along the perimeter of what had been the target zone, looking for some sign of his friend.

Had J.B. been caught in the crystallization process? Was he trapped inside with the creature? Or had the creature managed to crush him at the last second, just before the transformation had occurred?

Doc prepared himself for the worst, even as he came upon another of his comrades.

"Doc!" Ricky spread his arms wide. "*Dios mio*, it's good to see you!"

Doc ran past him. "Where is he? Where in Jehovah's name is he?"

"Where's who?" Ricky ran alongside him. "Who're you looking for?"

"J.B.! Did he get out? Did he make it in time?"

Just as he said it, they turned a corner of the pyramid and saw Mildred.

"My dear Mildred! Where is he? Where's J.B.?"

"I don't know," she replied. "I was just going to look for him."

Doc ran past her without another word. His stomach twisted, and feverish chills swept through his body. Had he lost someone after all?

After rounding the next corner of the pyramid, he and Ricky—and Mildred, who'd joined them—came across Jak, who was lying on his back on the ground.

"Jak!" Doc cried. "Where's J.B.?"

"Hey, Doc," Jak said. "Glad finally found you."

Doc, Ricky and Mildred kept running. After the next corner, they spotted Ryan and Krysty.

"Good to see you, Doc." Krysty mustered a smile, but she looked bad. Whatever she'd been through since Doc had last seen her had taken a toll.

Ryan was keeping her upright with an arm around her back. "Glad to have you back in one piece, Doc," he said.

"J.B. Where is he?" Doc asked.

Ryan shrugged, and Krysty shook her head.

Doc and the others moved on to the fourth corner. But when they turned it, there was no one up ahead.

Doc stopped running and slumped. "Blessed heavens." His head was spinning. He'd been around the entire pyramid, and J.B. was nowhere to be found.

Mildred stepped up and touched the back of a hand to his forehead. "You're looking pretty pale there, Doc. Why don't you sit down?"

"We have lost him." Doc wagged his head slowly as harsh reality settled in. "He must have gotten caught in the transformation."

"Who's that?"

Doc looked up, all misery fled. He instantly recognized that voice.

"So who got caught?" J.B. shook the sand off his fedora.

"You, my dear J.B. At least I thought so," Doc said, relief evident in his voice. "I could not find you anywhere."

"Because I was off doing something nice for you." J.B. held out Doc's sword. "But if you don't want this, I'll find someone who does."

Doc smiled and accepted the sword, which the Armorer handed to him. "Of course I want it."

"Union dropped it when Ryan shot her," J.B. explained. "I just ran over to pick it up for you before some mutie got hold of it. Had to wipe some blood off the top, but it looks good as new."

"Ryan's got the sheath," Ricky added. "He found it in that ginormous mat-trans in the redoubt."

"Good to know." Doc nodded as he gazed at the silver lion's head, fighting to hold back a tear.

"Your blaster's over there somewhere, too." J.B. gestured at the sandy ground between the pyramid and the core. "Not sure exactly where."

"Yes, well…" Doc still felt that tear fighting to get out.

"Thought we ought to get your gear back," J.B. added, "now that we've got you back, finally."

"Many thanks." Doc started to reach for a handshake,

then stopped. "It is good to be back, my friends." Then he couldn't hold that tear back anymore, or the ones that came after it.

And he couldn't hold himself back from hugging J.B.— and then each of the others, one by one—either. He was so caught up in the moment that he didn't even notice the earthquakes had finally stopped.

Chapter Fifty-Six

"Get lost, you bunch of idiots," Hammersmith said as he flicked a spent marijuana roach onto the sand in front of the not-so-secret front door of the core redoubt. "I'm sick to death of lookin' at your faces."

"Don't worry, Dr. H." Krysty threw her arms around him and gave him a hug. "We love you, too."

Hammersmith rolled his eyes. "Get the fuck off me," he snarled, but he didn't seem to be in any hurry to break off the hug.

The rest of the companions went on loading their gear into the wag they'd commandeered from the redoubt. It had been two days since the battle of the core, and they were finally recovered from the ordeal and ready to move on.

The wag wasn't much, just a weathered Humvee from what was left of the redoubt's motor pool, but it would be better than marching on foot. The dome light shone like a little beacon in the gritty gray predawn glow, flashing to life every time someone opened a door.

"You sure this bucket of bolts will get us where we're going?" J.B. asked as he heaved a crate of MREs and canned goods in the back.

"Out of the Shift? Hell yes." Hammersmith managed a grateful nod to Krysty as she ended the hug. "But if you keep up your bitching about the wag, I'll toss the keys and let you walk."

"Other Doc not talk like that." Jak grinned as he loaded ammo boxes in the back. "Good thing you stay here."

Hammersmith flipped him the bird. "You couldn't pay me enough to come along with you bastards."

"Good!" Jak snapped. "Not invited!"

Everyone laughed.

Ryan started the engine and let the Humvee idle while they finished loading. The sun was just rising, and the companions wanted to get an early start.

That sunrise, in fact, was of particular interest to Doc. He stood apart from the others and watched it in progress, admiring the pink, orange and gold colors of the wispy chem clouds drifting over the horizon.

Ryan walked over to join him. For a moment, neither man said a word; they just let the stately movement flow before them, clouds and sun and planet ticking along like some magnificent cosmic clockwork.

Ryan was the one who finally broke the silence. "Krysty says she's all clear. No more headaches."

Doc nodded. "Good." Sometime after the defeat of Union and her creature, Hammersmith had shut down the modified mat-trans unit. He'd trashed it, making sure it could never be switched on again. Since then, the Shift had stopped shifting. No more transformations, meaning no more early warnings for Krysty or Doc…so far anyway.

"So how're you doing?" Ryan asked. "Shaking it off, I hope?"

Doc sighed. "Of course, my dear Ryan. What choice do I have?"

"Same as the rest of us." Ryan put a hand on Doc's shoulder. "Same as every other morning. Survive or die."

"Agreed." Doc watched as the sun bobbed up over the horizon, appearing in full for the first time that day. How many other sunrises would he see in this life of his? Not many, perhaps, given the deadly lands he was traversing. Yet, somehow, that made each one all the sweeter.

"It's beautiful, isn't it?" Ryan gave Doc's shoulder a squeeze. "I'm glad you're here to share it with us again."

"There have been times, you know." Doc frowned. "Times when I have wished my life was…otherwise. When I would rather have been anywhere else but here." He cleared his throat softly. "Or nowhere at all."

Ryan nodded. "I know the feeling."

"But now…" Doc hesitated, considering his words. "I was given a choice. Be a victim, resign myself or fight to get back to my friends." He nodded over his shoulder at the rest of the companions, working at the Humvee. "And I fought, Ryan. I fought my way back, because I realized this is worth fighting for." He reached out a hand. "We are worth fighting for."

Ryan took that hand and shook it. "Damn straight."

"I would still give anything, you know," Doc said quietly, "to have them back. My wife and children. But I would give anything to have this family back, as well." He released Ryan's hand and turned to watch his comrades loading the wag, their shared moment over.

As families went, the companions had their occasional disagreements; they didn't always enjoy one another's company.

But when one was hurt, the others rallied to help him or her. And when Doc dwelled too long on the nightmare his life had become, on the people and things he had lost because of fate's cruel vagaries, his companions did the very best thing they could do for him.

They made him laugh. They helped him forget. They kept him human in a world full of inhumanity.

Sometimes it helped to be reminded.

"Looks as though they're almost done packing the wag," Ryan said. "What do you say we get the hell out of here, Doc?"

"Where to? Where are we headed?"

"The redoubt from our last jump, mebbe." Ryan shrugged. "Away from here, that's all I know for sure. Anywhere else will be better."

"My dear Ryan, I would follow you to the gates of hell. Lay on, Macduff!"

* * * * *

COMING SOON FROM

GOLD EAGLE®

Available October 6, 2015

GOLD EAGLE EXECUTIONER®
UNCUT TERROR – *Don Pendleton*

Mack Bolan sets out to even the score when a legendary Kremlin assassin slaughters an American defector before he can be repatriated. His first target leads him to discover a Russian scheme to crash the Western economy and kill hundreds of innocent people. Only one man can stop it—the Executioner.

GOLD EAGLE STONY MAN®
DEATH MINUS ZERO – *Don Pendleton*

Washington goes on full alert when Chinese operatives kidnap the creator of a vital US defense system. While Phoenix Force tracks the missing scientist, Able Team uncovers a plot to take over the system's mission control. Now both teams must stop America's enemies from holding the country hostage.

GOLD EAGLE SUPERBOLAN™
DEAD RECKONING – *Don Pendleton*

A US consulate is bombed, its staff mercilessly killed. The terrorists scatter to hideouts around the globe, but Mack Bolan hunts them down three by three. When the last one vanishes, the world's leaders are caught in the crosshairs and the Executioner must stop the terrorists' global deathblow.

COMING SOON FROM

GOLD EAGLE®

Available November 3, 2015

GOLD EAGLE EXECUTIONER®
DARK SAVIOR – *Don Pendleton*
Cornered at a mountain monastery in the middle of an epic winter storm, Mack Bolan will need both his combat and survival skills to protect a key witness in a money-laundering case from cartel killers.

GOLD EAGLE DEATHLANDS®
DEVIL'S VORTEX – *James Axler*
When a group of outcasts kidnaps an orphan with a deadly mutation for their own agenda, Ryan and the companions must protect her without perishing in her violent wake.

GOLD EAGLE OUTLANDERS®
APOCALYPSE UNSEEN – *James Axler*
The Cerberus rebels face a depraved Mesopotamian god bent on harnessing the power of light to lock humanity in the blackness of eternal damnation.

GOLD EAGLE ROGUE ANGEL™
Mystic Warrior – *Alex Archer*
Archaeologist Annja Creed must face down a malevolent group of mystic warriors when she discovers an ancient document that could lead to lost treasure.

SPECIAL EXCERPT FROM

JAMES AXLER

DEATHLANDS.

Check out this sneak preview of
DEVIL'S VORTEX
by James Axler!

"Get down!" J.B. yelled.

Ryan ducked into the ditch. Cool water splashed him as several of his companions dove for the same side.

He heard a snarl of several blasters on full auto. Bullets kicked up dirt along the bank and thudded into the bare dirt of the far side. An engine whined by, no more than twenty yards away.

Ryan popped up again as the wag's passenger door opened. A coldheart in a black vest with colorful bandannas tied around both arms tried to dive out. Krysty, closer to the truck than Ryan, stood up and fired a burst from her Glock-18, holding the pistol in a two-hand combat grip. The coldheart yowled like a startled bobcat and fell to the ground.

Mildred and Doc also rose to open fire. Ricky and Jak started shooting at a wag swinging in on the north side.

Ryan heard fire answering from the coldheart vehicle. Risking a bullet in the back, he let the Scout fall to hang by its sling as he came up to a crouch, taking his handblaster in both hands.

A female coldheart with black hair stood in the Sierra's bed, pointing an M16 at Krysty, who was just ducking back down into cover. Ryan lined up the sights of his SIG on the black-haired woman's shirt and double-tapped her right below the pistol grip of her longblaster. She folded down out of sight into the truck bed. The longblaster toppled over the side.

Six—no seven—other wags were cruising along the ditch, their beds overstuffed with coldhearts waving blasters. At least thirty or forty of them.

"Right," he called to his friends, firing a couple shots toward the cab of a passing truck and hunkering down.

"Our one chance is to grab that wag with its nose hanging over the ditch and try to power out of here. First, reload, then pop up and back the bastards off!"

He shouted a three count, then "Go!"

Ryan rose again. To find himself facing what looked like a field of bright yellow wildflowers, viewed from above. If the "flowers" were blooms of fire. And death.

"Down!" he screamed. He followed his own command. As a lead shit-storm broke out above his head.

Don't miss
DEVIL'S VORTEX by James Axler,
available November 2015 wherever
Gold Eagle® books and ebooks are sold.

Check out this sneak preview of
APOCALYPSE UNSEEN
by James Axler!

Kane began to turn, and as he did so something illuminated behind him, at the opposite end of the chamber. Kane saw the figure sitting there as the shadows were bleached away, something that looked half alive, half dead—and all lizard. It was clearly an Annunaki, one of the cruel race of aliens who had tried to subjugate the people of the Earth and turn them into slaves. It wore a few strips of material like bandages but most of its russet-colored scales were on show. Its skin had dark patches on it, like fungus on a tree's bark, and the typically defined muscles of the Annunaki were nowhere to be seen. Instead this Annunaki appeared to be wasting away.

But its face, its head…that was another matter. As Kane turned he realized the brightness was emanating from the creature's head, a great ball of white lightning propped atop its neck. As Kane looked, the intensity increased, until it was not just dazzling but absolutely blinding. His eyes seemed to scream inside his head as his vision winked out like a television switching to standby, and for a few agonizing seconds, the brightness was so overpowering it seemed to make a sound as he tried to process it.

Beside Kane, Brigid Baptiste was holding her hand up against the growing luminance of the Annunaki's skull, but already her eyes were hurting, her vision wiped out in a cluster of sudden, painful seconds.

Mariah saw what was happening, but it was too late to respond. Even as she tried to turn away, the world went from bleached to blurred to a wash of orange and yellow, as though she were looking at the sun through closed eyelids. She dropped to the floor, her hands reaching up for her face.

Even Grant, who had not turned, was caught in the sudden display of brilliance, unable to avoid its spread as the rays bathed the room and its diamond-encrusted walls with sheer radiance. He heard his colleagues drop to the floor almost in unison. "What's happening?" Grant asked, screwing his eyelids closed against the magnificent glare.

But his eyelids could not protect him against a light so pure it burned itself into the very surface of the retina.

Don't miss
APOCALYPSE UNSEEN by James Axler,
available November 2015 wherever
Gold Eagle® books and ebooks are sold.

GEOEXP75